ALSO BY
JORDON GREENE

To Watch You Bleed
The Reserve
A Mark on My Soul
Watching for Comets
Every Word You Never Said
The No Repeat Policy

WITH
YAYIRA DZAMESI

Snowflake Kisses

WITH
KALOB DÀNIEL

This I Promise You

AUTHOR NOTE

The magic in this book is a real-to-life portrayal of witchcraft in a YA contemporary romance story as opposed to Hollywood magic or fantasy. You can look forward to spells with candles of all colors, scented herbs, incantations, chosen gods, and of course, crystals. Get ready for cute love spells, blessings on their baking (they're a kitchen witch), and appeals to the old Norse gods. I hope you enjoy it!

TRIGGER WARNINGS

Underage drinking and smoking, parent death (in the past and off page), depression, accident involving physical trauma on page

JORDON GREENE

Copyright © 2026 by Jordon Greene

Visit the author's website at
www.jordongreene.com

This is a work of fiction. Names, characters, places, and incidents are products of the author's imagination or are used fictionally and are not to be construed as real. Any resemblance to actual events, locations, organizations, or persons living or dead, is entirely coincidental.

All rights reserved.

Published by F/K Teen
An imprint of Franklin/Kerr Press
Kannapolis, NC

Edited by Christie Stratos
Cover illustrations and design by Yayira Dzamesi
Interior design by Jordon Greene
Author photograph by Bob Clark

Printed in the United States of America

FIRST EDITION

Hardcover ISBN 979-8-218-45611-5
Paperback ISBN 979-8-9887979-4-4
Audiobook ISBN 978-8-9887979-5-1

Library of Congress Control Number: 2025916969

Fiction: Romance
Fiction: Contemporary
Fiction: LGBT/Gay

To Dawn Evans,
my second mother and friend.

IF I HAVE TO wipe up one more glob of caramel, I'm quitting. I promise. I swear it by the Allfather. I'll walk right out the front door, not a second thought.

"Could you not, maybe"—I twirl a finger in the air at Kaitlynn—"make a mess?"

"Me?" She feigns pouty eyes and intentionally misses the cup while coating the counter with cinnamon. Ladies, gents, and theys, my best friend, the one and only essential bane to my existence, Kaitlynn May Miller.

She dusts the mess onto the floor, as if that's better, and I roll my eyes to hide my amusement. I pop a lid on the drink I whipped up for one of our regulars and shake my head. A mess. That's what she is, but she's my mess, I guess.

"What?" She acts innocent.

"Really?" I ask. "Come on, less mess means less cleanup, and I still have to finish the pumpkin bread before we close, or Dawn is going to freak."

Dawn practically begged Kaitlynn and me in the work group chat earlier to get all the extra stuff done so she could focus on baking the many Thanksgiving orders in the morning. There were lots of pouty emojis. She really likes emojis.

"Yeah, yeah, I know," Kaity groans. "Gotta have a—"

"Have you seen Hayden yet?" I interrupt as if I'm only now thinking of it. I'm not. It's been on my mind the last hour. He's a… Well, he's a guy who comes into Woodsy Café & Cakes a lot. Okay, not just a guy, he's *the* guy.

"No." Kaitlynn grins, brown eyes squinting with amused accusation under pinned-up blonde hair, and shakes her head. "You miss your man?"

My man? I deflect by turning around, a plastic cup in hand marked GUNTER. Hayden is not *my* man. I wish he was, but he isn't. I'm one hundred percent not that fortunate. He's probably super straight anyway, which rules me out entirely. Besides, he doesn't even know I exist. Okay, he *does* know I exist, but... You know what, stop. Just focus on the now.

"Mr. Franz," I call out across the counter. It's a rule to always call out the customer's name on the cup, but I refuse to call him Gunter. It's Mr. Franz. Unlike some, he isn't weird and flirty with Kaitlynn, and he has this cool hint of a waning European accent. I want to say it's German—my mom is German—but it might be something else, like Polish or Danish. He's just one of the sweetest old men I've ever met, and until he says otherwise, it's Mr. Franz.

"Here," Mr. Franz answers, one hand on a thin wooden cane, the other reaching for his drink. His fingers are rough when he takes it from me. "Thank you, Mackenzie."

"Of course." I nod. "Hope you enjoy it."

My friends call me Kenzie, but my name badge says MACKENZIE in brown letters. I don't usually hear my full name unless I'm in trouble at home, but there's a warmth to the way he says it.

"Is that a new skirt?" Mr. Franz's head ticks to the left. His movements tend to be a little abrupt.

"It is!" I let my shoulders bounce and I do a little curtsy. The light mocha fabric shuffles around my legs. I only recently started wearing skirts last semester. Mom didn't care, and Kaity thought it was great, but I knew not everyone would, especially at school, and that wasn't how I wanted to spend my freshman year. We live in one of *those* towns where the high school dress code changed to let dudes wear skirts, but people's acceptance didn't change with it.

Last week even, Mr. Franz saw someone give me a weird look while I was working, probably because of my outfit, and he made a point to compliment me right in front of them. He might be old, but he's far from old-school.

"Looks good." He nods and starts toward the door. "Have a good night, you two."

"Thanks! We'll see you tomorrow," I say, and walk around the counter. Kaitlynn yells her goodbye as the door settles shut behind him.

I walk past her, slapping the counter as I swish around it. "I'll be in the back if you need me," I say, and stop at the prep station.

Away from the shades of browns and grays, the old farmhouse-style lantern lights and eclectic gathering of wooden tables, couches, armchairs, and stools, I uncover loaves of pumpkin bread under a harsh fluorescent bulb. A nutty, spicy scent wafts up to greet my nose. I take a deep breath of it and sigh. It's one of my favorite things about my job, even if after a few months of pumpkin spice I know I'll be so ready for the flavor to go out of season. It's amazing.

"Perfect," I say to myself before starting on the bread that Landon put out earlier. I steady my thoughts while I start to slice. Chest relaxed, I pull in a new breath and whisper a blessing over the bread.

"Whosoever eats of these cakes,

may prosperity find them,

may good health be with them,

may happiness shine on them,

and no harm befall them.

Oh, and may their Thanksgiving be bright...I mean happy."

As soon as I finish the blessing I start again. My thoughts weave around the regulars I imagine will be here tomorrow as I speak the words. Mr. Franz in particular.

Seems he's staying in my mind. I hope he has family to see. A whole big bunch of them. I dip my knife in the maple butter icing and slather it on a piece of warm bread from thick stacks while images of Mr. Franz pop behind my eyes like a photo reel from the '80s. He's sitting by an old rock-framed fireplace with a toddler bouncing atop his knee. A young woman laughs at his side while others gather around to listen to some story he's telling. He talks to a brother, or maybe a cousin, by the oven with his wife, or it could be a sister, who shoos them from the kitchen. The thoughts warm me and simultaneously fill me with a tinge of envy. I don't even know if he has that and I'm jealous.

I grumble and push the feeling away before it consumes me again. *Breathe slowly, Kenzie.* In and out. In and out. *Please, Freyja, take this out of my mind.* Still, the tendril of jealousy holds tight, refusing to let me forget. I want that type of holiday, that type of life. All I have is Mom, and sometimes that's not even true.

"I will have a wonderful Thanksgiving. I will have a wonderful Thanksgiving," I tell myself, and then switch to what really looms over my head. "Mom is going to feel great. Mom is going to feel great."

She's a good mom, I promise. It's just that sometimes she gets depressed. I know she tries, but she's been like this since Dad died—since I can remember. I was six when it happened, I think, so he's this mostly blurry figure in my memory. It's weird missing someone you never really knew, but it's even harder missing your mom from across the dinner table. The meds help, but it's just us. I faintly remember there being people around when I was younger. Family gatherings and holidays with people whose names I can't remember, people who one by one vanished from our lives.

"Kenzie!" Kaitlynn yells around the corner in German, "Notfall!"

I snap out of it. It's how we say *get the hell up here and help me* without saying *get the hell up here and help me* in front of customers. It's German for *emergency*.

"Ich komme," I yell back and cover the cakes before I exit the kitchen.

When I round the corner, the line is four deep from the counter. Kaitlynn is taking cash from the customer at the register when she looks back and asks, "Could you make drinks? I'll take orders?"

"Sure."

She hands me an order slip and I go for the cups. It's a large white chocolate latte with an extra shot of espresso for…I check the slip again. *TOBY*. I could probably make this in the dark, so by the time Kaity passes back the next order, I hand off the drink to an average-height ginger with full facial hair and a massive coat who happens to reply when I call out *Toby*.

I steal a look past the counter. Hmm, no sign of him. Usually Hayden comes in around now. No, I'm not obsessed with him. He's just handsome. I turn around and get back to making drinks, and twenty minutes later we're down to one customer and still no Hayden.

"You look sour." Kaitlynn bumps me with her thigh.

"Shut up," I mutter and grab a miniature pumpkin pie to-go for Sheila. I take another glance at the glass entrance. Seriously? Where is he? I mean, he doesn't have to come, but it's just weird, and maybe I do want to see those gray eyes. I hand over the little pie and half notice Sheila leaving because I'm too focused on who's not here yet.

"I'm going to go finish up those breads," I tell Kaitlynn, since there's no reason for me to be up front anymore, and I start for the back. He always comes for his iced caramel latte with cinnamon. "Always," I huff under my breath.

"I'll get..." she starts as the door chime rings. "Actually..."

I wheel around and run to stand next to her by the register. There is only *one* thing that could mean. I freeze at the counter as *he* walks in, and suddenly the inch I lack on Kaity feels massive. Are my hands clean? Do I still have that smudge on my apron? I glance down. Yep. Still there. It's too late to clean it off, he's already here, gorgeous smoky eyes switching between Kaitlynn and me. They settle on me for a little longer though, I swear it.

Hayden Marcus. *The* man of my dreams. He's tall, so tall. I'm talking over six foot even without the black-and-white-checked Kobe sneakers. His smile is intoxicating. His hair is a luscious mess of short, dark brown that I've dreamt of running my fingers through way more than once. It looks so soft. And well, the rest...gawd, just makes me melt. Hard jawline. Small upturned nose with a faint freckled bridge between gray eyes. He's also captain of the Mitchell High varsity basketball team. They're my school's rivals, but I'll root for them no matter what.

I just have to find out if he's into the theys. That's my current hurdle, besides how I can barely function around him. I swear it. I'm *going* to be his one day, no matter what Kaitlynn says.

"Hey." Hayden's voice envelops my senses in a savory gruffness.

"Hey there," I say back, all grins and nervous energy.

This might be ridiculous, but there is this piece of me, like this tiny little sliver of my brain, that thinks he might be into me. It's a long shot, but why else does he talk to me first when he comes in? And despite what Kaitlynn says, it's not because I'll talk to literally anyone. She isn't exactly Miss Shy. There's just no way he likes our drinks that much.

I'm about to lose my balance when something solid kicks into my ankle, and Kaitlynn forces a cough. Oh hell. Have I been staring?

"Uh, sorry...what, uh..." I start, but movement outside catches my eye. There's someone lurking by the entrance.

"Sorry, that's my little brother," Hayden says dismissively.

"He doesn't want to come in?" Kaitlynn asks. "It's cold."

"Yeah, it's cold," I echo.

"Nah, he's weird. Says he hates the smell of coffee." Hayden shrugs.

Hates the smell of coffee?

"Oh." I grunt. "Sorry. What can I…uh…can I get for you, Hayden?" I stutter, and throw in his name. Should I have said his name? Is that too much? No. It can't be. We call customers by their names all the time. We know all the regulars. It's okay.

As he opens his mouth, I clench my teeth together so I don't speed scream his entire order at him before he can get the words out himself.

Hayden grins. "I'll just take an iced caramel latte with cinnamon."

I pause, I know there's more. While I give him a second, I steal a glance around Hayden. His brother hates the smell of coffee that much?

"And how about a Cinnacake Roll too?" he asks.

"Of course." There it is.

I finish ringing him up while Kaitlynn puts his drink together. Now's the hard part. He always uses cash, which means I have to take it from him, which means I might have to touch his hand. I want to, but it's so awkward. There's this electricity inside me when I think about it, but my head says it'll freak him out. I stop myself from taking a big breath when he extends his hand toward me. I reach for the money, and of course I fail. The side of my thumb brushes his palm and a flutter springs through my hand and jumps past my wrist. I squeeze my mouth shut and give him my most "natural"-looking tight-lipped grin.

"Let me get your roll," I finally breathe.

"Thanks," he says.

I go to the display case and select the largest of the Cinnacake Rolls. We call them Sinnercakes when customers aren't around because they're sinfully large and sugary. They're basically a diabetic coma in roll form. From the other side of the display case the large white *M*, for *Mountaineers*, stamped across the breast of his deep purple letter jacket catches my attention. It fits him well. How the hell does he look so good and eat these? I'm certain he's got a six-pack under that shirt. I refocus on the roll and drop it into a bag as Kaitlynn finishes his drink and I meet her back at the counter.

He takes the cup and I pass him the pastry bag. I feel super awkward. I want to say something else, maybe compliment him, but I don't know how. Like there isn't anything else to say, and to be like, *Hey, your eyes look pretty tonight* as he walks out the door is just weird, plus I bet he doesn't want to be pretty. Ugh! *Handsome, Kenzie. Tough dudes like to be called handsome.*

"Thanks again!" Hayden says. "I'll see you two tomorrow."

"Kaitlynn won't be here tomorrow. I will," I blurt in one long breath, literally pointing at myself like some absolute fool. I want to disappear, but it's done. It's out there. I keep my shoulders high and my smile higher.

"Oh, okay." Hayden shrugs, and I think he laughs. Was that a nervous laugh? "Guess I'll see *you* tomorrow then. Have a good Thanksgiving, Kaity."

"Thanks, you too. Night!" Kaitlynn waves as he twists about and heads for the door. "Tell you brother we said happy Thanksgiving too."

"See ya." I nearly gasp, ignoring Kaity. He'll see me tomorrow. He even said it. He literally said it. "Bye!"

He's out the door, his silhouette disappearing around the

corner along with his brother's before I can get it out. My eyes are stuck on the back of the Open/Closed sign dangling from the door.

I let myself breathe again and look at Kaitlynn.

"I *am* going to be his one day."

2

MY TIRES CRUNCH TO a stop next to Mom's car. Headlights splash against brick and then beam through the forest, catching endless bare branches and a few evergreens. The occasional yellow or red leaf flitters in the wind, but most have already fallen.

"Here we go." I pump myself up for the cold and pull my hood over my curls. I take in a breath, hand on the key, not quite ready to let go of the heat blasting from the vents. "Summer. I just want summer!"

I switch off the engine and the world goes silent as the warmth is sucked away from me. My fingers fumble for the door handle and I step out with my arms wrapped tight around my chest. Chilly wind whips at my face and bites at my nostrils. The soles of my shoes crunch against gravel as I sprint for the front door, interrupted by the slow chirps and trills of crickets and grasshoppers and the occasional rattle of a katydid. I glimpse the thinning gray crescent against a diamond-studded sky. If it weren't so cold I'd take my time out here. It's beautiful.

Not too bad a night for a spell though. It's almost the dark moon.

I march up the single step and slip my key into the lock. It clicks and I rush inside, happy for the heat to wrap me up like an invisible blanket. I pause. It's quiet. Mom must already be asleep, which isn't a surprise. Past the tiny foyer to the right sets the kitchen—my domain—and an open space with our old wooden dining room table and four overly decorative chairs, most of which haven't cradled more than a stack of books in years. There are dishes in the sink and a large, uncorked, slender-necked bottle on the counter.

I huff.

Off to the left, splotches of flashing light escape into the hallway. She left the TV on again. It's been worse the past few weeks. She's slept so much and drunk more. The holidays are always hard for her. Me too, if I'm being honest, but I try to be strong for her.

I pick up the bottle and shake it. It's light in my hand. Empty.

"Mom." I sigh and close my eyes.

I deposit the bottle back on the counter and leave the kitchen. The volume is off, but the TV still covers the room in a kaleidoscope of colors, including my mom's face. She's on the couch with a throw blanket barely draping over her legs and her arms pulled in, eyes closed. There's a nearly empty wine glass on the end table. I don't understand how she falls asleep there. It's old and firm, we got it used.

"Hey, Mom," I whisper and pull the throw blanket over her shoulders. "Hope you had a good day."

I know she didn't, but I say it anyway. This is how I find her on her *less than* days. She doesn't like calling them bad days. That would mean there was something wrong. There is, but it's not that easy. It's been nearly a decade since Dad died, but for her I think it still hits like yesterday. She never moved on, never opened herself up to finding someone else. She says there isn't anyone like him, no one who would make her feel joy like he did. I don't know. I've never had that, but I wish she would try. It doesn't help that Dad's entire family went radio silent a few years after he died, and Mom's family is in Germany. All she has is me.

I lean over and kiss her forehead. "Night, Mom. Hab dich lieb."

I walk back into the kitchen and fill up the sink to soak the dirty plates while I tie up the trash bag and walk it out the rickety back door. Its bent metal frame slaps back into place when the wind catches it, just before biting at my uncovered face and ears as I run down the wooden stairs. There's little more than dim moonlight to illuminate the concrete slab that doubles as a back porch, and I toss the trash in the gray receptacle as fast as I can and race back inside. It's so freaking cold. I let the door slap shut behind me and immediately regret it. I squint, grimacing at the bang and waiting to see if I woke Mom. I don't hear anything, so I think I'm good.

Back in the kitchen I get to scrubbing the dishes left in the sink. I've been the kid who sticks around home, whether it's cleaning up after dinner or making dinner, for years, ever since Mom started drinking. I don't mind, really. It's not like I don't enjoy the kitchen, and I'd rather it get done than bother her. There is something about having a spatula in hand, or my fingers coated in batter, or a sweet aroma wafting from the oven. It's calming. I think that's why I chose the bakery as my first job, it's a lot like this, and if I weren't thinking about nursing or maybe psychology, I'd probably consider opening my own bakery one day.

That's all a long way away though. First, I need to get through my last year and a half of high school. I have plenty of time to figure it out, but I do have a plan.

I'M IN MY BROWN pajamas with the inscription from the One Ring printed down the leg in gold lettering. I'm sitting on the floor with my legs crossed in front of my altar. My version of an altar at least.

It's a simple rustic wooden table with a forest-green cloth on top, sort of like a table runner. There's a small bouquet of wildflowers. I pick them every few days from the woods behind the house. I don't know them all by name yet, I'm still learning, but my favorite are the three red columbine blossoms, the white petals and yellow anthers of a few thimbleweed flowers, stalks of lavender, and one lone sunflower towering over the rest. Next to them is a calming satchel of ground-up kola nut, a clear crystal, and a rough piece of yellow tiger's eye I found myself at the Emerald Hollow Mine down in Hiddenite on a school field trip when I was twelve. A small polished amber stone, a black tourmaline, a pointed chunk of polished sodalite sit around and between my candles.

I've already said my intentions for Mom, now it's time for the thing I wish for most. From the small chest next to the altar I take a piece of browning paper and place it in the center before setting a simple silver candle plate on top of it. Next is a thick, half-melted red pillar candle. The top half was pink before it melted away during the first three days of the spell. It's one of the old Valentine's Day candles I bought when they went on sale.

It's already charged and coated in oil, so I skip that step and sprinkle a mixture of lavender petals, nutmeg, ylang-ylang petals, tonka bean, and cinnamon from another satchel around the base and on the candle itself. I position the sodalite near the base before fumbling a tiny smooth rose quartz from my drawer of stones and setting it on the base opposite the sodalite.

It's for my love spell. I haven't told anyone about it except Kaitlynn because I feel pathetic thinking I need to use a spell to find love or to get Hayden to love me, but I want it so bad. I know I can't make him love me. That's not how it works, but I'm going to use whatever I can to help nudge it that way. That's why I added cinnamon to my love herbs — he loves cinnamon.

I let out all the air in my lungs and work on grounding myself. The hardest part is ridding myself of all the negative self-talk. I have to calm my mind, let all the self-deprecating thoughts leave. My focus has to be right. I breathe in a long gulp of air and I start by lighting the two black candles at the edge of my altar.

"I am letting go of all doubt and embracing what may come," I say calmly, letting the words vibrate through my body. "I am letting go of all doubt and embracing what may come."

I close my eyes and repeat it two more times before snuffing out the candles. I sniffle when the smoke touches my nose. Keeping my calm is hard while I imagine what I'm aiming for: Hayden Marcus. I have to be still, at peace. I don't think I can really screw up a spell, not like in a way that'll harm me or anything, but still.

I take a breath, close my eyes again, and center my thoughts. Stars in the sky. A warm summer breeze rushing through the tall grass. Hayden's smiling face. A drop of water. The scent of cinnamon rolls fresh out of the oven.

"Okay, Hayden, I need a boyfriend," I say, and pick up the long-necked grill lighter. It didn't take me long to learn that I'm not good with matches or the little lighters. Too many seared fingertips.

I click the trigger and a flame comes to life. I light the wick on the Valentine's Day candle and wait for the first bit of wax to start melting.

"Me and my smoky-eyed man, we are meant to be," I quote the words written on paper under the candle, my mind focused on those gray eyes. "So it is."

I say it again, letting my eyes close. Sweet notes of lavender and the woody spice of warmed nutmeg greet my senses. I imagine arms around me, hugging me, warming me. I say it again, a third time, then a fourth. I open my eyes. The candle has almost melted to the next notch. I focus on the flame and say the words two more times.

"Me and my smoky-eyed man, we are meant to be. So it is. Me and my smoky-eyed man, we are meant to be. So it is."

With the last word I lean in and blow out the flame and trim the wick.

"So it is," I say one more time, hoping that my intent was clear.

3

"YOU'RE NOT BLACK FRIDAY shopping?" Landon side-eyes me.

"Nah," I say, leaning against the counter opposite the register.

We've had nothing to do for nearly an hour. I thought it'd be busier today, being Thanksgiving and all. I thought we'd have a line until we closed and have to shove people out the door. I mean, I didn't want to be stuck here after five, but this is ridiculous. The upside is we've stayed on top of the cleaning, which means we might get to leave right after close. Mom said she's cooking a ham with her amazing pineapple sauce, my favorite. I know it depends on how she's feeling. That part was unspoken, but it's always there. Regardless, I'm bringing home a key lime pie and I'll probably end up making some of the sides, but it's just us.

"That's what *they* want," I continue. He didn't ask for this, but if he's going to sound incredulous about me not partaking in the annual anti-Thanksgiving capitalist slugfest that is Black Friday, I'm going to explain. "They want you to come to their stores in droves. To fight your neighbors for an extra five dollars off a shitty version of a product they're making a fortune off. People are literally having Thanksgiving tonight. *Tonight!* They're being all 'thankful' and warm and fuzzy, but then tomorrow...tomorrow the same people would cut your throat for a set of one-thousand-thread-count bedsheets."

He's just staring at me, saying nothing, lips skewed like I've lost my mind, but *I'm* not the guy fighting an old grandma type at Walmart for the one-thousand-thread-count bedsheet set. Yeah, I saw that happen a few years ago. It was surreal. He didn't cut her throat, but that's not the point. I'm just trying to be thankful right now, even though Hayden hasn't come by yet.

"Sooo big no, then." Landon nods and laughs.

I shrug. "Nope. What are you getting though?"

Maybe I don't participate, but that doesn't mean I can't spectate. Who hasn't watched the Black Friday videos from the 2000s on YouTube? People stampeding into stores and over each other. Men fighting women and guys half their size for a gaming system. Camping outside stores for a TV or baby doll.

"*Tekken 8!*" he yells.

Thank the old gods we have no customers right now.

"*Tekken?*" I ask. A video game. I should have known. The only games I play are *The Sims* and *Tetris*, otherwise my computer is useless. I don't even own a gaming console.

"Yeah," Landon says. "It's a fighting game. Sort of like—"

"I know what it is." I roll my eyes while the wheels grind in his head. Landon goes to Mitchell High, the same school as Hayden. I met him when I started working here, and we've gotten along well. "It's like…like *Mortal Kombat*."

"Uh…no." His face contorts into what I think is dismay. "It's not a gore-fest, and—"

"I get it, it's a fighting game," I say.

"Yeah, yeah, but they added a heat gauge, and they're bringing back the Rage Drive!" Landon starts listing things I've no clue about. He keeps going. Something about how cool the stage destruction is going to be and something else about a new character. "I mean, technically it's an upgraded character. It's Jack-8. He's getting a laser cannon and giant drill this time!"

"Ah." I nod.

"So what are you doing instead?" he asks.

"Nothing…" I shrug. "Sleeping in. I'm definitely sleeping in.

Maybe play some *Sims*. Oh! And I might go up to Waterrock Knob. Check out the crashed Cessna up there again."

"Trespass. You mean trespass?" Landon grins.

"No." I roll my eyes. How can it be trespassing? It's just the wreckage of a plane that crashed years ago. It's not a house.

"Sure. Why did they never clear that up anyway?" Landon asks.

"I don't know. That was what, like twenty years ago, right?" I think. It was before I was born at least.

"I think." Landon shrugs. He stands up and heads to the back. "Speaking of twenty, it's twenty till closing. I'm going to mop the dining room."

"Good idea," I say, and grab a cup. "I'm going to make myself a drink before I clean the machines. You want anything?"

He rounds the corner with the mop and bucket. "Sure. Give me a peanut butter frappe."

"Coming right up," I say in my best mock customer service voice, which is basically my voice, but an octave lower. He laughs and slaps the mop on the floor. I can hear the water splashing across the hardwood as he sloshes it around.

I pull another cup and my mind goes into autopilot. Milk, a little finely ground coffee, the blender, then pour into a cup. I start again for Landon's drink, and as I'm drizzling peanut butter around the cup, the front door chime rings and the door creaks open.

We were *this* close to closing. I'll let Landon handle it. I *am* making *his* drink after all.

"Oh, hey." Landon greets whoever it is like he knows them. Must be a regular. "Just be careful, the floor is wet."

Whoever it is grunt-laughs in response as Landon comes back around the counter. I ignore it and pour his peanut butter blend into a cup.

"Kenzie," Landon says. His voice raises to this awkward tone. "What was it you said about that tall guy who always comes by late?"

"You mean Mr. Dreamy?" Hayden's face blossoms like a movie reel in my head. "Have you seen his eyes?"

I sigh longingly and shake the compressed whipped cream container. Gods, his eyes. Never before have I seen such gorgeous grays. I know it's cliché to say they sparkle, but seriously, they do.

"Yeah, him." Landon clears his throat.

"What about—" I turn.

My fingers clench around the canister. It's Hayden! Oh my gods, it's Hayden. And I was just saying…shit. I flinch, and cream squirts from between my fingers like fireworks. It rains down, splashing on the countertop and my chin. Hayden's eyes widen, and he starts to laugh. Instead of letting go, my body tenses again from the sudden cold froth on my skin, and another stream of whipped cream flies through the air and coats my shirt. Shit!

"Uh…" I release my grip and let the can clack freely on the wooden floor while I scramble to fix this. It can burst into flames for all I care, burn this whole place down, after all that. "W-what can I, I mean, *we* get you?"

I shuffle next to Landon to wait for Hayden's order like I'm not covered in globs of whipped cream, as if this type of thing is completely normal.

"You good, bro?" Hayden takes a step toward the counter now that the danger is gone.

"Yeah, all good here! Of course! All good." I grab a napkin and start wiping the mess from my shirt and face. Why me?

"Okay…I know y'all are about to close, sorry for coming so late." Hayden settles his elbows on the counter, eyes jumping past us to the menu, like he doesn't already know what he's going to get. It's always the same.

"It's—" Landon starts, but I've already opened my mouth.

"You're good. Perfectly fine," I ramble. "Promise."

"All right. I think I'll have an iced caramel latte with cinnamon on top, and…" He leans to our right and eyes the display case. So far it's his normal. "How about a slice of that maple butter pumpkin bread. I'm guessing y'all won't have that much longer. Might as well try it."

Something new. Wow! That's never happened since I've known him. I scoot into Landon, nudging him to the side, and start ringing up Hayden's order. He gets the hint and retreats to the coffee station to make Hayden's drink.

"Your total is ten sixteen." I smile at him.

"One second." He fishes his card from his wallet and hands it to me. "Uh… You've got a…a bit of whipped cream on your face still."

The look in his gray eyes says he's trying so hard not to laugh. I reach up and wipe at my cheek, but he shakes his head. I try again. Nope.

"Let me help," he says, and reaches across the counter.

Quicker than I've ever moved, I swipe my hands across my face. There is no way I'm letting him touch my face. It's not happening. I don't think I could handle it. I might faint, or worse, cease to exist. He raises his hands in defeat and settles back with a faint laugh.

"Did I get it?" I ask sheepishly.

"Yeah, you did that time." He shakes his head.

"You are so pathetic," Landon whispers as I turn around and breathe for what feels like the first time in minutes.

"Shut up," I whisper back.

"Your pumpkin bread!" I spout. Anything to change the subject as I awkwardly slide over to the baked goods case, barely avoiding slipping on the whipped cream on the floor.

"Y'all have plans for Thanksgiving?" Hayden asks from behind.

Why does he want to know? Does he want me to...no. No, he doesn't want that. *Stop it, Kenzie!* He's just making small talk, that's it.

"Dinner with the family, 'bout it," Landon says, and swings around with Hayden's drink ready.

"Same." I snap the word out.

I dare eye contact with Hayden again while Landon takes the bag with the pumpkin bread from me and hands over it and the drink. It's better than me making a fool of myself even more. It's too much though, so I look away.

"I hope you both have a great Thanksgiving." Hayden starts walking backward toward the door. "I got to get home. The fam—"

He slips. There's a squeak of rubber on wet wood. Then a yelp as he tries to swing himself around. I race around the corner to help, but he's too far. His hand flies out, grabbing at the nearest chair, but it's no match for gravity and comes tumbling after him as the back of Hayden's head smashes against the edge of a table.

Smack! I wince at the unsettling sound of bone crashing against an unforgiving surface. My body freezes in place.

"Hayden!" I yell as he tumbles away from the table and downward.

By the time I'm moving, he's on the floor. I gulp at the sight of blood dripping over his forehead. Oh my gods! Hayden!

"Is he?" Landon backs up, speaking the question I refuse to even allow into my head.

"No, no, no!" I yell back as I drop to my knees without stopping and crawl to Hayden's side.

His eyes are open, but they're not...present. They look adrift somewhere else, somewhere distant and foreign. He moves, eliciting a pained groan, but before he can get a word out, his body starts to quake and his limbs lock up.

"What the hell?" I stammer. I think…is he? "Is he having a…"

"I'm going to jail. I'm going to fucking jail!" Landon starts yelling and pacing from one end of the bar to the other. "I just know it! I'm going to jail!"

Hayden's eyes roll back and his head shakes violently. It smacks the floor once before I get my hand under him. What do I do? What the hell do I do?

"Shut up, Landon, and get over here," I yell. He's not going to jail, at least I don't think he is, but if we don't do something, I don't know what's going to happen to Hayden! And if he dies in my arms, then jail is the last thing Landon has to worry about because I'll end him.

"What do we do?" Landon kneels next to me.

I reach out like I'm going to grab Hayden's body to steady him, but I don't know if I should. Isn't that what you do when this happens? I don't know. I'm a teen! I'm a student! Hell, I'll admit it, *I'm a kid*. This type of thing isn't supposed to happen around me.

We have to do something though.

"Get some towels," I command.

Landon runs off.

This is so bad. "I'm so sorry, Hayden! I'm so sorry!"

I don't know what I'm sorry for exactly, but I'm still sorry. I guess it's that this is happening. My mind races as his body continues to thrash. Did we do something wrong? Was the Wet Floor sign out? Is Landon right? Are we going to jail? Suddenly Landon's back and hands me the towel. I throw it under Hayden's head and let it take the blows.

Then all at once it stops. His body goes still and his eyes flutter open and closed again. He lets out a breath. Is he okay? He's still breathing, but he's also bleeding.

"Hayden," I lean closer and whisper, begging him to open his eyes. I need to know he's okay. "Hayden!"

Finally, his eyelids flick open. They're dazed, still distant, but searching. He shakes his head and takes in a deep breath. Then those gray beauties lock on me.

"Hey," he says, like he's surprised to see me, but his tone is soft and warm.

"Hey," I say back, but the way he's looking at me, like I'm all he sees, chokes me from saying more.

Then, as quickly as he'd come to, his eyes slink shut and his body goes limp.

"Did he just die?!" Landon yells. "Please tell me he didn't just die. I didn't kill him, did I? Right?"

For a moment, the same thoughts shoot through my head. Is he dead? Please don't be dead! No! He can't be dead. I'm supposed to date him first! I put my hand to his neck like they do in the movies, hoping to feel something. I've never actually checked anyone's pulse, but I have the idea, I think. I should be able to feel it somewhere in his neck. At first there's nothing, and my anxiety begins to spike, but I move my finger up maybe an inch, and finally there's something. A quick sudden thump under my finger, pumping beneath his skin.

"He's alive!" I scream.

"Thank God." Landon gulps.

"But we need to get him to the hospital."

4

TEN MINUTES LATER, AFTER a furor of red lights, paramedics, stretchers, and Landon acting like he was composed the entire time, my tires screech to a halt in the ED parking lot. The ambulance is at the entrance, its back doors swung open, and there's Hayden, unconscious, being rolled out on a stretcher. I jump out of the car and chase after the first responders through the double glass sliding doors under EMERGENCY DEPARTMENT.

I'm in a daze, and honestly I'm not sure why I'm here. Something made me move. I didn't want to leave Hayden when they got to the bakery, so I told Landon I'd let him know what happens and I took off after the ambulance. I want to be there when he wakes up so I know he's all right.

Inside, the hospital staff roll his stretcher into a large lobby and keep moving. I'm hard on their heels, and I barely notice Regina approaching. Before I can get through the swiftly closing double doors, she puts her hands up and stops me.

"Only family and partners beyond this point," Regina says. She's a younger nurse, dressed in her usual deep green scrubs. I know her from my summer internship. I know most of them here, but still, for a second I almost ignore her.

"But..." I start, my eyes darting between her and the closing doors. "I..."

"Kenzie!" she says like she just recognized me. "I didn't realize it was you. Do you know him?"

"He's...uh... He's my boyfriend..."

EVERY TIME THAT DOOR swings open, I pivot to attention. My nerves are ready to ignite. Is he all right? How bad is it? I need to know!

My watch—the cool old type with the hands on a blue background—says it's been four minutes since Regina made me wait out here and said she'd *see what she could do*. It feels like hours. It has to have been hours. Come on, Regina! Work your magic. If Marcia were here, I'd already be back there. She would have found a way.

I grip my necklace. It's a half-moon affixed to a small jar filled with the tiniest little amethyst stone, a sliver of cedarwood, horsetail, and lavender. My anxiety jar. It stays around my neck twenty-four seven.

Everything is going to be okay.
I have no reason to worry.
I am at peace.

Be calm. It's all going to be fine…but isn't the best intention the one followed up by action? I bite my lip and eye the door leading farther into the hospital. I know the hospital, sort of. Benefits of interning here. I could go back. Say hey to a few nurses if they're here. Who knows, maybe I'll happen across a certain guy's room. I shrug and before I know it, I'm on my feet.

The problem is getting through the first set of double doors and into Triage without being noticed. I could ask if Lenore is working, see if they'll let me go back to talk to her. She usually worked the evening shift. It could work. Maybe.

I get up and start toward the greeter's desk at the front of the ED entrance check-in. The nurse is younger, probably in her early twenties, straight black hair well past her shoulders, deep brown cheeks under green eyes. There is a security guard next to the desk, bent over with his elbows propped on its surface, back facing me. I can't make out more than his midnight-blue uniform with SECURITY in large bold letters across the back.

"Is Lenore here tonight?" I whisper, practicing as I cross the waiting room. I'm close. All that separates me from the desk is a row of chairs with a few ill-appearing people waiting to be seen. I practice again, "Is Lenore here? Can I go—"

A man's voice stops me in my tracks.

"Help! I think she's having a heart attack!" he yells, tugging a woman through the sliding glass doors and into the entrance of the ED while holding her under his arm. His face is taut, and dark circles hang under his eyes. He's struggling to keep the woman up, and our eyes meet. "Help!"

I'm closest, and for the second time tonight I rush forward to help a stranger. Looping my arm under her arm, I hoist up and move forward with him. I don't know this person. But here I am. The back of her shirt is wet; she's sweating and her breathing is shallow. She's heavy in our grip.

"She's barely breathing," he pleads as the nurse jumps into action and rounds the corner of the desk. Another comes out of nowhere with a wheelchair and starts calmly giving instructions.

"Here, sit her down." She motions to us as we keep moving. "Andrea, have Dalton turn a room, quick."

"On it." The nurse who was just behind the counter, Andrea, runs back to her post as we wheel who-knows-who past the ED doors and into the back of the ED.

A few steps in, Dalton—I assume—motions us into an empty room. In a whirlwind of structured chaos, the wheelchair is parked beside the stretcher and the men have hoisted the woman up and laid her onto the stretcher.

"Thank you." The nurse puts a hand on my shoulder. "You can go back to the waiting room and they will assist you there."

I don't move, but she's too worried about the patient to notice. Then as suddenly as it all happened, it hits me. I'm in the back of the ED. Did I just get back here without having to make up an excuse? I did. Oh my gods, I did! For a brief second I forget why I wanted to make it back here, but it comes rushing back in an instant. Hayden! And with it, the worry and dread. Please be okay, Hayden!

Where would he be? Trauma comes to mind, but I don't want to think it's that bad, so I wait long enough for the nurse with the wheelchair to disappear around the corner before I take the same route. I flatten against the wall and slide to the edge. A quick peek around the corner reveals a line of open doors along the right wall and an open desk on the other side. I think there were two nurses.

Just act natural and no one will question it. You can do it. Breathe, Kenzie.

Everyone says I'm a thrill seeker, especially Mom, and she hates it, but this isn't it. This is like go-to-jail-level thrill. Then again, trespassing abandoned buildings I guess is too…hmm…but still, it isn't the same. There aren't people there who I have to avoid. It's quiet, and empty, and eerie, not patrolled, and sterile, and in danger of violating HIPAA. Shit. This was such a bad idea.

You're here now. Just commit.

I suck in a big gulp of air and not at all stiffly swing around the corner and start down the hall. Walking has never felt this difficult before. *Right foot. Left foot. Right foot. Left foot. Don't make eye contact.* A set of nurses approach on my left, so I keep my eyes diverted, a little too interested in the posters about washing your hands and getting your flu vaccination. Look casu—

"Kenzie?" one of the nurses calls out just as I'm passing.

Shit. Uh…wait…is that…

"Amanda!" I yell, having to shove down the volume. *Remember. Hospital.*

She's one of the nurses I worked with over the summer. One of the more eclectic of the group, so she sucked me in immediately. Her blue-streaked hair is wrapped into a tight bun, and cute bat-shaped earrings frame a big smile and bright brown eyes.

"What are you doing here?" she asks.

"I...uh..." *Calm down, Kenzie. She's not suspicious, she's just asking.* What do I say though? I'm not supposed to be back here...but wait. She doesn't know that, and I *am* back here. "I'm trying to find my friend. I forgot the room number. Hayden...Hayden Marcus."

"Oh." She shrugs and starts typing at her computer. "Little young to be forgetting stuff, but we'll figure it out. How you been though?"

"Good." I nod too quickly. It's more like a spasm than a nod. "Just working and school."

"You a senior?" she asks, eyes flicking between me and the computer screen.

"I wish." I grin. "I'm a junior."

"Don't know why I keep thinking you're a senior," Amanda grunts. "Found them. He's in room 124."

She's reading something, so I spout a quick thanks and take off. I'm not letting any second thoughts keep me from getting to Hayden. A quick scan of the doors to my right tells me to keep going down the hall. I'm close. Only a few more rooms, but with each one I pass, the pressure in my chest builds. Is he okay? He wasn't conscious when they wheeled him away from me, and the bandage on his head was soaked in red. Please be okay!

Finally I find 124 stamped next to a big wooden door. I stop in front of it and pause, staring at the number like a stone statue. Is this a mistake? I shouldn't be here...right? A piece of me wants

How (Not) to Conjure a Boyfriend

to turn and run. But he's in there, and it's because of me. I didn't warn him about the floor when he was leaving, and he obviously didn't remember it was wet. I should have said something. I fill my lungs with air and let it slowly slip out between my lips just before I turn the doorknob and push it open.

The room is brightly lit. Sterile and white. Machines beep and whir. I think I hear a pump. Then there he is. Hayden. His eyes are closed, and he's laid out on his back on an inclined hospital bed under white and blue sheets that look much too cold. A bandage is wrapped around his forehead, and his left eye is swollen and purple.

My mouth gapes. No. Oh my gods, I'm so sorry, Hayden!

Instinct says to turn and run, to get this image of him out of my head, but I can't. I won't leave him like this. My eyes jump between his groggy swollen face, the leads attached to his forehead leading into some machine next to the bed, and the door as it closes behind me. I grip my necklace again. *Calm down. Take it slow. Breathe. Be intentional.*

I squeeze my necklace harder and walk to the bedside. He's so still and peaceful, and if it weren't for the bloated eye and bandages, I'd think he was just having a good nap. I want to say something, but what? Instead, I grip the metal railing on the bed. Should I touch his hand to let him know I'm here? No! Stop. That's just my head. It's not appropriate. He probably needs to sleep. *Just say something, but don't wake him.*

"Hey there, Hayden," I mumble, struggling to make eye contact even with his eyes closed. I focus on the clear tube hanging from one of the machines and follow it down to his arm. "It's Kenzie. Well, you probably know me as Mackenzie. You know, from the bakery…uh, Woodsy Café & Cakes. I'm the short one who usually makes your drinks."

What else can I say? How do I make sure he knows who I am? What am I thinking? He's asleep. He can't hear a word I'm saying. I roll my eyes at myself and go on anyway. I need to say something.

"U-uh, I'm the one with, uh, two different e-eye colors, green and blue. You might not have noticed that though," I say. Most people do, but I probably shouldn't assume. I think it freaks some people out. I'll catch their pupils darting from right to left, not sure which color to focus on. Do I focus on the bluish-gray one on the right or the muted sage green one on the left? "Most people call me Kenzie. Oh, I already said that. Sorry."

It's odd talking to someone who doesn't seem to be listening. Even if that someone is absolutely amazing and has the kindest smile, except he's not really smiling right now either.

"Sorry about what happened. I should have warned you. It's my fault. I'm so sorry. And I swear Landon didn't mean for you to slip," I tell him, leaning in closer to whisper. "Please don't sue him. He's horrified he's going to jail."

The thought makes me giggle, and I manage to look at Hayden's stoic face. He's so calm, and so am I now, as long as I don't focus on the purple bruise and bandages.

"You're still beautiful, even like this, you know?" I blush again. I can't believe I just said that to his literal face. "We've not *really* talked before, so I don't know what to say, but—"

"My baby." A woman's coarse voice shoots into the room followed by a stampede of feet.

"Hayden." An old gruff voice.

"Calm down, he's sleeping," an older lady says more quietly.

"He's in a coma, of course he's asleep," a small sarcastic voice replies.

A what? A coma?

I turn in time to see who's talking. She's young, super pale, a

How (Not) to Conjure a Boyfriend 31

blonde preteen at best. She darts for the bedside, and five more people pile into the room, focused on Hayden. An older gentleman who reminds me of the old actor in that Pedro Pascal comedy where they're trying to stop a drug lord while attempting to make a movie. A middle-aged woman with long nearly black hair, probably his mother, races to Hayden's bedside and clamps her fingers around the bedrail.

I shuffle back and cower in the corner. I don't know these people and they definitely don't know me. Did they even see me? And did she really say a coma? Is Hayden in a coma?! It can't be.

I contemplate running. They haven't seen me yet, and Mom's waiting for me at home for Thanksgiving dinner. She's probably blowing up my phone by now. I'm going to be in so much trouble. I eke a foot across the tan floor, trying not to make a noise. Only a few steps and I'll be out of trouble. One more step, another.

"Ahem."

I freeze, eyes locked on the group in front of me. They haven't noticed me yet. I manage to unfreeze just before I find Regina staring me down. Her eyes narrow, and I do the only thing I know to do. I smile. One of those big oops-you-caught-me grins. I half expect her to grab me by the arm and pull me out into the hallway, but instead she sighs and shakes her head, although a gentle rise in her cheek belies a subtle smile. Before I can mouth a silent *thank you*, the tall slender middle-aged woman starts up.

"My poor baby boy." She leans against Hayden's bed, cupping his head in her palm. She's pretty. Her hair hangs in long wavy strands of black. From a glance, her eyes are dark-dark brown. Is that Mrs. Marcus? His mom? "Mama's here."

Yep.

"Who's that?" The preteen's voice pierces the room. She's pointing directly at me, arm stretched out like she's pointing out a witch in Salem. Okay, I am a witch, but we're not burning them nowadays.

"Uh, I-I..." I stutter.

"Who are you?" That must be Mr. Marcus. I'm frozen again. He's distinguished. Shorter than Hayden's mom, but that might be the high heels she's wearing. His blue eyes shine with confusion. His tone isn't angry like I expected, just confused.

"I'm...uh..." I try again, but the words aren't coming to me. Why did I come? This was such a bad idea!

"They're Mackenzie. Hayden's boyfriend," Regina says so very matter-of-factly, I almost break my neck to look at her. I freeze up again.

What? No, Regina! It isn't true. How? Why would you think I'm his enbyfriend, boyfriend, whatever? Like, I never said that...or...oh shit. Okay, maybe I did. Yeah, I did say he was my boyfriend, didn't I? And I did tell them about him over the summer... Shit. Okay, fine, but in my defense I also told them there wasn't a chance in Niflhel that it would happen. People say that all the time about their crushes. No one believes me when I say I'm going to marry Pedro Pascal or that *he's* my boyfriend. So why now? Fine, but what do I do? What do I say? Before I can decide, the oldest lady in the room speaks up.

"Hayden went for a handsome one." She's smiling from ear to ear, and now I'm blushing like a rose. Grandmother maybe?

"Right?" A short and plump, oddly familiar-looking woman with nearly midnight-black skin nods at me and grins. I swear I've seen her before.

"Well...I u-uh..." I keep stuttering. *Dammit, Kenzie, pull it together*. "Actually, I'm his enbyfriend."

Shit! No!

"Sorry, right." Regina nods. "I should have known that."

"It's okay," I tell her. "Easy mistake. It doesn't bother me."

"Enbyfriend, boyfriend, girlfriend." His dad, Mr. Marcus, lists, his eyes blinking rapidly. "Hayden didn't have a—"

"Person." Ms. Familiar speaks up quickly. Her expression morphing from stern into a smile as she looks my way again, knowingly. And that accent! New Orleans? Maybe a Baton Rouge backstory I'd like to figure out. Wait... The apothecary! It's her! She works at The Good Hex. I remember now! I go there all the time, and she's super sweet, funny even, and now she's here.

I can feel the color drain from my face.

"Huh? Oh, yeah." Mr. Marcus nods. "Person. Did he?"

He locks eyes with Mrs. Marcus and she frowns. "I-uh... Not that he told me."

"He wasn't ready to yet," I blurt. *Gods, Kenzie, why can't you just keep your mouth shut.* "He wanted to be s-sure...uh... Sure that you would approve. You know, of him...being with me."

It's a lie. It's a bold-faced bona fide Grade A lie. Loki might even be proud, but what the hell am I thinking? I'm not. It's like my mouth is running without giving the tiniest thought as to what it's going to get me into. I'm just a helpless passenger.

"Oh, honey." Mrs. Marcus looks back at Hayden and puts a palm on his cheek. "You can date whoever you want—"

"As long as they're not forty or a murderer," the older blonde lady, Grandma maybe, says.

"Or a Duke fan." The man whose arm is intertwined with hers laughs. She jabs his side, and he grunts.

For a second it breaks the pit in my stomach and allows a grin to replace the tight straight line along my lips. It's probably safe to guess that's his grandpa.

Mr. Marcus rolls his eyes.

"You're the kid from the café, aren't you?" the apothecary lady says, and I want to disappear into nothing. What is her name? I know this!

"Yes, ma'am," I whisper.

"That's great," she says to me and then addresses the rest of the crowd. "They're a sweet one. They come to the shop a lot."

"You two know each other?" the young girl asks. It could be his sister, if he has one.

I nod now that it's out there. Eliza! That's her name.

"More like acquaintances."

"Oh." Mrs. Marcus seems bewildered. I can't blame her. First your kid is in a coma—I think that's what they said—and then you learn he has a supposed enbyfriend. She looks from Eliza to her husband, worry etching creases in her cheeks. "We didn't know about, you know... Why wouldn't he tell us?"

"I don't know. Maybe..." Mr. Marcus stumbles, "...he *wasn't* ready?"

"They also saved his life," the doctor interrupts out of nowhere. I hadn't noticed her enter, but she's giving me a warm smile, so I'll let it pass. I use the moment to check her name tag. Dr. Melody Kline. Okay, Melody, doctor, *saved his life* might be a stretch. I should have warned him so it never even happened. "Had they not acted so fast, the damage could have been much worse."

It's like Dr. Kline is trying to butter me up for Hayden's family. Help lessen the impact and make all this new information more palatable.

"You saved his life?" Grandma tilts her head and smiles at me. "That's good enough for me."

"I'm sorry, I just thought... You know what? It doesn't matter." Mrs. Marcus steps toward me. "If Hayden loves you, then you're family."

Loves? That's a bit much. We could have just started dating.

Loves? That's much too big a step. My head feels like it's beginning to wobble. *Breathe, Kenzie.* I feel myself sinking deeper into the pit. Which is weird, because I've wanted to be Hayden's for months, but this? I wasn't planning on this.

"It's okay." I squirm. What do I say to that? And a coma? The thought is racing through my head. Like an actual coma? "Thank you."

Suddenly I'm an introvert. This is so not me. Sure, when Hayden walks in the shop I get cold feet and my words make no sense, but that's because it's him. This never happens otherwise. I can talk to anyone. But here I am, completely at a loss for what to say. And worse, why am I going along? It's not true. This is going to blow up so bad in a second. Plus, I'm supposed to be home. I have to go. That's it. That's how I get out of here.

"I gotta go." I start stepping toward the door. "My mom's waiting on me."

"Can I get your number, dear?" his mom asks, and holds her phone out.

I pause.

"So I can keep you up on how he's doing," Mrs. Marcus says. Her head tilts and her dark brown eyes glint suspicion. Or maybe that's just my head talking.

Should I just make an excuse and leave? No, that would be rude. *Just do it.* I grin nervously and accept the phone. I am in so much trouble. I take her phone and tap in my number.

"I think he'd want us to keep you in the know," she says as I hand back the phone.

I nod and scoot backward.

"Thank you," I say, dipping my eyes to the floor. "I really have to go now."

5

"**YOU'RE NOT GOING TO** believe what happened tonight!" I yell at my phone.

Kaitlynn's on the screen. She's lying in bed with her face propped between her hands. Immediately I get the side-eye.

"What did you do?" she asks.

"What did *I* do?" I adjust my hold on my phone so she can see the string of photo cards hanging from my bedposts and the K-pop light sticks arranged along the wall. It looks better than the nightstand. Especially with Nicholas from &TEAM's soul-piercing gaze in the middle. "What do you mean, what did *I* do? Why do you assume I did something?"

She raises an eyebrow and stares me down. Finally she breaks. "Please tell me you didn't destroy the espresso machine. I can't deal with that when I open tomorrow."

"No, no!" I wave it off. I am clumsy, but come on. I roll my eyes and brace myself before revealing what actually happened. "I, well...I'm Hayden's enbyfriend now?"

The video chat goes silent. Kaitlynn raises her chin from her hands and squints. She pooches her lips, then opens her mouth but stops short of speaking. Then again. And again.

Just say it! Whatever it is, just say it! Please!

"Was that supposed to be a question?" she asks.

"I mean, sort of." I shrug.

She stares me down again, still squinting.

"I'm sorry," Kaitlynn blurts into the quiet and puts her pointer finger to her lips like she's in deep thought. "Okay, but...like... How?"

It's rare to see Kaity at a loss for words, but here we are. I'm not sure if I should be hurt or amused.

"That's a whole story," I tell her, scratching the side of my head. On my phone, in the little space that shows me, I notice my curly hair is a little out of place, so I run a hand through it. Better.

She wiggles and settles back onto her hands. "It's tea time then."

I take a deep breath, trying to remember everything that went down tonight. It feels like a lot. I'm still trying to make sense of it all. Sitting through Thanksgiving dinner with Mom in near silence except for the occasional, and very awkwardly timed, question about school was excruciating. She did ask where I'd been, and I told her. I just left out some key details. Such as the boyfriend part. I didn't dare bring that up. She knows I've been crushing on Hayden, but she would have had too many questions I don't have answers to.

"So..." I drag it out as you do at the beginning of any good story, and this one's a doozy. "Hayden came to the shop—"

"Like he always does," Kaitlynn interrupts.

I let her finish before continuing, "—before we closed. Yeah. But tonight was different. Like he *talk* talked to me."

"*To* you?" Kaitlynn questions.

"Yes!" I defend my words, then backtrack. "I mean, to us. Me and Landon."

"Right," she sighs.

I roll my eyes. "That's just the beginning. He was really sweet and— Oh, and he got something different tonight instead of his Sinnercake. He got one of the pumpkin breads that *I* made. Yeah, but like I said, he was sweet and even told me, well *us*, to have a good Thanksgiving—"

"Like any half-decent human being," Kaitlynn cuts in again. "When does this get interesting?"

"Can I just tell my story?" I beg.

She looks away all sus and pops her eyes wide. It's her way of saying, *Damn, fine*. I make a mental note to try to cut it down a little. I do have a tendency to ramble sometimes.

"*As* I was saying," I start back up. "He wished us a good Thanksgiving and then was about to leave. But Landon had mopped the dining area. Hayden slipped and fell. Like hard."

The way Kaitlynn's eyes pop is probably about like mine when it happened. "Oh!"

"Yeah. He fell and hit his head on a table. I think he had a seizure. I held him so he wouldn't hurt his head any worse, and then I ended up at the hospital with him."

"Wait, you held him?" she asks.

I can't help but smile. "Yeah. But not, like, romantic or anything."

"Of course," she laughs.

I left out the part about Landon freaking out, but it's not important to the story and she's already impatient enough.

"Where was I? You distracted me." I grin, the thought of my hands wrapped around him for that brief moment running through my head, trying to ignore the fact that he was shaking uncontrollably.

"You went to the hospital with him..."

"Yes." I nod. "Well, they took him back but wouldn't let me go with them at first. But I snuck back and Regina—she's one of the nurses I worked with over the summer, remember?" I ask but don't wait for a reply. "Well, she thought I was his boyfriend, which is sort of my fault, but—"

"Nope, enbyfriend," Kaitlynn says before I get a chance to tell her I did correct them.

"Yeah, exactly. So his family came and she told them!"

"Oh." Kaitlynn's eyes bloom even larger. "They think...you're his enbyfriend."

I nod. "And now he's in a coma, and they want me to—"

"Whoa, wait, he's in a what?" Kaity interrupts.

"—come to Thanksgiving." *Okay, slow down, Kenzie.* "A coma, he's asleep, like involuntarily."

"I know what a coma is, bitch, I've just never known anyone in one," she comes back.

"Yeah, it's crazy. I feel so bad because it happened at the shop," I tell her. "But then his whole family arrived."

"Oh wow." A smile creeps across her face with this knowing pleasure that I must have been horrified.

"Yeah, yeah, shut up. It was horrifying!" I tell her. "They didn't have a clue who I was, and one of them...gods, I can't remember who, I think it was one of the grand...no! It was some girl who's younger than us. She asked who I was, and then everyone was looking at me."

"Dayum," Kaitlynn laughs. "All eyes on you, babe!"

I ignore her. "They were confused at first, but then it was like boom, hey, Hayden's enbyfriend, you're now part of the family."

Hold on a second. I didn't see Hayden's brother there. Wonder where he was? It's no matter. Whatever.

"Are you serious?" Kaitlynn sounds totally befuddled.

"I know, right?" I lean back on my pillow. "I still can't believe it."

"But wait." Kaitlynn stops me and smacks her lips. "You two aren't dating though, right? Like I didn't miss something, did I? Did he ask you out before he hit his head?"

"That's where things go off the tracks," I tell her, looking away and letting a mouthful of air explode from between my lips. "We *aren't* dating. I mean not officially. He never asked—"

"And you never asked." She just has to bring it up too.

"Yeah, but we are now...sort of."

It's a technicality, really. Everyone thinks we are. He just doesn't know it yet. Oh gods. Am I a horrible person? I give my necklace a squeeze.

"Sort of? So you're *not*." She's right. She's one hundred percent right, but his family still thinks I am, and even worse, I'm supposed to have dinner with them tomorrow.

"Yeah, true," I say as my shoulders deflate. "I know. But, like, they all think I am. And I actually got to *talk*-talk to him tonight. They say he can hear."

"So he's probably screaming for everyone not to listen to you," Kaitlynn laughs. "Bad witch."

I ignore it and instead try to think how I'd even go about telling his family the truth without sounding like a total and complete asshole. Nothing comes to mind.

"But, like, how do I break it to them? Now they think their son was a closeted gay, or bi, or something, pan maybe, I guess. I don't know." I start to ramble, and I know it, but oh well. "They think he was afraid to tell them. And they think I was his secret lover because I saved—"

"Whoa! Saved him might be a bit much." Kaity knocks me down a notch. "You just called an ambu—"

"*And* stayed with him at the hospital," I stress.

"—lance." She laughs again.

"Bitch," I giggle. "Still. Now I'm supposed to have a late Thanksgiving dinner with them tomorrow."

Before I got home, Hayden's mom, Mary-Anne as I now know her, sent me a text inviting me to their Thanksgiving tomorrow night. I was not expecting that, and instead of thinking it over, I immediately texted back that I'd be there. "Oh! And you know the pretty New Orleans woman who works at The Good Hex, right?"

"Uh, not like personally, but yeah. What's she got to do with this?" she asks.

"She's Hayden's aunt!" I squeal.

"Excuse me?" Kaitlynn yelps. "Did she recognize you? And Thanksgiving dinner? With *them*? *Tomorrow night*? Bitch, you were supposed to do that at my house tomorrow."

"Yeah, she did, and uh, about that…" I start to whisper. I'm going to have to do a protection spell for myself tonight after this bit. "They didn't get to have their Thanksgiving because they got called to the hospital. And when his mom texted me about it, I freaked out. How could I say no?"

"Uh… No. Or maybe no in Spanish, nada, or nein, or non. See? There's a bunch of ways." She eyes me down through my phone screen.

"Kaity," I whine. Yeah, I should have said no, but I couldn't.

"Ugh!" she growls. "Fine. Ditch me for your new fake boyfriend's family. He'd be *your* boyfriend, right? Only you're *his* enbyfriend? Like, *if* it were real."

"Yes." I huff and roll my eyes. I'm doing that a lot tonight.

"Honestly." Kaitlynn rolls her eyes back. "You'd be stupid if you didn't try to make this work somehow, right?"

"Really?" I beam.

"Probably not, but maybe. Who gets to date their crush without being asked out? This is crazy. But this doesn't mean you get to keep ditching me."

I smile and put my free hand into view with only my pinky finger up.

"Pinky promise," I tell her, and she does the same.

"Pinky promise."

Once the screen goes blank, I fall back against my pillow and laugh for no reason at all. This is really happening. It's not just a dream. At least, I don't think it is. And so far, it's a good dream with just a little dash of anxiety.

6

LIL WOOZI—my car, because like Woozi, it's a little thing—is squealing. *Please don't blow a gasket, whatever that is.* The engine is whining so loudly, I can barely hear XG's intense voices, and the volume is maxed out. I have the pedal to the floor just to keep him at fifty-five. After a quarter million miles, I think he's on his last good days. Although *good days* might be a bit too optimistic.

What doesn't help is living in the literal mountains and Hayden's family living even farther up them than I do. If someone had told me that it'd take forty minutes to get from my place to theirs, I might have reconsidered. That's just shy of a full hour for my anxiety to wreak havoc on my stomach. My phone says it's only another five minutes, but there's no sign of a home yet. It's all the same up here. Road, grass, trees, repeat. Nothing is close up here.

I tried to get Kaitlynn to come with me. Okay, I begged her, but she flat-out refused. Something about me needing to get to know my "boyfriend's" parents by myself. That hasn't stopped my head from waffling between scenarios. Maybe this is all some weird sort of awful/cool dream, or maybe it's real somehow—but then the existential dread sets in full force—or maybe my potions the other night had something a little bit stronger in them than I realized.

Either way I nearly turned around ten minutes ago. I was so close to saying forget it, but instead I'm driving under endless barren trees and a dark and puffy sky. I relish every glimpse of the moon when its paper-thin sliver manages to get through. Its faint glow is a glint of reassurance that it's going to be okay, even though the road looks never-ending and disappears into a black nothing beyond the reach of my headlights.

A minute later my headlights reflect against something up ahead. I blink as if that'll help, and finally see a little hanging sign. It swings in the wind as I draw closer, my engine still fighting for air. This is why I don't drive too late, if possible. I'd wake people up, plus all the lights have halos around them at night. I squint. The lettering goes from blurry to finely engraved silver lines that read *MARCUS ESTATE*.

"Estate?" What the hell? I knew Hayden wasn't poor—he drives a nice *new* black truck—but I didn't assume he was *estate* wealthy. "Wow."

I turn down the driveway. My tires clonk along the washed gray stone drive while a charcoal-gray barrier rises to my left, shielding my view of a drop-off. Ahead I catch lights, and then the shape of a house starts to form, but it's not what I expect. My mind had conjured up one of those old money Southern homes with perfect symmetry, lots of ornately framed windows, most likely a chimney or two, maybe some columns, and either lots of brick or a lot of white paint.

That's not at all what's forming ahead though. It's not quaint or old-fashioned. It's modern AF. Black monolithic pillars jut into the air, framing large glass panes with sheer ivory curtains standing guard between wooden walls. Gray concrete barriers are erected around parts of the perimeter with outdoor lounge furniture under towering evergreen trees. There are no slopes or shingles. It's built in hard lines, flat roofs, like a bunch of cubes laid one next to another, but it's gorgeous. And the road adjacent to the house is filled with cars. It seems the others are all here already, so reluctantly I brake and my tires come to a mostly smooth stop.

"Wow." I gawk at the house. It's pristine and ethereal, surrounded by towering trees under a sky that's threatening rain. Like a fortress, but one that still feels...I don't know. Calming? I lean toward the rearview mirror and check my makeup. It's simple. I had to give my face a little color to cover up all the pale, and my winged black eyeliner is actually looking really good.

"What am I doing? This is so stupid." My heart is pounding. I shouldn't be here. This is wrong. I don't belong with Hayden's family inside *that* house. I just don't.

I close my eyes and shift Lil Woozi into reverse. The engine shudders but follows my lead. *Just go.* I turn to look over my shoulder, and I'm so close to pressing the accelerator when headlights flash around the bend and settle in behind me. "Shit."

Now I'm stuck. I face forward and fall back against my seat. What do I do now?

"Kenzie!"

I jump. They're already standing at my window, bent down looking at me. It's Eliza. That was quick and stealthy! I face my window and smile. It's only partially fake. I pull the handle and pop my door open. The window motor has been out a few months and I don't exactly have window repair money sitting around.

"Hi." I lean out from under the doorframe to meet her eyes.

"Trying to escape already?" she asks.

"Huh?" I play confused. "What?"

"I usually wait until after dinner," she tells me. "Randall thinks everyone wants to hear about his cases—no one has the heart to tell that poor man they don't."

She shrugs and huffs. I laugh. It sounds fake, but it's funny that she's dissing one of them to the new person right before Thanksgiving dinner. And cases? Who is Randall?

Eliza nods toward the house. "You ready to go in?"

"U-uh...yeah," I say, but don't immediately get out of the car.

"One second, I brought something."

I take a quick moment to pinch my necklace between my fingers and ask Freyja to calm me down while I reach across the center console. I scoop up the covered plate I brought and get out.

"That's sweet of you. Mary-Anne *is* going to protest, but still sweet," Eliza says.

Mary-Anne? Right, the mom. Gods, this is going to end badly. I don't know most of their names, but I have to act like I do, or at least that they sound familiar. I would have heard them *if* I were dating Hayden, right?

"Oops," I laugh. "I wasn't sure what to bring, so I made a batch of pecan pie brownies. Hope no one else did."

"That sounds amazing. They'll love that." Eliza grins and I follow her to the front door.

Unlike the rest of the house, there's a stone slab with a sliver of a window down the middle. A wooden-plank door sets to the left of the slab with a long, vertical brushed-metal bar nearly my height along the face. It's so modern. Eliza pulls the bar and the door swings open without a sound.

This is *so* out of my league.

My nose is blessed by a scent of apple mingled with the smell of so many different foods. Sweet potatoes for sure. I sniff and catch a whiff of something salty—green beans maybe?

"Kenzie!" My name becomes a chorus of voices.

The first I notice is Mr. Marcus standing behind a large tan sofa behind Grandpa, who hasn't noticed me yet. He's caught up in the football game playing on a massive screen. If this is the living room, it's almost the size of my entire house. Then Grandma in a sleek but somehow cushy-looking armchair next to an adorable, even older lady I haven't met before. His sister is at the other edge of the large room with some tall blonde-haired guy who looks to be about the same age as Mr. Marcus. Eliza walks up to him and hooks his arm in hers.

"Kenzie!" Grandpa's gruff voice yanks me away from the horror of more unknown faces.

"Hey, everyone." I nod nervously. I can't remember a time I've entered a room and had my name yelled out.

"I must be chopped liver," Eliza grumbles, but she's smiling.

"Aw, no you're not, honey." The blonde guy pulls Eliza closer and kisses her check. So maybe Eliza and whoever he is are the aunt and uncle?

"There are children present." The little girl rolls her eyes.

He leans in and starts to peck her cheeks over and over again.

Eliza mumbles something he finds funny apparently, then turns and throws me a lifeline. "I'm guessing you're not too sure who's who."

It's like she read my mind. I grin big and shake my head.

"Okay then." She squeezes blondie. "This here is my man, Hayden's Uncle Jeffrey. Hands off."

Of course, it's all framed by Hayden. But that's great, because I'd have a time mapping out the entire family dynamic otherwise. I laugh at her comment. She's without a doubt my favorite.

"This is Randall" — she points to the man I've been calling Mr. Marcus — "Hayden's dad. He likes to talk."

"I have lots to discuss." Mr. Marcus, or Randall, comes back with an amused smile still planted on his face.

"This is Randall Sr." She points to Grandpa. "Randall's dad, Hayden's grandfather. We call him Gramps."

"Welcome, sonny." Gramps nods. Gruff. Balding head, peppered hair. Blue eyes that seem to run in the family — minus Hayden — and a small budding gut. I wish I could place the actor's name I have in my head. Nick comes to mind, but that's it.

"They're nonbinary, Gramps." The only other kid in the room speaks up, looking at me apologetically. I grin back but don't say anything.

"She's mine." Eliza grins proudly at the girl.

"I'm Catina." The girl throws her hand up like it's roll call, with a big smile showing perfect white teeth between dimples that redden her brown cheeks.

"Huh? So what's that mean? He don't eat meat?" Gramps asks, not an ounce of sarcasm in his voice.

I bite my lips to keep from bursting into laughter. The girl is visibly holding back too, as well as Jeffrey. Eliza's lips are turned inward as she breathes in a deeply. The smell of sweet potatoes is almost too much now. Overriding the moment for just a split second. I'm hungry.

"Moving on." Eliza ignores the question while Gramps peers around the room in obvious confusion. I, for one, am not answering that question. "This is Gramps's wife, Kristi, grand—"

"You can call me Kiki," Grandmother interrupts, her voice high and proper like her meticulously styled dyed-blonde hair. She gives off very esteemed matriarchal vibes.

"Or Grandma," Eliza whispers. I nod at Kiki, yeah, probably Grandma for me.

Eliza moves on to the oldest person in the room. She's seated in a comfy-looking black armchair by a floor-to-ceiling glass pane. There's something interesting in her blue eyes, something mischievous. Maybe it's her big drooping smile, or the way she bobs back and forth, or maybe it's the piece of fabric looped about her long wavy gray hair. She screams eccentric, or maybe it's just fun. "This is Gran. She's Mary-Anne's mom, Hayden's grandmother."

"Call me Gran, cutie!" she trills, repeating exactly what Eliza already said. I smile and nod, again trying not to laugh. She sounds like she might have been a smoker back in her day but managed to bypass its ills. "Or if you like, you can call me Super Old Gran like Hayden and Zachary."

"S-super old?" I sputter. And Zachary? Is that Hayden's brother? The one who wouldn't come into the shop?

"That's Randall's fault." Mrs. Marcus comes walking into the room, rubbing her hands on a small kitchen towel. The apron she's wearing sashays gracefully around her hips as she steps next to her husband.

"I like it," Gran croaks. "It's cute."

"And this is Mary-Anne, Hayden's mom." Eliza holds out her hand toward Mrs. Marcus.

Honestly, I think I'm still going with Mr. and Mrs. Marcus, but at least now I'll know who they're talking about.

"And I'm Holly!" The little blonde girl cuddled up next to Mr. Marcus waves frantically at me.

"Hayden's sister." Eliza giggles as I wave back and smile. "Thought you might already know them."

She can't be more than twelve or thirteen. I've always wanted a little sister or little brother. I'm already jealous.

"That's everyone except Zachary." Mrs. Marcus looks to Eliza and then me. "He's on his way back from the hospital right now."

"It's wonderful to meet you all...again?" I question, hoping it might break some of the tension in my chest.

There are a few grunts and laughs while Eliza directs me around the sofa. "It helps to put names with faces. I'm sure Hayden's mentioned at least a few of us."

That'd be a great assumption *if* I were actually his enbyfriend. I fight the impulse to puff and lower my head. Instead I nod and smile. Looks like I'm going to be doing a lot of that tonight. I don't want to say, nah, he never mentioned any of y'all. It'd be easiest, plus the truth, but it feels cheap and mean. So instead I deflect.

"Where would you like me to put these?" I hold up the plate of brownies.

Mrs. Marcus stands straighter. "Oh! You really didn't need to bring anything."

Eliza nudges my arm and the tiniest of amused grins slips on my face. "It was no trouble. I promise. I love to cook."

"Now it makes sense." Mr. Marcus, Randall, laughs to himself. "Hayden would fall for a cook."

"I guess that's all right then." Mrs. Marcus laughs at him and walks over to take the plate from me. "I'll take them to the kitchen. You sit down. Food *is* ready, *but* we're waiting for Zachary."

"Have a seat. Get comfy." Mr. Marcus pats an empty spot on the smoke-gray sofa next to theirs.

There is so much room in here. Oddly, somehow, it doesn't feel empty with all the empty space, just open and clean. *Very* clean. I take a seat. The stiff but comfortable leather gives under me and cradles my back.

"Thank you for having me." I bow my head. "Y'all have such a beautiful place."

I cross one leg over the other with my hands clasped on my knee, and I'm suddenly feeling overdressed. Everyone else is in flannels and jeans or something casual, except Kiki, who's sporting a fitted white long-sleeved shirt with frills down the chest. Maybe I should have asked what the dress code was going to be. I ended up in black skinny jeans held up by a fake Valentino belt with its fancy golden buckle, and then my favorite black sleeveless turtleneck along with a set of black arm socks. My bare shoulders are freezing, but I look cute so that's what matters. Plus, I need to make a good first impression here.

"Thank you." Mr. Marcus nods and settles back on the couch.

"And all thanks to the divorcees and—"

"Stop!" Mrs. Marcus grumbles as she walks away. "It sounds so bad when you say that."

And what? Now I want to know. Divorcees? Kiki sees the confusion on my face, I guess, because she leans over and pats my back.

"Randall, Jr. here is a family and personal injury lawyer," Kiki, or Granny, or whatever I was supposed to call her, explains. I think I know why Mary-Anne wanted him to stop now. "He uses humor to cope with all the shady lawyer junk."

Shady lawyer junk? Okay, what have I gotten myself into? They seemed so normal at the hospital, but are they? I mean, this house is huge, it's elegant. Hayden's dad is a lawyer and, unless I'm taking it all wrong, shady?

"Uh..." I hesitate.

"You're making me sound like some sleazy lawyer, Mom, come on." Mr. Marcus shakes his head, but he's smiling.

"Okay, he's not *that* shady." Kiki smiles at him and then me before putting her hand up, fist closed, with her pointer finger and thumb out, barely touching. "Just a little."

Hayden's dad rolls his eyes and sighs. "At least my work doesn't give me back problems."

Gramps shrugs. I'm guessing there's something I'm not catching. Does Gramps still work? How old is he?

A few minutes go by and the conversation goes from the house to Holly's last softball season at the middle school. The coach at Mitchell High School is already asking about her. I guess that's a good sign for her. My world of sports only goes as far as spectating an occasional football or basketball game and then rallying at Cook Out until one in the morning with Kaitlynn and a horde of others from school.

How (Not) to Conjure a Boyfriend   51

"Mackenzie, tell us a little about you." Kiki angles her head and fastens her regal gaze on me. Her words are like a refined coo. There's something calming in them.

"Well, there isn't much to tell." I start off on a negative note, the way you're one hundred percent not supposed to with your boyfriend's family. I resist the urge to cough back an imaginary knot in my throat. "I work at the Woodsy Café."

"In downtown? Over by The Good Hex?" Kiki questions in one of the most polite tones I've ever heard.

I nod. "Yep. I go to school at Mount Laurel. I root for Mitchell though."

"There you go. That's a good one," Mr. Marcus roars, fist pumping toward me.

Joke is I don't follow any sports unless Hayden's playing. I couldn't care less otherwise.

"Got to cheer on my —" I'm about get it out, but a voice interrupts me.

"We eating or not?" A boy I've only seen from a distance behind a pane of glass glides around the corner and stops between us and the kitchen. That must be Zachary. Hold the hell up. The brother's hot too? Fuck my life. He's shorter than Hayden, not like way shorter, but I'd say he's under six foot with the same amazing eyes. Those gorgeous smoky grays, but they're darker and there's a sheen to them I don't remember in Hayden's. Almost a metallic gray. They're gorgeous.

"Thank God." Gramps fumbles out of his chair and starts past Zachary. "I was about to revert to cannibalism had your ass not shown up sooner."

My eyes widen. Did he just say *ass*? In front of us? A grin sneaks across my face. I like Gramps.

"I gotcha, Gramps," Zachary says just as his gaze meets mine and the smile lifting up his cheeks disappears.

Oh! What did I do?

"Language, Dad!" Mr. Marcus says while *his* dad throws a hand back. "We don't need Kenzie thinking we're barbarians."

"It's okay," I say. This is great.

"Eh!" Gramps waves him off and lumbers on, grabbing Zachary up in a big hug.

Kiki grins at me while Mr. Marcus sighs. *Focus on Kiki*.

"If *I'm* not allowed to say *bad* words, then you can't either, Gramps," Holly whines and races him to the kitchen.

"How's Hayden?" Mary-Anne leans around the corner as we all get up.

"Alive? I think," Zachary says.

"Zachary Elliot!" Mary-Anne chides.

"He's in a coma." He shrugs. "I guess he's good."

Mary-Anne grunts and turns around with an annoyance-glazed smile. "Dig in, everyone."

Gramps and Holly hadn't waited. He's already at the edge of the large center island with the beautiful butcher's block top, plate in hand, scooping a generous helping of baked beans. I glance back to get another look at Zachary. Hayden never wore pants like that. Tight around the thighs and shaping. Hayden's hair is more brown. Zachary's is nearly black and whooshed back with product, where Hayden's bursts over the front of his forehead in soft plumes.

I overhear Catina asking what a dish near the center is, and Mary-Anne takes a quick look before saying it's broccoli casserole. My eyes widen and I involuntarily lick my lips. I love broccoli casserole. I ground myself back on the food, until I spot the turkey and ham set at the start of the line next to bowls of gravy and pineapple glaze. My mouth is watering from the smell alone. If it tastes anywhere near as good as it all looks, I'm going to be in pain tonight.

How (Not) to Conjure a Boyfriend

Before I can get in line behind Gran, a spindly arm wraps around the crook of my elbow and pulls. Holly. I don't know what to do, so I just follow. The food will still be there in another minute.

"This is Kenzie," Holly says, presenting me to Zachary like I'm some cool animal she found outside. She looks up at me and nods toward Zachary. "This is Zach, he's annoying."

"I'm not annoying. You're just whiny," Zachary scoffs, and pokes Holly's shoulder. She squeals playfully as he retracts and looks at me. "And I know who they are. Wasn't hard to figure out."

What? He knows who I am? And he said *they*, not *he*? I fight back a curious squint.

"Hey," I say, hoping this is over quick so I can stop focusing so hard on making eye contact. His eyes are so gorgeous it's literally intimidating. Why can't he be an ugly brother?

"So, you're Hayden's enbyfriend, huh?" Zach asks, but it's not a simple question. There's accusation in his voice.

"Yeah." I bounce my shoulders as if to say *so what?* I need to make myself believe it if I'm going to survive here. That's part of selling the lie, right? Gods, I'm a horrible person, but he's got me on edge. Everyone else just went with it. He's challenging it with nothing more than inflection.

A moment goes by and he doesn't respond, he doesn't say a word. He just stands there, eyes boring into my very being. If they weren't so pretty and my outrageous lie didn't depend on it right now, I'd look away. Say something, Zach. I'd rather you accuse me in front of everyone than to have a stare-down. I'm about to buckle when he squints harder and his lips move.

"What's his favorite sport?"

"Huh?" I'm thrown off by the sudden question.

"Sport. What's Hayden's favorite sport?" Zachary asks again, his words thicker.

"Uh…" I stumble. Trivia? About Hayden? You want to quiz me to make sure I'm who I say I am. I know this though. "Basketball. He plays for Mitchell."

"Okay." Zach rocks his head from side to side, eyes searching for another question. "When's his birthday?"

I start to open my mouth, but stop. Was it May or April? I remember this. He came in with a friend, some oddly tall guy I think he called Anthony, on his birthday this year, and I put it in my phone. Okay, maybe that's a little weird, but it was a fact about him I wanted to keep. But when was it? I know it was on the twenty-second, but was it April or May?

A grin rises on Zachary's face. He knows he's got me, but I'm not getting outed for not remembering Hayden's birthday! I'm about to blurt May, but Mary-Anne speaks first.

"Zach, what's gotten into you?" Mary-Anne scolds while I try to determine how bad getting it wrong would actually be. Just because I get it wrong doesn't necessarily mean we're not a couple, just that we're not *there* yet. Right?

"Nothing. I'm good." Zachary puts a hand up.

If I did that, my mom would be doing more right now than giving me a grimace. Must be nice.

"The twenty-second," I blurt. I have to say something quick or they'll all get suspicious, and I don't want tonight to end that way. I want to have dinner with a nice family and feel like I belong, then get the hell out of Dodge. "Of May."

Yes! That's it. Because it was close to Memorial Day when they came in and his friend bought him a whole-ass cake for his birthday.

"O—" Zachary starts, but his mom cuts in.

"What is going on?" Mary-Anne shrugs, leaning over the kitchen island.

"Nothing, just a little fun quizzing. That's it." He squints at me then slaps my shoulder and smiles. "You pass."

I don't know whether to scream, cry, or laugh. Maybe it would've been better had I gotten it wrong and they all figured it out now. That way I could have run out the door, sped home, and rocked myself to sleep in tears, but it would be over. Now I have to keep it up. Is that so bad though? I glance around the room at all the happy faces and I'm reminded of all that I'm missing in life. I huff and return Zach's smile, hoping it comes off as genuine. *Just get this over with.*

Zachary starts toward the line, but not before scooting in closer and whispering in my ear, "I still don't believe you."

Before I can panic, I grip my necklace and breathe while putting on an annoyed face just for him. Something that hopefully says he's being unreasonable. Something to convince him he's wrong about being right. He waves his hand toward the line, like some southern gentleman with a side of deviousness, and I get back in line. He falls in behind. I swear to the gods I can feel his eyes lasering into the back of my head, trying to search for that clue he needs to out me as a fraud. *Just breathe, Kenzie. Breathe.*

Plate full, I take a seat at the family's massive pine table. It's so large it seats six people per side, and a pale sandy-brown cloth runner splits it down the center. Yet somehow, Zachary still manages to get a seat across from me. He's staring me down, but I refuse to make eye contact. No matter how much I can feel him looking at me, judging me, I'm making the best of this super weird situation.

"Dad, would you say grace for us?" Mr. Marcus asks as I'm about to dig in.

I drop my spoon heaped full of broccoli casserole back to my plate and droop my shoulders, mostly involuntarily. Gods, I probably look sheepish. Usually I'd just bless my own food and dive in. The rest of my friends aren't religious, so they don't even bother, and group dinners... I've not had one of those in a while. I about yelp when Super Old Gran's cold soft hand grabs mine and holds it atop the table. Then Catina reaches out to me and does the same. I let her, giving her my best attempt at a gracious, not-at-all-horrified smile. The others do the same, forming a chain of people around the table.

"Let us say grace." Gramps bows his head. The others mimic him and close their eyes.

For a moment I stare around the table, awkward and unsure if I should follow along or not. I'm not exactly religious, and I'm definitely not Christian, or Jewish, or Muslim, or whatever they are. Probably Christian, but you never know. That doesn't matter anyway, people can be whatever they want and believe what they want, I'm just not in other people's personal spaces enough to see it, I guess.

I bow my head and close my eyes. There's nothing wrong with respecting their faith as long as they don't use it to hurt me, and I don't see them being the type. So I quiet my mind and listen as Gramps prays.

"Lord, we come to you on this Thanksgiving day to give thanks for all that you have provided us, for the health you've given us, and for the joy of family that you've blessed us with."

He goes on, speaking each request and thanks in that gruff old country voice. I learn that Holly had gotten better from an episode of bronchitis a few weeks ago — Mr. Marcus joined in on that one with a sighed, "Amen" — Zachary got his first ever raise at work this week, someone named Delilah had beaten breast cancer years ago and a recent scan confirmed she was still cancer-free. It took me a second to realize Delilah must be Super Old Gran. Then come the words I was expecting.

"And Lord, please be with Hayden in this hard time. We know

you know what he needs, and we trust and pray that you'll see him through this coma and bring him back to us better than before." Gramps coughs and continues his prayer. *I know these can go on for a while, but there is hot food waiting for me, Gramps, so let's speed it up.* Immediately I regret the thought. "Lord, we also would be remiss not to thank you for sending Kenzie into our Hayden's life, and for putting him in the right place at the right time to look over him. May you please bless them both."

That last part brings a smile to my face, despite Gramps calling me a *he*. I can let that pass. At the same time, it causes a lump of guilt to build below my Adam's apple.

Gramps says, "Amen" and my eyes open to everyone else raising their heads and letting go of each other's hands.

There's no delay between the prayer and the family digging in, and honestly, now that I've finally sampled the broccoli casserole I understand why. As quickly as hands go for their forks, conversations start up around the table. I try not to be nosy, but little bits of their exchanges drift over the table and right into my ear. Something about a cousin stealing a television from the local electronics store. Mr. Marcus says he's in jail now. Oh wow. I try to tune out that conversation. Holly's telling Catina she thinks her mom might have gotten her a new phone for Christmas.

"He's a piece of shit," Super Old Gran blurts, grabbing my attention.

I clamp my teeth together. Super Old Gran? I can't say I expected anything like that to come out of her mouth. She looks so innocent and sweet.

"Grandma!" Mary-Anne eyes her down.

My eyes slip to Zachary sitting next to her. He scoops another helping of green beans, not fazed in the slightest. He sees me looking, though, and his brow raises. I yank my eyes away, back to Mary-Anne and Super Old Gran.

"He is, we all know it, y'all just don't say it." Super Old Gran shrugs, and like Zachary, goes back to eating.

"But we have"—Mr. Marcus alludes to me—"company."

Yep, me. Super Old Gran looks at me and grins.

"I'm sure you have some lowlifes in your family too, darling," she says.

At first, I'm not one hundred percent sure how to answer. It has all eyes on me at once, and I definitely know lowlifes—Dad's side of the family is full of them—but how do I answer?

"Mother," Kiki scolds, patting her hand across the table. "Maybe not now."

"I do," I blurt finally. "I do. My dad's side of the family. Most of them."

Smiles transform into grimaces around the table, and I catch a few *awws*. I'm past needing sympathy, but I don't mind calling them out now and then. Is that spiteful?

"They all abandoned us after my dad died." I hold back a grimace of my own. Why did I decide that would be the first thing I talk about tonight? It's a real downer topic. Today is a celebration of Thanksgiving. You're supposed to be thankful. Especially around Hayden's family.

"I'm so sorry, Kenzie," Mary-Anne says in a calm, soothing tone, smiling warmly.

"No, no. It's okay." I try to be upbeat and bring things back around. "It was a long time ago. I'm over it."

A few nods make their way around the table, and before anyone else can say something—or worse, ask about my mom's side of the family—I divert the conversation.

"So how long have y'all lived here?" I look around to signify the house. It still amazes me I'm in such a place. "It's beautiful."

How (Not) to Conjure a Boyfriend 59

"We built it in 2011. Hayden was only four back then." Mr. Marcus smiles, reminiscing about when his sleeping boy was a child. Hayden as a toddler. I can't imagine it. In my head he's only ever been the dreamy six-foot-tall guy who could throw me around.

"He was three, actually," Mary-Anne interjects. "We started building in March that year."

"Ah yes." Mr. Marcus nods thoughtfully, and part of me wishes I hadn't brought it up now. I hit a *spot*, I think. "That's back when we thought he was a terror. Nah, that was this one."

Mary-Anne points directly at Zachary.

"What?" He shrugs.

"You were a handful," Mary-Anne says.

"No, he wasn't," Kiki says.

The smirk on Mary-Anne's face says Mr. Marcus might be on to something.

"You just always had a soft spot for him, Kristi," Super Old Gran croaks. "He near burned down my house."

"That was an accident," Mary-Anne reminds her grandmother with little emotion.

"I know, but I'm still going to give him hell for it." Super Old Gran leans over and eyes Zachary with a big mischievous smile. "You were a little pyromaniac."

"I don't remember any of this." Zachary raises his hands in surrender.

"Likely story," Mary-Anne giggles.

"I don't!"

"Hayden was always the athletic one. He wanted to play baseball or basketball. Wanted to chase you around the field playing tag. Anything that exhausted the crap out of me." Mr. Marcus is smiling so wholesomely, like the memory of being out of breath is one of his favorites. "Zachary…now Zachary was a whole other animal."

I glance Zachary's way to find his mouth is gaping, but that doesn't stop them. I say keep going, this is getting good.

"He didn't mind being outside, but he always wanted to be making something. Which was great until he discovered fire was a thing he could use." Mr. Marcus laughs and turns to Zachary. "You remember that model jet we got you for Christmas? What was it? F-22?"

"Yeah, yeah." Zachary rolls his eyes, but he's all smiles. He even smiles at me for a second, and I have to look away.

"This one here thought he could use some fireworks he'd stolen from our little Fourth of July haul the previous summer to build makeshift engines for the model to make it *fly*," Mr. Marcus explains. Everyone at the table, except Holly, is shaking their heads.

"Did it work?" I ask. Then it hits me that maybe that wasn't the question to ask, but I want to know. Did it?

"Sort of," Zachary laughs. "It moved like five feet, then just blew up for like a minute straight. It was cool."

"Fortunately, he was smart enough then to wear eye protection and get away once he lit the fuse, but God." Mr. Marcus shakes his head. "You've probably taken years off my life scaring me with that stuff."

"Nah, I just strengthened your heart." Zachary grins.

"He knows better now." Mary-Anne raises a brow. "At least he better."

Zachary grins and nods, then leans in toward the table and whispers toward me, but loud enough so all can hear it. "She's right. I keep a fire extinguisher around now."

So Zachary's an asshole but funny. Noted.

7

A DROP OF WATER pelts my curls and a chilled wind clips at my exposed arms as I walk under the local music store's awning. The scent of early morning showers hangs in the air. It just stopped raining minutes ago, and the water is still beading off the rooftops into little puddles on the sidewalk. I step over one of them and turn in to The Good Hex.

Chimes sing as the door closes behind me, and I breathe in the calming aromas of sage, spices, and earth. I love it here.

The store is a mix between a cute little clothing boutique and a metaphysical shop, but it's mostly clothes. Right up front it features an eclectic collection of skirts and gowns that I plan to look through before I leave. To my left is a clearance rack with literally every color of the rainbow on display. The other racks are more muted with earth tones and soft fabrics that my fingers will one hundred percent be feeling. Everything from jeans to scarves and belts, to turtlenecks and tunics, a rack of printed tees with funny sayings — my favorites — and so many pieces of jewelry. I've bought a few outfits here, like the flowy fern-green dress that's in my closet. It's super cute, but I didn't realize it was so sheer when I first tried it on.

I pass between the eye-level racks of clothing and a wooden display case filled with earrings and pendants while music that could have easily been in an episode of *Shadow and Bone* or one of the old *Lord of the Rings* movies whispers overhead. What I'm looking for is nearer the back, almost like it's purposefully partitioned off from the rest of the store. The metaphysical part.

I reach the back and a wonderful world opens up. Candles line the wall and wooden buckets sit beneath them, stacked two deep. Each one is filled to the brim with crystals. Clear quartz, moonstone, sodalite—one of my favorites for balancing out my emotions—agate, amazonite, and so many more. The colors range from solid black to twisting bands of purple and white, and hodgepodges of turquoise and browns, and deep blood-reds and celestial-looking blues.

"Let's see." I lean in and examine the various shapes and sizes.

I need a citrine stone and some selenite after this week. Citrine to attract some prosperity, maybe get Hayden to *actually* like me when he wakes up, and in case that doesn't work, the selenite is to stop me from making poor-ass decisions. And give me some calm when it all does hit the fan, because oh, it's going to.

"Pretty." I see a slender piece of citrine behind a bucket of sky-blue celestite. It's perfect. I reach to grab it off the top before a familiar voice stops me.

"Did it pick you?" they ask with that leftover Cajun accent. I look to my right and Eliza's eyes light up with recognition.

"Eliza!" My voice raises at least two octaves.

"Kenzie!" Eliza throws her arms out and engulfs me in a big warm hug. "Didn't think I'd be seeing you again so soon."

"My neither," I gasp. It completely left my mind that she could be here. "Still can't seem to process that you're Hayden's aunt and you work here."

"No, darling, this is my shop. Was my mama's before me, rest her soul." Eliza dips her head briefly.

"Oh." I drop my chin, sorry to bring that up, even if I didn't ask.

"It's okay." She grins again. "Was many years back."

"I didn't know you owned The Good Hex," I say.

"Well I do," Eliza chuckles. "You're one of my few regulars."

How (Not) to Conjure a Boyfriend 63

Then she knows I get witchy stuff! Suddenly I'm worried Hayden's parents might find out I'm a witch and hate me. What would they say? They prayed over their meal yesterday. A lot of people don't understand us. They think we're wicked, or out of our minds, or something in between those. They don't realize that Christian witches are a real thing too, not that I am one, but still. However, they did seem good with Eliza, and she owns this place. I'm just overreacting. That has to be all.

"I'm not a…" I stop short of saying it. Hell, it'd be a lie, like a recanting of who I am, what I am. I can't really say a recanting of my faith because, well, it isn't religion exactly for me. Not exactly, at least. I try again. "I'm…a…I—"

"You're what?" Eliza eyes me, but there is no malice or condemnation in her eyes.

"Uh…" I don't know what to say, so I just blurt it. "I'm a witch!"

Eliza shrugs. "Me too. A green kitchen witch."

Oh. She's a… She's one too. I've never met another witch. I thought I was the only one in a hundred miles. Something in the revelation feels like a weight lifted.

"Really?" I can't contain my excitement. "I seriously thought I was the only one up here."

"No, no, dear." Eliza shakes her head. "You're not the only one. We're only two of a handful, but we're not alone."

"That's so cool! And I just met you this week because…" Oh shit! It can't be. Could it? Could this all be happening because of my love spell? I clamp those thoughts behind my lips as she smiles so kindly. "It's like fate."

"Maybe." Eliza nods cheerily and then looks toward the buckets of crystals. "So, were you looking for something in particular?"

"Yes, actually." I nod and point toward the citrine stones I'd been looking at. "I need some citrine and selenite, and some basil too."

"Well, the herbs are over here." She points behind us, where there's another cluster of wooden buckets surrounding a circular table to our right made from an old wooden wheel covered in trinkets. "Of course, you know that already."

"It's okay, thank you!" I go again to pick up the citrine stone I'd eyed earlier.

"Ah, one already picked you?" she asks, and I stop short of touching it.

"Uh…" I shrug. I've heard it said that your crystals and stones should pick you, they should call out to you, but after over a year of practicing I don't get it. "Actually…what do you mean? I've never understood what people mean when they say that. How does it pick me?"

"It's different for everybody." Her perpetual smile rises. "For some it's just a feeling, others intuition. Me, I seek guidance from my goddess and see which stone calls out to me. But that depends on you. Maybe it's just your intuition."

"Calls out to you?" I ask.

"Yes." She comes a step closer and holds out her left hand above the bucket of green jade without touching any of the stones. "I don't touch them at first. I just let my hand hover and feel for any pull. If one tugs at my senses, then that's the one."

"What if you don't feel a tug?" I ask. This means a lot to me and I don't want to waste time down the wrong path.

"Then just pick one," Eliza says. "It doesn't have to be some big gotcha or ritual every time. You probably know this already, but witchcraft is all about the individual, it's you figuring out what works for you."

I nod. I've been trying to tell myself that for months, but I always feel like I'm doing it wrong. Am I using the right stone? Does the website I'm looking at have a clue what energies they actually hold? Should I mix those herbs or not? Did I say my intent right? The questions run ablaze half the time, and usually it's just me and the internet trying to figure it out.

"Okay," I say, when I should thank her. Just that one piece of advice from an actual witch did more in my heart to soothe my questioning than a hundred internet searches or any of the books I've read.

I turn to the pile of citrine and hold my left hand over it, less than an inch from their polished surfaces. Did I just feel something? I squint and try to focus, but Hayden's face, complete with the tube running under his nose and feeding tube in his arm, eclipses my focus. Shit! My concentration breaks, but I keep my hand in place. I'm literally standing here trying to get a hope and prosperity stone to call out to me in front of his aunt while I keep up the lie that I'm his person. Now the only feeling rushing through my hand and entire body is guilt. Guilt for staying in the hospital room. Guilt for not correcting them. Guilt for sitting at their table for Thanksgiving. Pure guilt.

"Give it some time if you need to," she says, but at the sound of her voice another set of gray eyes flash in my mind, and I snatch up the stone closest to my fingers and back up.

"This one!" I gasp.

"Oh." Eliza forms a tiny O-shape with her lips and nods. "Very good."

I focus and slow my breathing. *Don't let her see.* To cover it, I put my hand over the selenite and wait a full point five seconds before snatching a random one off the top.

"Looks like you have this down," Eliza says.

You know what? I can get herbs later.

"I gotta go," I tell her.

"You don't need the basil too?" she asks.

Ugh. Yes, but I'd rather leave. Gods, I do have to pay for this though.

"Oh, yes, that too," I say, trying my hardest to hide my nerves. I take off toward the herbs and grab a satchel labeled BASIL and show it to her.

"That it?" she asks.

Gods, I hope so.

8

WHY AM I HERE?

I blow an exaggerated breath through pooched lips and walk inside. Machines beep and whir, with tubes draping between them and the bed. And there he is. My dream. My cinnamon make-believe lover, out cold on a hospital bed for only the gods know how long. And here I am, staring at him, wishing some of that old exciting flare would pop through my veins. Instead, dread stalks their passages, and I'm stuck trying to figure out what to say to a sleeping husk. Someone really does need to fix his hair though.

"Uh, Hayden," I start, then stop and swallow. *He can't hear you, Kenzie. Why the hell are you doing this? What is it going to solve?* I'm hopeless. Fine, whatever. I step closer and run a single finger through his hair to get it out of his face. I yank back when my finger touches his forehead. Did he move? No. It's just me. Nothing. Not a flinch.

A minute passes and I do little more than stand. My mind's been going crazy ever since leaving The Good Hex. Did I really cause all of this? Is my spell to blame? And if it is, what did I do wrong? This isn't what I wanted. I never hoped he'd get hurt just so I could be his. I'd even rather he never know me than for him to get hurt because of me.

My eyes flit from his closed lids to the bag of fluid suspended next to him. Back and forth like suddenly he'll be awake and tell me how to get out of this mess. Gods, no! That would be horrible. Please, Odin, don't let that happen! He'd be horrified to hear what's going on out here in the real world. Like let him wake up, but I don't want to be here when it happens.

"Kenzie?" A woman's voice comes from behind.

I stiffen and swing around on my toes.

"Doctor..." I try, but her name is not coming to me. Kaine? No. Carroll maybe? Neither feels right.

"Kline." She smiles.

"Right. Dr. Kline. Sorry." I nod apologetically.

"Did you come to talk with him?" She goes on without acknowledging it.

"I-I, uh..." And now I'm stuttering, dammit. Yes, I came to talk to him, but I don't want to now. It was a lame idea. "Yeah."

I can stick around and say a few random things to him. Maybe tell him how icky the weather is, or that Tae Hyun is putting out a new record in like a week. I'm so excited... but I'm betting Hayden doesn't even know who that is. Probably couldn't give a shit. He may not be as nice as I think he is either. He is a jock, right? He'd probably hate that I brought up K-pop music and laugh me out of the room.

Why did I obsess over him? Oh wait. I steal a look at him and immediately remember. Oh. Yeah.

"Good. It's nice for them." Dr. Kline angles her head but keeps eye contact. "He might not react, and he might not remember — he most likely won't — but it still is good for him."

She can see the confusion in my face, it's clear. So he can or can't remember what I say?

Dr. Kline smiles. "It's not like he's actively listening, but hearing someone talk to him keeps his brain alert. He can still hear. And we think it's even more helpful for him to hear stories he's familiar with from his past, from family. Think of the brain as a powerful circuit board. When he hears those stories, it exercises some circuits in the brain that can help bring him out of the coma."

That's cool, but I don't know any of those stories. And I'm not sure he'd even know my voice, to be honest. He's heard it every time I've taken his order, but that can't come close to hearing his family. Plus, I bet my perspective of his trips to the coffee shop are much different than his.

"Oh," is all I manage.

"I'll leave you with him," Dr. Kline says, and walks out.

I take another breath and blow it out. *It's just you and me again, Hayden.* I throw my eyes up to the ceiling and drag them back down. He shouldn't remember anything I say, and it'd be good for him, right? Maybe me too. Get it off my chest.

"Fine," I say out loud before locking my eyes on his closed eyelids. "Hey, Hayden. It's me. Kenzie. You probably know me as *the coffee shop person*, or maybe *that barista*."

I stop. *That barista?* Ugh.

"I don't know. It doesn't matter. I just wanted to come check on you. See how you're doing. Since it's probably my fault and all that you're here," I say. I'd be more than content to leave it there and be gone, but I don't. I put my hand on the plastic guardrail along his bed. "What I really needed to say — and please, for the love of all the gods, don't remember this — is that, well…uh…you see. I'm not your enbyfriend."

Immediately I roll my eyes. Really? Of course he doesn't think I'm his enbyfriend. What a stupid thing to say. He probably doesn't even know I'm non-binary. He probably thinks I'm just some dude who wears dresses sometimes. Hell, he probably doesn't even know what enbyfriend means. Yet, that's what I confess to him.

"Okay," I grunt, and psych myself up. "Let's try this again. You see, Hayden, I might have, well, actually Regina — you know, the nurse — *might* have assumed I was your enbyfriend. Okay, that's not entirely accurate either. I told her that." I huff. "And I also sort of cast a spell."

I check his eyelids. No signs of movement. I'm still not one hundred percent convinced it was the spell that did this. I did everything right, I think, but it did happen literally the next day.

"So yeah, I'm not. Obviously." I laugh and glance away, my eyes trailing down to the blue and white sheets over his chest. "Most of your family was there when it happened. So they might sort of…well, they all *do* think I'm your enbyfriend."

I laugh as if a sleeping guy is going to chuckle back at my little dilemma. If he did, I'd be out of here so fast.

"I didn't mean for this to happen. I swear." I throw my hands up, palms out and fingers splayed to make it clear, you know, like he can see it. "But…" I grimace and let out a defeated breath. "I just didn't say no."

That's it. I *didn't* do what I should have. It's that simple. But the real problem is that I *keep* not doing what I should.

"Gods. Hayden, I'm going to need you not to wake up until I figure this junk out," I blurt, and my eyes go wide. "Oh no. I didn't mean that. That's so bad. No. No! I want you to wake up. I do! You're honestly amazing and gorgeous, and you deserve to be here. Not like *here* here, in the hospital, but awake, you know? Yeah, awake. You have such an awesome family."

I need to stop talking, but I don't. I do slow down though.

"Your family is pretty great. Your mom is beautiful," I say. I've finally pinned down who she reminds me of. Sally in *Practical Magic*, Sandra Bullock. "Your dad sort of scares me. Not a lot, just a little. And your sister—Holly, right?—is adorable. Your aunt is a witch like me. Did you know that? Of course you did." What an inept question. "And Gramps is great. Super Old Gran, Kiki. I'm jealous, actually."

I stop. What am I doing? This is pointless. I need to get out of here. My hand grips my necklace and I say a quick chant under my breath.

"Everything is going to be okay. I have no reason to worry." I breathe out. "I am at peace."

I grind my heels into the ground and twist around, and suddenly I'm *not* at peace.

"Ah!" My fingers clasp my mouth to hold back the rest of the scream. "Eliza!"

"Oh," Eliza squawks.

"Sorry! I didn't mean—"

"No, no. It's okay. It's my fault. I didn't intend to scare you like that." She covers her chest and breathes in dramatically. "I didn't know you were going to be here."

"Uh…" An answer refuses to come forward. I fight back the urge to run. How much of what I said did she hear? Does she know? Did she hear me confessing to him? Please, no! I can't do that right now!

"How long have you…been here?" I ask, not at all sketchily.

"Just got here, darling," she says.

That calms my nerves a bit. Not as much as I'd like, but I guess it'll do.

"Oh, okay," I say. *Act natural, Kenzie! Act natural.* "I gotta go, Mom's waiting for me."

And I take off.

9

"YOU MAKING AN AMERICANO?" Landon leans over my shoulder.

"Yeah," I say, repeating *no whipped cream, no whipped cream.* I always forget they don't get any.

"'Kay, I'll get the maple latte," he comes back.

Kaitlynn is busy at the pastry station loading up bags with sweets and baked items for our Sunday afternoon rush, complete with a long line reaching the entrance: tucked-in polos and button-ups, long flowy dresses, and dress boots topped off in thick jackets, all waiting impatiently. The local churches must have let out.

I clamp a lid on the cup and do a half spin to end up next to Dawn at the register. She's greeting customers with her perpetual smile while I plop the Americano on the counter.

"Daniel," I yell over the chitchat and scuffling, and wait long enough for a middle-aged man with spectacles to walk over and nod before leaving the cup unattended.

Back at the prep counter, a new order receipt prints out. I tear it off and put it on the line behind four others without glancing at what's on the paper. I check the next ticket, slap two cups on the line, and twist around to Kaitlynn.

"I need a slice of pumpkin pie with crème, a slice of key lime, and two sugar cookies, for here," I tell her, but I don't stop there. "And I need you to save me from this crap show."

I'm not talking about the chaos in the dining area or the powdered mess Landon and I are making, including a few sticky globs of caramel under the collection of flavored syrups. Landon's contribution. Kaitlynn understands immediately though.

"It's *your* crap show, not mine." She grins and swings back around.

"Not the point." I roll my eyes and go back to prepping my cups. I really want to say "shit show," but Dawn says we have to consider our clientele.

"You could have just…oh, I don't know — not lied. Ever thought of that?"

"It's not…" I stop. I want to deny it, but I can't. So I redirect. "It's not that simple. How could I have said no?"

"No," Landon and Kaity say in unison. Smart-asses, both of them. Then Kaitlynn keeps going. "You say, *I'm not. Didn't happen. Just a friend. Sorry.* I don't know. Lots of ways! How many times are you going to ask me that?"

"Until you give me an answer I like." I huff and drop a shot of espresso into a cup. "Plus, it's a little late for that. So what do I do *now*?"

"Tell them." Dawn throws her voice into the conversation without looking back. She overheard us talking about it earlier and so yeah, she's now *in* on my terrible life choices. I blame Kaity's big mouth for that one.

"That," Kaitlynn agrees. "Do that."

"You want me to just walk up and say, 'Hey Mrs. Marcus, I lied to your face. I'm not your son's person'?!" I say it with as much sarcasm as I can muster without being too obvious to customers.

"Not li—" Kaitlynn starts, but Dawn interrupts her.

"How about y'all talk about this little drama once this rush stops." She grins and nods at us expectantly. "Okay?"

I nod and go silent. This is the only thing on my mind right now, so I have nothing else to say. Ten minutes later the crowd has lightened, and I nudge Kaitlynn.

"So…"

"Kenzie," Kaitlynn sighs. "I'm not some Buddha. I don't know!"

"Yeah, but—"

"No! No buts." Kaitlynn shakes her head. "Do what—"

"But they like butts," Landon says, thinking he has something.

"Uh… Nah. They're more a—" Kaitlynn begins, but there is no way I'm letting this be said in front of Dawn. No way in hell.

"La la la," I sing. It's the best I've got, and she stops and stares me down with a crooked grin, so it works. I raise my brow and she gives me a knowing smile back.

"You just have to find a way to tell them." Dawn leans her back against the baked goods container. "And at the right time. But make it soon. The longer you put it off, the harder it's going to get, and the worse it's going to look."

"I know." I drop my head in defeat. "I'll do it."

"Good." Kaitlynn sounds satisfied.

"Good? You didn't contribute anything," I complain, and turn to grab a new ticket.

Unlike before, it's the only one on the line. I take it a little slower and try to relax. I concentrate more on the ingredients. Espresso, hazelnut, and chocolate syrup. It's simple, not enough to keep me from worrying.

"I helped," Kaity whines.

"Sure." I shake my head and wrap my fingers around my necklace. I say my usual prayer for when I'm anxious. The words flow noiselessly in my head.

Dear Freyja, Queen of the Valkyries, I know I have no reason to worry. Your shield-maidens watch over me. But please give me the peace of home within my head.

I breathe in, then out, and pop a lid on top of the iced latte in front of me. I grab the cold plastic cup and call out the name written on it, "Billie!"

When I turn to put the cup on the counter, I freeze.

"Oh no," I mumble.

"Huh?" Kaitlynn asks, looking down my line of sight at the mom, dad, and daughter that just walked in. Mary-Anne, Randall, and Holly Marcus.

"That's his family," I whisper.

"His?"

"Hayden's. It's Hayden's family." I whisper it like it's the biggest secret of the twenty-first century.

"Oh." Her lip skews to the right and she grunts evilly, "Have fun."

"Lots of help, thanks," I throw my voice after her as she walks into the back, probably to eavesdrop, and Mrs. Marcus walks up.

"Kenzie!" she squeals.

I fake excitement, baring all of my teeth and hoping the horror isn't showing in my face.

"I'm so glad you're here." She doesn't stop. "We wanted to come by the shop. See where Hayden met you."

"Ah, yeah, that." I nod nervously, glancing back at Kaitlynn. Hoping she'll get that I need saving. She doesn't—or well, she does but does nothing about it. "It's just where I work."

Obvi. They know I work here, and if they hadn't already, me standing behind the counter should be a good giveaway.

"It's a nice place. I don't think we've ever come in before." Mr. Marcus looks around the space. "Sort of odd, actually. I've lived here all my life, and I've never been here."

"I have." Holly speaks up, eyes barely breaching the countertop.

"Really?" Mr. Marcus asks.

"Uh-huh. With Hayden," she answers.

It must have been a time I wasn't here, because the first time I saw Holly was at the hospital, and I can't remember a time when

Hayden came to the shop with anyone but some guy friend or his devastatingly handsome brother. Oh! Shit. I didn't mean it like that. What is going on with me?

"You weren't here though." Holly looks at me.

"Makes sense." I nod and decide to switch to customer service mode. Maybe that'll expedite this. "Can I get y'all anything? We make a great peanut butter frappe. It's my favorite."

"Please, Mom." Holly's eyes light up like Christmas.

"Is that what you want, then? You sure?" Mary-Anne asks.

Holly nods, and Mary-Anne looks back at me. Before she can say anything I ring it up.

"And two macchiatos," she adds.

"Okay." I put in the other drinks and place the order under *Marcus*. She pays and I instinctively give her the standard thanks. "Thank you so much. Your items will be ready in a few minutes."

I try to escape to the bar to make their drinks, but Mary-Anne raises her hand above the counter.

"Kenzie," she says.

"Yes, ma'am." I swing around. It's an impulse at this point. Too many times a customer has done the same to add something to their order or tell us how to make a drink we already know how to make.

"We were wondering if you might come by the house this afternoon. When do you get off?" she asks.

"Two," I tell her, my voice shadowed in a little more caution than I intended. What is up now?

Did they figure it out?

"That's perfect." Mary-Anne grins. Randall's standing in silence. He's still the hardest to read. "Hayden and Zachary usually play basketball after church. I thought maybe you'd like to come. It's just Zachary, and I think he's a little more down about his

How (Not) to Conjure a Boyfriend

brother than he admits."

Okay, first, why is she telling me all of this about Zachary? Isn't that a little oversharing? Maybe Zachary doesn't want people to know that.

"Oh, I'm—" I start to come up with an excuse. It was going to be something about how badly my mother needed me home to take care of the cat we don't have. But Holly interrupts.

"Please!" Holly smiles big.

"I…uh," I stumble. Why am I like this? "Sure. Yeah. I can do that."

10

THE CLOCK ON THE wall hits 1:53. I've had almost two hours to regret my decision. Two hours to try to find a way out, to come up with an excuse.

"Please, Kaity," I beg with my best pity eyes. "All you have to do is agree I was supposed to come to your place. That's all."

"I'm not doing that! You already told them you're coming," Kaitlynn refuses. "You got into this, you can get *yourself* out of it. Why don't you just say you're not feeling good?"

"Because…" I stop before saying *that's a lie*. So is the rest. "Because this is easier."

"Blaming me is easier?" She scowls.

Okay, yeah. It's sort of low, but that way I can blame it on someone else, and it won't just be me bowing out. It's easier that way.

"Yeah." I stretch out the word, hoping it'll smooth it over.

Kaitlynn laughs. "Such a bitch."

"Hey!" I scoff sarcastically. "I'll owe you one."

"Why do you not want to go so bad?" she asks. "Didn't you say they live in, like, some big high-end modern house? They probably have a full basketball court. A gym! Theater! All of it."

"So? I don't play basketball," I remind her. She knows that! A real-deal home theater sounds pretty dope though. "I watch."

"There *is* that, but still." She smirks. "You get to hang out at a mansion. With another hot dude!"

"It's not a mansion, and no! We're not talking about his brother." I stop her.

"But he is hot. Didn't you say he was?" she asks.

How (Not) to Conjure a Boyfriend

Ugh! Fine! Yes, I might have said that, but still, he interrogated me. "Not the point. I don't want to play basketball with *Zachary*."

She gives me the side-eye. "And why not? Why don't you want to play with Zachary?"

"'Cause I don't play basketball," I say again.

"No, you said *Zachary* real suspicious-like." She's squinting. Too curious for her own good. "Why don't you want to play *specifically* with Zachary?"

I huff and fall against the bar. "I think he knows."

"Knows?" Kaitlynn squints.

"Yeah, *knows* knows."

"*Knows*, like he knows you're a liar?" she digs.

I roll my eyes. That's not how I'd phrase it.

"That I'm not his brother's enbyfriend." I rephrase it for her. She makes me sound so bad.

"So, a liar." Kaitlynn grins.

"Not my fault," I say.

"Technicalities."

"WELCOME TO THE MARCUS residence, we'll be right with you," a recording of Mary-Anne's voice responds when I push the doorbell, and I immediately reach for my necklace.

My legs are crisscrossed as if I could twist around and make a run for it. This is so awkward. I'm awkward. I hate waiting at doors. I don't even want to be here. I should be at home with Mom, well, I mean hanging out in my room playing *Sims*, dancing around my bed to Seventeen and XLOV, or watching one of my many BL dramas for the hundredth time. Not standing here, waiting to play a sport I'd rather watch with a guy I essentially don't know who thinks I'm sus anyway.

A latch clacks and the big door swings inward. It's Mary-Anne. She's smiling widely.

"You came!"

Did you not expect me to? I scoff at the doubt inside my head. I said I would. I didn't want to, but I said I would. I'm not a li— Okay, maybe.

I shrug. "Of course."

Sometimes I want to smack myself. Is it really that hard *not* to dig my hole deeper? By the time I'm done they'll be able to drop me inside with a few others and still bury us six feet deep.

"Zachary's out back already. Do you know where the court is?" Mrs. Marcus asks.

Do I know where the court is? Like basketball court? Was Kaity right? Do they seriously have a whole-ass basketball court?

"No, ma'am." I shake my head.

"If you drive around back, you'll…" She puts up a hand. "Actually, no. It'd be quicker to cut through here. Just follow me."

I almost had an excuse to get in my car and make a run for it. I was this close! Instead, I nod and she invites me in.

"How was work?" Hayden's mom asks, leading me through the kitchen to places I've not yet been. I wonder how big this place really is.

"It was fine," I say. Not sure what else to say about it. It's work.

She takes a left and we head down a set of steps. We don't have a basement at my house, or another level, whichever it is here, so this is cool. This must be their game room. Foosball, billiards, table hockey, a dartboard. There's a round table on the other side surrounded by cushioned wooden chairs, and a sitting area off to the right.

"Is that girl you were working with a friend?" Mary-Anne takes a look behind her to smile.

"Yes, that's Kaitlynn." I brighten. "She's been my best friend since, like...forever."

"She seems nice," Mary-Anne says, and opens the door at the back of the room.

Sunlight rushes in and coats my face. The sound of the ball smacking pavement reaches my ears, and I strain to adjust to the outside light again.

"Zachary," Mary-Anne calls.

My eyes clear, and there he is. For a second I think I'm looking at Hayden, but the features are different. They're softer. The cut of his jaw is less pronounced, his arms might not be muscular, but those shoulders are perfect, and the eyes, gods. They're the same ashy gray as Hayden's, but they're bigger, more puppy-dog-like.

"Ye—" he starts, but his voice cuts off when he sees me. "Uh, hey."

I raise my hand and wave.

"I asked Kenzie to come by and play basketball with you," his mom says. "Thought you might like someone to play with."

It sounds like we're kindergarteners in need of a friend the way she says it, and she leaves out the part about it being because Hayden's not here. From the telltale look on his face, he didn't know she asked me to come. I'm not sure if it's shock or anger in his eyes, but he tilts his head and looks off into the woods, lips skewed. Then his mouth opens, but he stops.

"Some company," Mary-Anne suggests, like she's trying to sell the idea to him.

"Uh-huh." Zachary nods and throws me the ball. "Think fast."

The ball smacks into my hip and I almost yelp the f-word as I bend over in shock. What the actual fuck?! I shoot my gaze at him, making it evil and kind all at the same time, eyes slit while I smile. I grunt and chase after the ball.

"Caught me off guard," I say, and throw it back to him.

"I'll leave you two to it," Mary-Anne says, and leaves without delay before disappearing inside again.

Zachary catches the ball and just stands there. He stares me down, eyes moving up and down my jeans and then my bare midriff. I fight the urge to cover my stomach. Is he really sizing me up? I can play basketball. I have. Like twice. Maybe more, but it was all in elementary school when they made me. I know the rules though.

"*You* play basketball?" Zachary asks. "And dressed like that?"

Oh the derision in his voice. Like come on.

"Sort of," I say.

"You're dating my brother, the main point guard for Mitchell, and you 'sort of' play?" His brow skews.

"Yeah, well, I mean, I watch more than play," I explain. "I go more for the scenery."

Why did I say that? Now he's going to think I'm checking him out.

"Ah." Zachary grins. "The scenery can be good. *That* I understand."

Hold up. Did he just agree? I was talking about the guys.

"You don't play much either?" I ask, trying to forget it.

"I do. But it's usually with Hayden." His face grows somber.

"Sorry." I bow my head and cough.

"It's not your fault, unless you tripped him or something." Zachary chuckles.

"Nah," I laugh. "I'm too clumsy for that."

Zachary laughs again and suddenly I'm smiling.

"So one-on-one?" He shrugs.

"Sure." This is going to be so bad. I'm going to get floored.

He turns and bounces the ball a few times between here and

How (Not) to Conjure a Boyfriend

the goal, stopping at the flat line under the round one. I don't have a clue what they're called, they're just random shapes to me. I stop at the crest of the rounded line. I think I'm going first.

"Ready?" Zachary asks.

"Y-yeah," I stutter, and suddenly the ball is rushing toward me. My reflexes kick in and leather smacks my palms instead of my face, thankfully. I clamp my fingers to the surface and... Nothing. Shit. What am I supposed to do?

"Uh..." Zachary frowns.

"Oh, right."

I drop the ball and start dribbling down the court. My feet move to the right, but Zachary matches me, so I switch to the left and try to sprint forward. He reassesses and is on me in a second.

"Double dribble! You can't do that. And again!" Zachary calls out. He stops and I take the opportunity to take a shot. It skims the white edge of the backboard and bounces off.

"Ah!" I grunt.

"Wouldn't have counted anyway," Zachary says. "You were double dribbling *so* much."

He eyes me, confusion riddling his face.

"Sorry..." How the hell am I so unaware? I know what that is, but I never really play. I didn't realize how hard it was not to do that.

"You sure you know how to play?" Zachary asks.

"Yeah, just been a while." I shrug and then mutter under my breath. "A really long while."

"'Kay, my ball," he says, and throws me the ball while he gets into position at the head of the circle.

I huff, running all I can remember about basketball through my head. No double dribbling, obviously, no walking—aka running without dribbling at all—stay inside the white lines around the court, no pushing or holding, fouls are bad, I think. I'm pretty sure those are the main ones.

"Ready?" He nods, feet planted outside the circle.

"Yeah." I nod and bounce him the ball.

I might not be good at sports, but I'm small, so I'm quick and I can be agile when I need to be. He lurches forward and I throw my hands out to swat at the ball. He diverts with ease and twists around me before smoking me for a successful shot.

"Score one for me!" Zachary hoots and does a quick shoulder shimmy dance.

I'm not sure if it's more amusing, adorable, or cringe. So I smile and shake my head. He motions for me to get in place again and we go back and forth like this for a few rounds. Mainly it's me shooting and missing spectacularly or breaking the rules. He really doesn't like it when I grab his arms to keep him from shooting.

"That's walking!" Zachary yells, but he's laughing all the same.

"Damn right it is," I say and shoot at the same time.

It hits the rim this time, which so far is an accomplishment for me.

"You rimmed it!" Zachary laughs. "You actually got close."

When I look back, he's grinning from ear to ear.

"Excuse me!" My mouth drops open.

"What?" His face skews.

"Yo—" I stop. That's not what he's thinking. *Don't think dirty, Kenzie.*

I let the word hang there and get the ball from the edge of the court. This place is pretty incredible. A basketball court behind the house bordering the forest. I one hundred percent wouldn't play here at night, but it's cool.

Zachary gives me a big hard-edged smile and shakes his head.

"You're making this too easy." Zachary then swoops forward, dribbling right at me.

How (Not) to Conjure a Boyfriend

"Huh?" I grunt, but he's already in front of me, swinging around, passing the ball from right to left in a flash.

In no time he's behind me, going in for another shot. He's a lot like his brother, especially the gray eyes. I think they're darker, or maybe the metallic sheen in them is just deeper. He is a little shorter, but still they're so much alike.

"What I don't get is…" Zachary's feet leave the ground and his arms shoot upward with perfect form. His wrist flicks and the basketball lobs effortlessly into the basket without touching metal. "One," he says when his feet touch the pavement again. "How I didn't know he was…not straight? And two…" He puts two fingers up. "Why wouldn't he tell his *gay* brother he's talking to you? He tells me everything! It's not like I'm competition. He's the basketball star."

"You're—" I snatch my mouth shut and swallow the rest of the stupid I about screamed. *You're gay?!* And am I sensing a bit of jealousy?

His head swings around and he squints. The surprise painted across my face says enough. I'm not finishing that thought for him.

"You good?" he asks.

"U-uh, yeah," I stutter.

You're telling me I've been crushing on the straight brother this whole time when there's a gay version?!

He's eyeing me. The silence is getting awkward. Even the birds decided to shut up at the wrong moment. I'm afraid if I open my mouth now, I might come clean. I mean, it isn't the worst thing that could happen. I'm literally standing here with a super cute guy who might actually consider me, but I'm "going out" with his straight brother who's in a literal coma. If I told him, he'd see me as nothing but a liar, and I'd get kicked out of the family. No more Super Old Gran actually sort of breaks my heart.

"Right? What are the chances?" I put on a fake smile. "Two brothers being gay, huh?"

I laugh like it's ridiculous.

"But here we are." I keep talking. "You're gay, he's gay, I'm gay. Just a bunch of gays."

"I guess." Zachary's wincing, it's like he's embarrassed for me.

Shut up, Kenzie. I pass him the ball. Anything to distract. "Your turn."

"You also don't seem like his type." Zachary keeps on, dribbling toward me, which hopefully means he'll put the questions behind him. "Hayden always goes for long hair and…smart."

He looks back at me questioningly.

"I'm smart!" I bite back. "And maybe his type in guys is different."

He laughs and keeps going as he dribbles around me.

"Usually brown eyes, maybe bright green. And you're…"

He stops just long enough to look at me, but he keeps dribbling.

"Are you *trying* to distract me?" I ask. Anything to get him to end this line of inquiry and thought.

"No, jus—" And he takes off around me and lands another perfect layup. The ball swishes through the net, and he's all smiles when he twists around bobbing his head. "You think I need to distract you to beat you?"

That audacity. I shake my head. "You—"

"No, seriously. I'm trying to figure out why," he says. "I could see him liking your eyes. I didn't realize they were different colors until you came to Thanksgiving. I'd only seen them from a distance before. They're actually pretty."

I swallow and use every inch of my willpower not to freeze in place. He noticed my eyes. And they're *pretty*? He thinks my eyes are pretty? Wait, what?

"A distance?" I tilt my head.

"Uh, forget about it." He nearly trips.

"Okay." I let it hang there. Weird. "You're not flirting with me, are you?"

Knowing me, I probably wouldn't realize it if he actually were. Isn't that a thought. Hayden's little brother flirting with his fake enbyfriend.

"What? No!" he blurts and straightens his back. He dribbles the ball again and goes back for another layup. When his feet hit the ground, he throws me the ball. "Of course not!"

"Good, because I like your brother." I put force into my words, trying my hardest not to cringe when I blurt the L word. *You didn't have to be so forceful about it.* "Maybe I'm not his quote-unquote perfect type, but we're fine. He likes me like I am. And I like him as he is!"

"Uh..." Zachary's eyes are astonished. I don't think he expected this from such a small package. "Sorry, I didn't mean to offend you."

"'Kay." I nod. "Let's just play, okay?"

"Yeah, sure." He nods.

When he turns to take up his spot at the goal line, I linger a little on his face and notice how plump his lips are. They're a calm pink with a natural pooch to them, and in a split second of uncontrolled thought, I wonder what they'd taste like.

"No!" I yelp.

"Huh?" Zachary jumps and throws the basketball.

It bounces off to my left and I'm left standing speechless in front of him, mouth clamped tightly shut, fists balled up and pressed against my sides. Shit. I didn't mean to scream it!

"N-no." I scramble to come up with something, anything. "Let me serve."

"I'm sorry, what?" His head twitches to the side and he smiles. "Serve? You want to serve the basketball?"

"Uh..." I'm struggling hard. I don't even know what sport you serve in, but I know it isn't basketball. Refusing to let the shame show on my face, I go stone-faced. "You know what I mean."

"Sure." He nods and passes me the ball.

I nod and pass him to get to the goal line. Suddenly it's all I can do to look away, as images I don't need flash in my head.

I grip my necklace just before turning to face him. Just play basketball.

Unknown: This is Zach Marcus. Wanted to apologize for Sunday.

Apologize?

A lone gray text bubble sits at the top of my screen under a phone number I've never seen before, but there's no mistaking who it is. Hayden's brother. Zachary. And he wants to apologize? That should probably be my job.

The words feel like they're haunting me, begging for a reply. I must be taking too long, because the bubbles start strobing at the bottom of the window.

Unknown: Hayden's brother.

I roll my eyes. I figured that out. It isn't that hard. I don't know too many Zach Marcuses. I grunt as my head meets the thickly painted white cinderblock wall at the back of the classroom. Mr. Shook, my ancient Biology teacher, drones on about how adaptations can take hundreds, thousands, or even millions of years. He was probably there when the peppered moths he has projected on the screen adapted back in the Industrial Revolution.

I tap the screen to start typing out a reply. I pause. What do I say though? *Okay* just seems blunt. Not to mention, what is he apologizing for?

Mackenzie: I know who you are. And apologize for what?

It takes a few seconds for the bubbles to start jumping and a new message to come through.

Zachary: For questioning you dating my brother.

Ah, that. Yes, and thank you. Even though you're right. I may never admit it, but you are. Who am I kidding? He's going to find out one day. *Oh no, he's going to find out one day!* What the hell am I doing? I grip my phone tighter. Maybe if I come clean right now, it'll all just blow over. Maybe they'll forgive it, and I'll get to go back to crushing on Hayden. Like normal.

I start to type a confession but stop after the first letter, "I". My chest tightens and my mind goes into rush hour. His family will hate me. They'll think I'm a cheap liar. I'll never get to talk to Hayden again, even if he does wake up. He'll hate me for making them think he's gay, or bi, or whatever, won't he? But if I don't come clean and he wakes up, I'm screwed too. I close my eyes and take in another deep breath.

Mackenzie: Apology excepted.

My eyelids drop and my head dips. I feel no better. My stomach is a mess, and I just dug my hole deeper. This isn't sustainable. My phone buzzes again and I'm horrified to look at it.

Zachary: Excepted? Is that some new way to say no?

The bell rings and I jump. *Calm down, Kenzie. Talk to Kaity about it. Maybe she can give you some plan to get out of all this before you end up in prison.* I throw my bag over my shoulder and take off. *I need you to have a plan, Kaity.*

Between a huff and annoyed groan I type.

Mackenzie: 🤦 Accepted.* Sorry. Damn autocorrect.

I barely get past two classrooms before my phone vibrates again.

Zachary: 😂😂 I get that. So can I make it up to you?

Make it up to me? Does that entail never seeing each other again? That seems fair, except his entire family still thinks his brother is in love with me, so that's a long shot. Whatever. A smile extends across my lips as a thought comes up. It's absurd, but it'll be funny to see what he says.

Mackenzie: You can come to my place and help me clean.

I hit send. I stop to see if he replies. If I were him, I'd either never text again or come up with some elaborate excuse. Which might be part of my problem, actually. I give it a few seconds, and there's nothing. Nice. I think I lost him. Maybe he got the—

Bubbles start fading in and out again on my screen, then boom, his reply.

Zachary: When? What's your address?

My eyes pop open. Uh... What?

"I...uh..." I look around the packed hall. I'm not dreaming, am I? Nightmare maybe? How am I supposed to follow that? I didn't mean it! He was supposed to say no! I don't need him coming to my house. Not after yesterday. Not ever! It's one bad idea on top of another, and I don't need any more bad ideas.

Hold up! This could be okay. I could make him do everything, make him work, and maybe he'd want to go home. The thought sits there for a moment, but then I feel bad for it. I can't do that, but how do I take it back?

Simple, Kenzie! Just write back that you were joking and that everything is okay.

Mackenzie: After school? When are you out?

Yeah. I effed up.

Zachary: 2:45

Admit you don't need him there. It's not that hard, Kenzie!

Mackenzie: 3 here. But I work until 8.

What am I doing?

I'M HOME IN RECORD time after work and somehow he still beat me. My headlights catch an unfamiliar truck. I don't know a lot about trucks, but I think it's lifted, a Toyota, newer, and it's flaming burnt orange. I stop behind it and a door swings open.

Zachary steps out. His hair isn't gelled in place today. It's tousled about his head and even over his forehead some. It's...nice. Plumes of dust cloud around red, white, and black Nikes in the glow of my beams. He waves, all smiles.

I half grin and wave back before unlatching my belt and getting out with my hoodie squeezed around my waist. Why did I invite him here? He's going to see that I'm poor.

"Hey." I start toward him, but then divert through the yard so I don't have to maneuver around him.

"Hey," he calls back as I make for the house without him. In the corner of my vision I think he crinkles his brow before taking off after me.

"You really didn't have to do this," I say. Maybe I should have said *I didn't mean it, why are you here?* But I had way too much time to cancel on him and I didn't.

"It's okay!" Zachary says. "I owe you."

"You *don't* owe me," I tell him. On the porch I stop and put up a hand to make sure Zachary understands.

"Just so you know. My mom is a little...down," I say. I don't want to say sick. That's not really it. And depressed...well, that sounds too sad. "She's okay, but like..."

"Oh, I'm sorry." He nods. I can see the understanding in both the kind curve of his cheeks and the way his eyes soften.

"Nah, just wanted you to know before you see her," I explain.

He nods and I unlock the door and push inside with him on my heels.

I groan when I lay my eyes on the inside. The usual brightness of the foyer's white walls and repeating flower pattern feels dingy and old. The kitchen seems out of date, aged. I notice all the little stains on the wallpaper. Even the cracked vase of flowers I put next to the door seems lackluster and screams that we're not like them.

How (Not) to Conjure a Boyfriend

"It feels so good in here!" He exhales and sheds his leather jacket.

I'm not quite ready to lose mine. I need more time to retain the heat. "Yeah. Sorry it's a mess."

"A mess? It's great. Where can I put my jacket?" Zachary asks.

Hmmm. We don't get lots of guests, and I usually throw mine over one of the dining room chairs, if I take it off at all. That feels poor though. He's probably expecting a coat rack or a whole-ass closet. My thoughts scramble for an answer, but I come up short.

"You can just throw it over one of these." I point at the closest chair in the dining room.

He doesn't question it. He simply steps over and deposits his jacket evenly over the first chair.

"So what are we cleaning?" he asks.

"Kitchen," I say, spreading my arms and spinning. Why does it feel so small now?

"That shouldn't be too hard," he comments.

He's not wrong. It's not dirty. I don't let my kitchen get dirty. Messy though, disorganized — that's another issue. Plus the boxes on the table. Packages from everywhere. Mom's comfort purchases. I don't bother asking what they are anymore, and sometimes I wonder if she needed any of them. It's not like we can afford it, but I try not to say much because it just makes her sadder. If nothing else, it's taught me to save.

"Hey, dear!" Mom appears around the corner like she knew I was thinking about her.

She's dressed in one of her work pantsuits, minus the coat. The collar frills around her neck and she's still got makeup on, which never happens. Any other day she'd have wiped it all away and switched into pj's before I got home, but I told her Zachary was coming over. I also finally filled her in about my new relationship status, all of it, even though it was all a lie. It went over about as well as I'd expected, but I had to say something. She wasn't happy. Disappointed sums it up best, and I think that's what hurt the most. She might be smiling now, but that's just a façade.

"Hey." I smile back and give her a hug. It's weird seeing her like this. All smiles. Cheerful. I like it, but I wish it was real. "This is Zachary. Zachary, my mom."

"Zachary." Mom smiles and reaches out to grapple him in a hug. Yeah, she's a hugger. It doesn't matter who you are. "Kenzie's told me all about you."

All about you? What the— What are you doing? I barely told you anything. Just that he's Hayden's brother, Hayden's in a coma, I'm *talking* to Hayden, and they're sort of wealthy. It seemed like all the important information at the time.

"Really?" Zachary's eyes go big. It could be the hug he's being smothered in or that she heard *all* about him. "Good to meet you."

"All right, we have to clean, so, uh…" I grin through tight locked lips at Mom.

"You two have fun. I'll be in the living room," Mom says, but before she leaves, she raises an eyebrow at me.

Stop it, Mom! Not now! Once she's gone, I turn to Zachary and switch to planning me. "Okay, so let's clear the counters and the table, and go from there. You get the counters and the dishes."

He doesn't ask questions. He immediately steps up to the sink and starts in on the dishes. I shrug, honestly surprised, and get to work on the dining room table. There isn't a ton to do, but that means I'll have more time tonight to FaceTime Kaitlynn, maybe play some *Sims*, or work on my tarot game. I really need to improve. I keep forgetting what the cards mean. Using the reference guide has to stop. What type of witch can't competently read tarot cards?

Five minutes later I've moved most of the boxes from the table to the floor and managed to sort the Amazon and Ulta packages. I might open a few of them and see what I can find a home for later.

"You always this quiet when you clean?" Zachary breaks the silence.

"I don't usually have help." I want to take it back the moment I say it. That makes it sound like Mom does nothing around the house, and that's not true, at least not always. I guess I do a lot of the cleaning, but she does too. Still, it was too quick an answer.

"Really?" He stops drying the plate in his hand.

"Yeah." I shrug.

His nose crinkles. It's sort of cute, but there's a question behind it. He doesn't say it, but I know what it is. I look behind me toward the hallway. The sound of the television is just loud enough to hear from the other room. He wants to know why I do the cleaning and not Mom. I bet his mom even cleans his room for him.

"She's busy with work a lot." I stretch the truth a bit. It isn't work that keeps her busy. It's all the junk in her head, but he doesn't need to know that. She's just not always... *here*. "So I help out. I don't mind. I like cleaning."

"Ah." He shrugs, wide-eyed.

"I take it you don't?" I ask.

"Not if I don't have to." Zachary laughs. "Do you usually clean in silence though? No music?"

"Oh! You want music?" I ask. I can play some music, I just didn't know what he'd like and honestly, I didn't want to ask.

"Please!" he begs. "The silence is killing me."

I roll my eyes and laugh at him before connecting my phone to the Bluetooth speaker by the sink and starting my usual playlist. He can deal with whatever comes on. I dare him to question it.

Zachary's eyes glow a little after the first few notes of TXT's

"Deja Vu" graces the kitchen air. He grins. "You like K-pop?"

"Yeah." I lean against one of the tall wooden dining table chairs, propping it on two legs. My eyes slim into slits and I eye him down. "You?"

He doesn't hit me as the type, more country boy. Not full-on country boy, but definitely country. He and Hayden both carry that twang most of us do up here, and there's the blue jeans and plaid, just like the red and white shirt he's wearing now. I used to get bullied for liking K-pop. It was a whole thing. One more that I had to build up a wall to and decide I was living for me and not them anyway.

"I love K-pop!" He jumps. "And no joke, you just turned on one of my favorites. Tomorrow X Together is amazing! Who's your bias? Mine's Taehyun—"

"Uh, Soobin, duh." I look at him like it's a stupid question before a massive grin covers my face. "I can't believe you like K-pop! I can't even get Kaity to listen to it. Who else do you listen to?"

"So many! RIIZE, BoyNextDoor, Jungkook, ATEEZ..." His eyes peer up toward the ceiling in thought. "AMPERS&ONE—"

"Really? I love them." I start to jump excitedly, but I stop myself with a firm grip on one of the dining room chairs. "All of them! And of course Seventeen and XG, and you can't forget the idol of idols."

"Taemin!" We yell at the same time.

"Whoa! Maybe you're not *so* bad," I say with literally no thought.

"Uh," he grunts, his shoulders deflating, and licks nervously at his lips. I should say I'm sorry. That was mean. Too mean, but I just can't. If I do, I might spill everything, and I'm not ready for that. Instead, I pick up another box, but before I can figure out where to put it, Zachary speaks up. "Sorry."

"Huh?" I freeze. Box in tow, I turn to face him.

"Sorry," he says again.

"You already said that," I tell him. This just feels awkward now.

"I know, but—"

"I mean earlier. You don't have—" I want him to stop. I don't want to feel bad for him.

"That was…" He grunts, sort of like a laugh but quieter, and shakes his head with a tiny reserved smile. "But that was on the phone. I need to apologize in person. I feel really bad about how I acted, I didn't mean to be an ass—"

He throws a hand over his mouth and his eyes burst wide.

A smile breaks across my face and I giggle.

"You're good. The TV's too loud," I assure him. "She ain't going to hear shit."

"Wooh," he breathes through O-shaped lips and finally laughs with me.

"You're okay though, I get it," I tell him. I'm the bad one here after all. Gods, I really am the bad one here.

"Okay. I don't want to be your boyfriend's asshole brother." Zachary grins.

TWO HOURS LATER, MOM and I are clearing the Chinese takeout from the table. I'm scrubbing the silverware while Mom rinses and puts them in the rack to dry. Zachary's at the table looking like a lost puppy.

He asked to help and I said he could do Mom's part, but she told him to sit back down. This is probably the most time I've spent with Mom in a while, actually doing something together other than watching TV. It's nice even if it is cleaning up after dinner.

Zachary's been pretty cool too. Oh, and he's a sci-fi and fantasy fan. Before Mom stole his attention, we were going on and on about *Rebel Moon*. It's epic, and he even agreed that Nemesis is the coolest character. Then he mentioned loving the fantasy parts, and Mom mentioned *Game of Thrones*, which he seems to love, and I became a silent bystander for a while. I've only seen a few seasons. Now they're going on about his cats, something I can fully get into. One is even named after one of the *GoT* dragons or something.

"Rhaenyra is a ragdoll. She's *so* fluffy," Zachary says.

"Aw," I sigh. They sound so cute.

"I love that name," Mom says. "And your other?"

"Artemis," he replies. "He's a Russian Blue."

"Those are gorgeous," Mom says, handing me the last cleaned fork.

The light in her eyes and the exuberance in her voice feels so foreign. I like it, but it's like some distant relative coming to visit. Someone I've not seen in ages who warms my heart. I wish she'd stay like this.

"Arty is a cutey. He's still a kitten too." Zachary is nearly cooing over the cat.

At least it isn't a snake, or worse, insects. I don't want to be ten feet from any *pet* insect.

"Have you met Arty?" Mom looks at me.

"Uh…n-no," I stutter.

"Maybe you can soon."

"Maybe," I say, giving Zachary a funny look.

He actually returns the expression and then gets up. "I need to get going, actually."

Oops! I didn't mean to make you uncomfortable. *Good job, Kenzie.*

"There's no rush, Zachary," Mom assures him.

"Yeah, you're good," I say.

"Nah, I need to get home. I've got homework," he tells us. His eyes settle on me. "But Mom did want me to invite you over for dinner tomorrow."

"Oh," I say. Suddenly I don't know how to respond. I don't need to keep going over there. Silence bounces loudly between us while we look awkwardly at each other until Mom nudges me with her elbow. What? Oh! "Uh, yeah. Sure. What time?"

"Think she said seven," Zachary says. "I'll make sure."

"Okay, yeah." I nod.

"Well, I'm going to get going," he says to me and then looks to my mom. "Thanks for dinner, ma'am."

"No problem," Mom says.

I slide between them. I swear it looks like she thinks I'm dating *him* instead of his brother, which…actually whatever. I grab his arm and pull him into the hallway and then to the front door.

"Thanks for the help," I tell him, trying to urge him to go before Mom can say something stupid. He stops and faces me, his hand on the knob. Okay, like why is his nose so cute and perfect? He smiles and I glance away.

"Of course." He nods and twists the knob. The click makes me jump just before the wind slips inside and chills my arms, and he crosses onto the porch. "I'll see you tomorrow."

"Yeah, see ya," I say and let the door shut behind him.

I huff. Okay. Fine. That wasn't as bad as I thought it was going to be. It could have been so much worse, but like…Mom! Wrong boy!

"He's cute," Mom says from behind me.

I swing around and spring my eyes open at her.

"Mom!" I say.

"What? He's your boyfriend, right?" She shrugs.

"Him? Zachary? No!" I blurt. Then I lie, which is feeling too normal at this point. Well, I tell the truth on top of a lie, I guess. "Hayden's my boyfriend! That's his *brother*!"

"Oh." She shakes her head. "That's right. The one who's…in a coma?"

"Yeah," I sigh. "A coma."

"You seem pretty uh…struck by Zachary though," Mom comments.

"What? Mom!"

"Sorry," she says. "They look alike?"

"Uh…I mean…" I grumble.

"Okay." Mom wobbles her head and shrugs. "Be careful, then. Don't go falling in love with the brother while your boyfriend is sleeping."

What the hell, Mom?

12

IT'S BEEN OVERCAST AND cold all day. Rain splotches my windshield, and brooding gray clouds hang over the treetops. They're threatening to bring a deluge down on the mountain. All I ask is that it doesn't flood. My little hatchback can't deal with that. Not to mention rain at night sucks.

Korean lyrics I don't understand are playing through my speakers as I pull into their driveway. I gasp again when Hayden's house comes into view. Not sure how long that's going to take to get used to. It's just so cool.

Out front, sitting in a low chair, is Eliza. Her white top and flared tan bottoms contrast with the rest of the porch. She always stands out. Catina, her daughter, sits next to her in a graphic tee and shorts. It's much too cold to be sitting outside period, much less in shorts.

I roll to a stop and grab the covered plate from the passenger seat before slipping out into the light drizzle. The tiny droplets are chilly against my neck and wrists. Little ice pricks, so I rush for the shelter of the covered porch.

"Hey, Eliza," I say, stepping up the stairs. "Catina."

"Hi!" Catina smiles.

"Kenzie." Eliza nods. "Sit with me a moment."

"Uh, shouldn't I take this in first?" I ask. I really want to get inside and out of this shitty weather.

"Catina can take it in for you." Eliza looks at her daughter, who doesn't seem too excited about it but doesn't question.

She takes the dish from me and disappears inside. "Okay.

Thanks," I say because I don't know what else to say. I take the seat Catina was previously occupying.

"I know how it is. To be on the outside." Eliza smiles calmingly at me.

Uh…say what? What is that supposed to mean?

I grin, but my nerves are suddenly on edge.

"It took a while for the family to accept me when I met Jeffrey down in New Orleans," she says. Am I about to get a whole family history lesson? "I wasn't just the first Black woman in the family, I was the first witch. It took them a bit to be alright with the witch part. They're good people though. So loving, and they have a way with understanding. I love them dearly."

Now my entire body is radiating nervous energy. Where is this going?

"That's really good." I grin. What are you getting at? Is this like the talk dads usually give their daughter's potential suitors? Is a shotgun about to come out? A Smith & Wesson story? Some Rodney Atkins song?

"It really is." Eliza nods and shifts to look at me directly. "I'd do anything for them. They're my family. So I'll get right to the point, Kenzie."

Okay…

Eliza leans forward, her smile somehow holding both a lightness and weight that's usually reserved for my least favorite conversations. Our eyes meet, and no matter how much I want to look away, I can't. Her dark browns bore into me, searching me. Yeah, I already don't like this.

"I know you and Hayden aren't dating," she says.

"What?!" I jump, taken aback by the accusation, the truth. How does she know? "How…I mean what?"

"I was in the hall the other day…at the hospital," she starts to explain. My stomach jumps into my throat and I fall back, letting my back smack against the black wooden slats. I thought she said she'd just arrived though! "When you were there talking to Hayden. I overheard."

Shit! Immediately I go into damage control mode.

"I'm so sorry! I didn't mean for this to happen. I really—"

"No, no. Calm down, Kenzie." Eliza pats my shoulder, her smile motherly. "I know. I heard. I could feel your conflict, how much you wanted to be truthful."

"I do, I really do!" I tell her. "I'm just...I don't know...I'm afraid of how they'll see me. How you'll see me. I don't even know if Hayden would date a guy."

She grunts at that last bit but doesn't seem too worried about it. "How much of what you said *is* true though?"

"Uh..." I pause. *Just breathe, Kenzie. You can't go back to five minutes ago. Just be honest.* "The rest, really. We *did* meet at the café. It's where I work, and he comes all the time. I just never *really* talked to him. I just took his order, but nothing else. I was too scared. Too much of a coward."

"Don't say that." Eliza purses her lips.

"It's true though," I tell her. "It was all a misunderstanding."

"A misunderstanding?" Eliza asks.

I huff again. This is too hard.

"Yes." I nod. "At the hospital they wouldn't let me go back and see him because I'm not family. I might have gotten ahead of myself and said he was my boyfriend. The nurses know me—I interned at the hospital this summer—so I thought it would help my chances of seeing him. I didn't think anything of it."

I stop and examine the palms of my hands. My fingers grip my amethyst.

"But when y'all came in the room and asked who I was. The

way y'all reacted…when the nurse said I was…uh…Hayden's enbyfriend. I couldn't say it wasn't true. I wanted it."

Gods. I wanted it so bad. To be *his*. And I *think* I still do, but is it worth lying to his family?

Eliza's face softens and she blinks slowly, never once letting go of my eyes. I was expecting something much different when this happened, but it's not there. The rage isn't there. The disbelief and disgust. None of it. Is this how the entire family would be?

"I see." Eliza looks away into the trees.

It's already so dark you can only see the first few before it fades into nothing. The rain is coming harder now, splatting along the walkway and at the edge of the porch.

The back of my throat is dry despite the humidity, and pinpricks run up my shoulder. What is she thinking? Does she hate me now? Am I a horrible person in her mind?

I am in mine.

"Mackenzie." Her voice is quiet and kind, but it feels like the friend equivalent of Mom calling me Mackenzie Nicholas Jackson. "I guess the real question is, do you care about him? Do you know Hayden enough to care about him?"

I snap my gaze away and crinkle my nose. Elegantly manicured ferns fill my vision against the stoic concrete barrier lining the front porch. My eyes lock on a single frond. Its toothy pear-green leaves along a single stalk are coated in water. One among a much larger thriving ecosystem. Together, but also alone. I get lost in its leaves until a droplet pelts my forehead.

"I don't know." I wipe the water from my head, annoyed by my response. I do know…I think, at least. "I mean yeah, but no. I want to."

"But do you?" she asks again.

I shrug. How can I know? The longest conversation we've ever had was that time he ordered snacks for his family and he had to keep repeating which cakes and pastries he wanted. That wasn't a conversation though. Not really.

"They deserve to know the truth." Eliza says it slowly, her words coated in Southern honey with a kick of Cajun.

"Yeah," I whisper. "I know."

What I don't know is how to break it to them. This wasn't how I'd expected anyone to find out, and I don't think I can just say it. I can't just bring it up. That's too hard.

"I'll tell them," I say anyway. Because it's right, even though my mind is in gridlock and my anxiety is through the roof.

"No." Eliza pats my knee. Wait, she said *no*?

"Huh?" I reel back. "No? Why not?"

"Maybe it'd be good to wait. Let me think about how best to break it to them," Eliza says, bunching her cheeks up in contemplation. "Delilah isn't called *Super Old* Gran for nothing. I don't want to shock her too much at once."

Excuse me? Are you saying I might kill Grandma? Don't say that! That's horrible! I couldn't deal with that. Super Old Gran is so fun! My stomach sinks. I think I'm going to be sick.

"Super Old Gran?" I frown.

"It's good. I'll figure it out," she assures me with a laugh. "I got you."

"I...I don't want to lose them though." I frown and look away. It's not really something I can control, but it's true. "All of you. I've never had a family like this."

Eliza's thoughtful expression morphs into a mother's warm grin. She sighs and squeezes my shoulder. "I see. I can't speak for them, but I always get good energy from you. Our faults don't have to define us, Kenzie, and even if some things take time, it doesn't mean they can't work out. Just give me some time."

"Thank you!" I breathe. Does part of me feel wrong for letting her take it on? Yes, yes it does. Does part of me adore her for doing this? Also yes.

Am I the problem? Definitely.

TO SAY DINNER IS awkward may be the understatement of my short life. I refuse to look at Eliza. Thank the gods for her, but the sight of her reminds me I'm on the edge of the cliff.

"Did you see the Mountaineers lost to Avery last night?" Jeffrey asks.

The Mountaineers are Hayden and Zachary's school. I've been to a few games to watch Hayden play. Okay, more than a few.

"Yeah," Mr. Marcus sighs. "Forty-eight to fifty-two."

"Beau said it was a tense one." Jeffrey droops his shoulders.

They've been going on about their favorite college basketball teams. Jeffrey's a Carolina fan. I bet he's got a blue Heels sticker on the back of his truck. Randall seems to root for the Trojans—I don't have a clue what school that is. And now, we've veered into high school basketball.

"If they'd had Hayden they might have made it. They haven't done as well since." Jeffrey slumps back.

"It won't be long," Mary-Anne says, but I can tell she's fighting back some deeper emotions with the way she twitches. They're the words of someone wishing out loud, like maybe if they say it, it'll come true. "He'll be back soon."

The room falls silent. No one knows what to say, and I'm not taking a chance. Instead, I take a gulp of water while I try to ignore the gut feeling that everyone is looking at me, like they know my secret. My head is screaming that they're all accusing me right now with every innocent glance. Gods, I want to duck under the table and disappear, to become nothing. On top of that, it's been hell having to be around Zachary. He's being too nice. I don't deserve that. Part of me would feel better, more in place, if he was still questioning me. I don't deserve to be here at all.

The quiet is too much. No one knows what to say, and all but one face is somber and soured by Hayden's absence. Super Old Gran is at the end of the table smiling away like nothing could be better, but she doesn't look entirely present.

"Have you seen Hayden's room?" Zachary speaks up from across the table.

It's a weird question, sudden for the middle of dinner, but there's an easy answer.

"No." I shrug.

"Let me show you." Zachary slides his chair back and gets up. His eyes look at me expectantly, and a second later I'm up. Why are you saving me from this awkwardness?

"Oh… O-okay," I stutter and look to his mom. For some reason I feel like I need to be excused first. She grins and dips her head, so I get up and meet him at the edge of the hallway.

I don't have a clue where I'm going, so I stay a step behind. Why does he want to show me Hayden's room? Is he trying to make me slip, to give myself away? I can't shake the feeling there's an alternative motive. Was it all a ruse to make me feel comfortable, to make me trust him so I might say something unreasonable?

"It was getting way too serious in there," Zachary says once we're out of earshot. "I had to get out."

"Yeah," I mutter. But still, why take me here? "I mean, I get it though."

"Sure." Zachary nods. "But still."

A meow squeaks around the corner before a little blue-gray kitten prances into view. Oh my gods, they're so cute. Then as quickly as it appeared, it sees me and runs the other direction.

"Ah," I sigh.

"He's skittish," Zachary says.

"And so cute! Is that Artemis?" I ask. I think I remember him telling Mom about his Russian Blue kitty cat being Artemis.

"Yeah." He grins. "Rhaenyra is around here somewhere."

"I love kitties," I squeal. I want one so bad, but Mom always says no.

"You like animals?" he asks.

"Uh, yeah. I need a cat familiar," I tell him. Every witch needs a familiar.

"Wait!" Zachary grins big and turns back around. "My room first, then."

"Uh...sure." I shrug and follow him back down the hall to the door we just passed.

I cross the threshold and...wait. *This* is his bedroom? It's massive. You could fit two—no, three of my rooms in here. And there's a skylight in the ceiling. It's like a moonroof in a car, but in his room. And it's so clean and tidy.

"You have a king-size bed?" My mouth hangs open.

"California king," he corrects me.

"Asshole." I shake my head. "I've got a twin. And it's from the consignment store."

"I..." Zachary tenses up, and immediately I realize what I've done.

"It's good, it's comfy. Your room is so cool though! It's so nice. And green."

There are plants everywhere. Ferns and shrubs, flowers and vines. Splatters of color dot the vegetation, from big purple orchid blooms and pink hyacinth to white daisies and some bright blue and white blossom I've never seen before. But somehow, despite the plants being everywhere, it doesn't look cluttered.

"A little." Zachary laughs and the weirdest thing happens. My nerves calm a little. It's gentle, like a springtime melody. "Yeah, I like plants…and gardening…and basically anything nature."

"You're in the perfect place then," I say. "Your house is surrounded by it."

"Isn't everyone's up here?" he smirks.

"Fair," I agree. Except the rest of ours are set within view of other houses, or power lines, or some state road. Here it's like you've stepped out of the world into a wholly separate universe. "Yours is cooler though."

"Eh." He shrugs, and his eyes dip toward my chest.

A tingle rises in my throat and I clamp my teeth together. What are you…

"I really like your necklace," Zachary says. "Are those amethysts inside it?"

"Huh?" I blurt. His eyes are back up again, and his smile is soft and kind. "Thank you. And, yeah. Just little tiny stones."

I'm about to tell him how it's my anxiety necklace. How the amethyst is packed inside with cedarwood, horsetail, and lavender, and how it gives me calming energy when I need it, but I stop. He doesn't care about all that.

"My Aunt Eliza wears a lot of jewelry like that. I love the crescent moon stuff," Zachary tells me.

Maybe he would know some about the metaphysical. His aunt is a witch too. He might have grown up learning about it, unless Mary-Anne and Randall didn't let him, but I don't know how all that works here.

"I have a bunch like these. With different crystals and herbs in them, but I usually wear this one," I admit. It's become a habit. I'm not sure if it's because it works or because it's my prettiest one, but I do love it.

"Wait." Zachary angles his cheek toward me and pooches his lips. "Are you a witch? Wiccan?"

"I am, but not Wiccan. Just a witch, well, a Norse witch, a Norse Kitchen Witch." I keep adding to it, hoping that he's good with it. Please be good with it.

"That's cool! Aunt Eliza is too. Except she's Wiccan, I think, and maybe a Green Witch…" Zachary seems excited. "I've never met a Norse witch though. Who are your gods?"

Did he just ask who my gods were? It wasn't, *Oh my God that's weird*, or *Norse, really?* Or, *A witch?* It was who are your gods. I might be in lo— No! Nope. Stop right there!

"Odin, Freyja, Heimdall, Odr, and others." I reel myself in. No one usually cares. "I pray mainly to Freyja though."

"That's so neat. Freyja's Thor's mom, right?" Zachary asks.

"No," I say. It's a common misconception. Thanks to Marvel everyone knows Thor and Odin, and the rest just get thrown around. "That's Frigg, Odin's wife. Freyja's the daughter of Njörðr—not sure I'm saying that right—and rules over Fólkvangr. She's the goddess of love, and beauty, and war, and future magic."

Zachary seems surprised. He did ask, so I feel no remorse for unloading it on him. I could go on. All about how Freyja's part of the Vanir, and she can use her cloak of falcon feathers to become a bird sometimes, and is charged with the Valkyries. Oh, and how half the dead go to Odin in Valhalla, while the other half go to the field of Fólkvangr where Freyja reigns, and not only Valhalla. I find it all fascinating. I love how she was venerated by all and equal to men in a time in Christendom when women weren't.

"You're really into it, aren't you?" he asks.

"Yeah, it's my faith," I tell him. Shouldn't I be?

"Of course! I didn't mean to belittle." Zachary waves his hands, palms out, horror written all over his face.

It's hard to bury the laugh building in my throat with the way his entire body is fidgeting and jumping. I manage it though.

"I know!" I grin.

"I'm sorry. I really think it's cool, I do!" Zachary says again and again.

"It's okay! Promise," I assure him, or at least attempt.

"Okay. Good. I didn't think how it sounded. Moving on though," he says, and just as quickly his eyes shoot to the other end of the room. "You're not afraid of spiders, are you?"

"I *most* definitely am," I say promptly. Bugs in general freak me out, but spiders are next level.

"Hmmm…" Zachary purses his lips and considers me a moment before turning and heading toward a large glass aquarium…with no water in it.

No. Don't you dare tell me I'm in the same room with a freaking pet spider! No!

His hand plunges over the aquarium's open top and fishes around a second. When he comes back up, he walks backward…toward me. My throat tightens. My arms pull back and I gulp. Please no, Zachary! But do I say it? No!

"Meet…" Zachary strings the word out and then suddenly swings around. "Teo!"

In a matter of a second I'm confronted with the biggest sand-brown spider I've ever seen in my life. I flail backward against the wall and claw for anything that I can get my hands on.

"Put it back! Put it back!" I beg.

The excitement in Zachary's eyes dims to shame. He yanks back and hurries to the aquarium. My body is shaking by the time he returns. He surprises me again when a palm lightly cups my arm. I flinch from the unexpected touch, but he holds on.

"I'm sorry, Mackenzie," he says. "I didn't think it'd..."

He doesn't finish the sentence and I find myself staring down at his hand. It's still there, lightly holding my arm. It's warm and soft, and I'm not shaking anymore. Then my brain floods with one singular question on repeat.

Why the hell is he touching me?

I yank my arm away as the adrenaline wears off, and he takes a step back. His face is blushed. Damn. I made him feel bad. Well serves you right, scaring me like that. I told you I was scared of them.

"I'm s—"

Involuntarily, a tiny giggle jumps into my mouth and escapes. I try to hold the next back, but it happens anyway. Zachary looks at me oddly, and I giggle again. Now I'm smiling because it's funny, even if I was just scared out of my mind. It's like a reflex for me. Something makes my adrenaline spike, then it fades and I giggle.

"Are you okay?" Zachary asks, a smile forming on his lips despite the confusion pouring from his eyes.

"Yeah, it's an adrenaline response," I tell him. "Weird. I know."

"It's cute. I mean okay. It's okay," he speeds over himself.

Okay... I'm not sure what to do with that.

"So, no Teo then." Zachary keeps talking. "I love spiders, he's my second, actually. But I get it. You and them don't mix."

"Two of them?" I ask, peering around him at the *open* aquarium. There's no lid. *It has no lid!* And I can't see the spider. Wait, it has a name? No, I knew that already. But where's the lid?

"Yeah, you just met—well, sort of—Teo. They're a tan jumping spider. I caught them a few months ago in the backyard." He sounds so proud of his catch, and despite how much I don't want to be in the same house as a spider, I can appreciate that. "I don't know if it's a boy or girl, so I just say they're non-binary like you."

"I never thought of spiders as non-binary," I admit. Although

How (Not) to Conjure a Boyfriend 113

most of the time when I think of spiders I'm thinking nasty, creepy, crawly things that deserve to be swallowed by the depths of hell. Sort of like yellow jackets. "I remember you telling Mom about them. Just didn't think I was going to meet them."

"Yeah." Zachary shrugs. "I named them after the Great Goddess of Teotihuacan. They also called her Spider Woman, so it sort of makes sense."

"Teotia-whaty?" I say.

"Exactly. That's why they're Teo." He smiles. "Before Teo, I had Aria — she was a black and white garden spider. She was bigger than Teo. I named her after the Celtic spider goddess."

Great Goddess of Teoti-something. Celtic goddess. Cats named Artemis and Rhaenyra. Okay, that last one isn't a mythological character, but she is fantasy. No wonder he was actually intrigued by Freyja.

"You have a thing for mythology and religions, don't you?" I ask. It wasn't really a question, but oh well.

"How'd you guess?"

He looks genuinely surprised.

"Really?" I ask, my giggle returning for a second. "All your…pets. They're named after gods and goddesses. And you actually seemed to be interested in my faith. No one ever is."

"I think it's neat! And yeah, they all are named after gods and goddesses, except Rhaenyra," he corrects me. "Mom named her. I wanted her to be Athena. Did you know she was one of only three virgin goddesses?"

"Nope. I hadn't a clue," I admit. I guess that gives me one thing in common with a goddess then.

He goes on about how she helped Perseus against Medusa, and made sure Odysseus got home, and how the city of Athens was named after her. Then he starts in on Artemis. This stuff is just cool. It's so intricate and exciting. And it sounds so much more interesting when he talks about it. It seems to really mean something to him.

A good ten minutes pass before he remembers why we came back here in the first place. To see Hayden's room. To see my "boyfriend's" room.

"I'll ramble forever about mythology if you don't stop me," he says as we walk down the hall and turn in to another room.

"I believe you," I laugh.

"So this is Hayden's room," he says.

It's nothing like Zachary's. There are trophies along one wall on a floating shelf, a few basketball jerseys in cases. I'm assuming until I'm told otherwise that they're real ones that the players wore because, I mean, look at this house. The bed is perfectly made, just like Zachary's, probably courtesy of Mrs. Marcus...or a maid. A few posters dot the walls, including a *Euphoria* poster just over his bed's headboard featuring a busty Sydney Sweeney with her signature blonde hair and low-cut, fitted dress.

Yeah. He's straight. Okay, no, he could be bi! Or maybe he is gay and just obsessed with her. I can't really rationalize that last one with all I know of him, but that's what I'm going with. I should really stop trying to figure it out.

"Definitely not as green," I comment nervously. I don't know what I'm supposed to be doing.

Does he expect me to rummage around Hayden's stuff? That seems rude since he doesn't actually know me, not like that. And I've already seen plenty.

"Hayden couldn't care less about plants," Zachary laughs.

"So that's your thing, then."

"And building junk," he says. "Uh, so what are you up to this weekend?"

This weekend? That was way out of nowhere. Work, obviously. I rarely get a full day off on the weekend, but why do you want to know?

"Nothing much." I shrug. He starts back into the hall and makes off toward the dining room. "Just work, maybe play some *Sims*—"

"You play *The Sims*?" Zachary asks.

"Yeah, you?" I ask, hopeful.

"Nah. I didn't know anyone did anymore." He grins.

I shake my head and nudge him. He lifts his hands in defense. "And I might go visit the old Harrell House."

"'Visit'?" Zachary makes finger air quotes. "You mean trespass."

I just smile. He's not wrong, but I'm going to leave it there. It's abandoned. Has been for like thirty years, I think, and I most definitely won't be the first person to visit since the signs went up. I've wanted to go since I heard about it freshman year. Mom doesn't want me going, but I'll worry about that later.

"Wanna come?" I surprise even myself, but when I consider taking the invite back, I can't. How rude that would sound.

"You want me to go?" Zachary asks, then dips his head. "Or are you just too scared to go by yourself?"

"Eff you," I say, not wanting to say the real word where his parents might hear. "I take it back. I'm going by myself."

"No, don't do that!" Zachary punches my shoulder. He's acting like he's known me a long time, and I'm not sure I know how to feel about that.

"Have no fear. I won't. I'm trying to make Kaity go," I tell him.

"Kaity?" He's bewildered by the name, and I have to remind myself he knows basically nothing about me...well, except he does know more about me than Hayden. Hell, he's met my mom!

"She's my best friend," I say.

"Oh, okay." He nods. "Probably safer if I went too though."

"Or just one more person to get in trouble," I say.

"Or one more person to keep an eye out." He raises his brow like he's on to something.

Seems like he actually wants to go. I let my head angle, curls falling just over my eyes, and shake my head at him and smile.

"I guess you're coming then," I huff.

"Yes!" He jumps.

Maybe this is okay. Since I hadn't actually asked Kaitlynn yet. Probably should ask her now.

13

IT'S COLDER UP HERE than I thought it would be. I've two jackets on over a pair of thermals and a T-shirt and I'm *still* freezing. This might have been my idea, but I didn't expect it to be the coldest day of the year.

"You expect us to jump *that* fence?" Zachary looks puzzled.

Ah yes. The fence. I forgot about that little detail. It's at least eight feet tall and built out of black wrought-iron bars. The top is well out of his reach, and *so* out of mine. Maybe we could help each other over, but there's also the problem of the thick spiky pieces of metal jutting from the top of each bar. It's almost like they didn't want anyone getting in.

"Are you sure the gate's locked? This place has been abandoned forever," Kaitlynn whines, which is against rule number one.

No complaining.

It took a lot of convincing to get her to come along, which somehow she spun into Zach and me needing a chaperone, not because I simply asked her to come, and in the end I had to lay down some ground rules. Number two was *Don't embarrass me*. She's the queen of that, maybe even thrives on it, but tonight is not that night. There's also a third I added later because she wouldn't shut up about it. *No calling Zachary my boyfriend*. She somehow got it in her head that's why he's coming. Hence us needing a "chaperone." It's not though.

"Of course," I say. "I checked last week."

"Really?" she sounds surprised.

"No, bitch." I roll my eyes. "I've never been here before."

"So…" Zachary smirks, steamy breath rolling from his mouth the moment it hits the chilled air.

I think he's trying to understand Kaitlynn and my dynamic before getting in the middle of it. Smart boy. She's a handful that he doesn't want to upset, not yet.

"I hate you. You know that, right?" Kaitlynn eyes me down.

I smile back and then nod to our right.

"The gate's that way," I tell them.

"So you *did* check it?" Zachary finally asks.

"No." I toss the word behind me and start off.

We ditched Zachary's truck back where the fence picked up, just in case there were cameras. We could be misidentified on camera, but a license plate…that's a little easier to catch. Not to mention Zachary's truck isn't that subtle. It's big and, well, very orange.

Plumes of steam billow from Kaitlynn's nose when I point my phone's light back toward her and we pass the vine-and-weed-wrapped fence. She's not the biggest fan of my little expeditions into the abandoned, but I drag her along anyway whenever I can manage. She loves me. It's mostly the dark that gets her, I think. Above us, the moon continues to wane into a thin crescent, and with all the clouds, it's nearly pitch black. It's so quiet I can hear every breath we take, especially Kaitlynn's, and the occasional insect singing its late autumn song to the coming winter. My trespassing sneakers — yes I have old shoes just for trespassing — squish and sink with each step, courtesy of today's morning rain. It's not a sound I particularly enjoy.

"Is there a story to this place?" Zachary asks. "Why's it abandoned?"

There wasn't much talking on the half-hour drive up. At least not with him. Kaitlynn wouldn't shut up as usual. I could barely

How (Not) to Conjure a Boyfriend

enjoy the music for her raving about the new season of *Siesta Key* and how Elijah looked at her in Math yesterday. She's determined he's in love with her. There wasn't time to talk about the house.

"From what I've heard, there was a family living here in the early '90s," I start relaying what little I know.

"That's forever ago," Kaitlynn mumbles.

"We weren't even born," Zachary whispers back to her.

"Yeah, major old." I laugh. "Well, they say it was a husband and wife and their two kids. Twins, I think, a boy and girl."

"That's rare," Zachary comments.

"The dad was an only child, and they say he was training his son to take over the farm," I say. "But—"

"This is a farm?" Zachary interrupts.

"Yeah." I look back and nod. We're at the gate. "So…"

I stop storytelling to stare at the chain links drooping from the gate with a massive rusted padlock hanging from it. I survey the gate. It's made of the same black wrought-iron bars, except it has a big *H* on each door and the spikes are taller. I pull at the lock to see if it'll budge, but get nothing. I don't think we're getting in this way.

"Locked," Kaitlynn says the obvious.

"No shit," I blurt.

"Is there another way in?" Zachary asks.

I shrug even though he's not looking at me. I honestly figured we'd have to jump a fence, but I hadn't expected it to be this tall. I had a fence I could look over in my mind, like a little white picket fence. Not a stay-the-hell-out iron monstrosity. And honestly, I expected the gate to just be open.

"Over?" I suggest, but the doubt is clear in my tone.

Zachary groans, eyes shooting to the spears topping the fence. "It's sort of tall, and spiky."

"Maybe there's a log around here somewhere we can use to stand on," I say, knowing all too well it's much too convenient. There's not going to be a random perfectly shaped piece of log just sitting around. "Or we could walk around and see if there are any openings?"

"Didn't you say this was a farm?" Kaitlynn's whining yet again.

"Yeah." I shrug and face them both.

"Um…" Zachary puts a finger in the air. "How big of a farm?"

"I don't know," I admit. "I didn't get the Zillow specs on the property before we came to view. Are we planning to buy or something?"

Okay, maybe it was a little spicy, more of a Kaitlynn thing to say, but this isn't working like I'd planned. We were supposed to be inside already, exploring, seeing if there are ghosts or cool old nineties relics.

Kaitlynn pooches her lips and shakes her head. "It's probably huge, then. And I'm not here to walk miles in the pitch black, in the woods, where there are bears. Big bears."

"I'm with her," Zachary says.

"Traitor." I aim my light at him.

"Well, I… I— Wait!" Zachary yells and shields his face from the sudden brightness. Then he shrinks back like he said something bad. "That was loud."

"Everything is loud out here," I tell him and then raise my eyebrows to say, *and?*

"I have this project I'm working on for school in the back of my truck. We could use it," he says.

"We going to *present* ourselves over the fence? Lecture it into submission?" Kaitlynn scowls.

I bite my lip to hold back a laugh, but my belly shakes anyway.

How (Not) to Conjure a Boyfriend

"No-o-o." Zachary strings it out and laughs it off. "My carpentry project. It's a bookshelf."

"Oh." I nod quickly. "How big a bookshelf are we talking?"

"Just three shelves," he says.

"That shouldn't be too hard to carry," Kaitlynn says.

"Well…" Zachary starts.

I don't like the sound of that.

"It'll take at least two of us." He looks at me, then grimaces. "Okay, maybe all three."

Kaitlynn giggles and nods at Zachary approvingly.

"No! That's not what I meant." Zachary's hands are flailing.

"Excuse me?" I widen my eyes. I'm not that puny.

"I swear, I didn't mean that," Zachary repeats, and then looks at Kaity and shrugs. "Okay, maybe I did a little."

"We doing this?" I growl and roll my eyes. I will not be doubted.

"Come on." Zachary waves and he's off toward his truck.

I huff and race to make up the lost ground. A few minutes later, we're standing at the back of Zachary's truck with the tailgate down and the cover lifted. He has to be kidding.

"That looks heavy as fuck," I blurt.

"Eh." Zachary shrugs and jumps into the truck bed. "It *is* solid wood. It's not finished yet though. I haven't put the trim on or etched out the decorative stuff, but it's sturdy." He grips the corner of the unstained wood and gives it a shake. It barely budges.

"Looks like it." Kaitlynn grimaces.

"I'll push it to you two and then y'all can ease it down," he tells us. "Ready?"

"Uh…sure." I shrug.

"Please don't break it," he says, and starts to push.

It slides to the edge quicker than I expect. Maybe it's not that heavy after all. When it gets to the edge, I grab my end while

Kaitlynn's fingers wrap around the little feet on the other side. This ain't so bad, nah, it's...oh shit! The full weight drops as it clears the tailgate, and I brace. This is heavy as crap. It drops several inches before I get my fingers back around it.

"Kenzie!" Kaitlynn yelps.

"Sorry!" I yell back. "I got it now."

"You sure, Mack?" Zachary doesn't look convinced yet. His arms are desperately wrapped around the top of the case.

"Yes, *Zachary*, I have it," I bite back.

"Mack?" Kaitlynn leans around and whispers at me.

"Shut up," I whisper back. No one calls me that, ever. It is a little weird to hear, like mac and cheese or something, but I'll let it pass until my life isn't on the line.

"All right, I'm putting all the weight on y'all now," Zachary says.

I'm sorry, what? The full weight? Only now?

I push forward as the case comes down. I struggle, but keep it from free-falling. This bitch is heavy AF! We finally get it to the ground and I let go.

"How are we getting that way over there?" I gulp in air.

"Ah, you'll make it." Kaitlynn pats my back.

I want to call her a bitch, but I don't.

Zachary jumps off the back. That's when I notice he's wearing boots. Okay, why do they look sort of hot on him? Nope. Focus. Focus, Kenzie!

"You can call me Zach, by the way," he says over Kaitlynn.

"Huh?" I stumble, but manage it.

"Zach—you can call me Zach. You know, short for Zachary, like Mack is short for Mackenzie." He acts like he's giving me a lesson.

I roll my eyes. "Let's just get this thing over there."

How (Not) to Conjure a Boyfriend

"Zach," Kaitlynn says a little louder than I'd like.

"Huh?" Zach asks.

Dammit. He heard her.

"Nothing, just getting used to the name," Kaitlynn says.

I press my lips together and beam at her. When she meets my eyes I mouth, *I will end you.* She giggles and steps back, coordinating with me, while Zachary lifts the other end on his own. I'm fine with this. I don't mind that he can lift it with ease. Makes our part easier.

"How far back was it?" I whine.

"Rule number one," Kaitlynn whispers next to me where Zach can't hear it. I ignore her and roll my eyes. Not like anyone else is here to see. Just like they won't see me when I die crushed under a massive school carpentry project.

"Dunno," Zach says, leading the way with his back to the bookshelf and fingers under it like a tow hitch. "It's not super far though, right?"

"Define super far?" I say, reminding myself not to attach *bitch* to the end of it because it's not Kaity, and remembering that *I'm* the one who should know how far it is. Luckily it's not as far as I thought. After an excruciating ten minutes, and four — no five — rest stops, we deposit the shelf next to the fence in a spot Kaity found where the ground rises a little. Every inch counts, right?

Between the bars, the house's brick structure is barely visible through a light fog. It coats everything.

"Gross." Kaitlynn frowns.

The wood sinks an inch into the dirt. The smushing noises are atrocious. Like, I didn't know *that* could sound *that* bad.

"Yay." Zach eyes the mud.

I lift a foot and examine the bottom of my shoe. It's caked in wet dirt and grass. I look up and show Zachary a cheesy toothy grin.

"God," he sighs. "If this stains, I'm blaming you."

"Fair." I keep grinning. "You first?"

I figure he should have the honors of ruining his project first. He grumbles, plants the messy bottom of a boot—that probably cost more than all the clothes on my body combined—on the first shelf and climbs to the top. Mud gushes between his boot and the wood. I'm so sorry. He's committed though. He pushes himself up, and his waist is now level with the top of the fence.

"This might actually work," Zach says.

Good. Now I don't feel *as* bad. He plants a foot between the spikes. There's just enough room, but it still has me worried.

"Careful," I urge. The last thing I need is to be the reason *this* brother gets impaled.

"I got it." He waves me off and starts to push off the steel fencing. He jumps, and for a moment he's airborne, like Hayden going in for a layup, graceful and intentional, but slow motion this time because instead of waiting for a basket, I'm hoping to Odin he doesn't fall back onto the spikes or face-plant in the mud. Then it ends. His feet plop into the thick mud, and something wet smacks my face. I wipe my cheek and dirt smears along my finger.

"Really?" I sigh.

"So glad I was behind you," Kaitlynn laughs. That's when I notice the splats of brown on my jacket and jeans.

I huff and roll my eyes. "Thanks."

"Who's next?" Zach giggles and I jump up before Kaitlynn can so that I'm not the one splattered again.

"Me!" Peering over the top, the entire house comes into focus behind the foggy veil.

It's an old place, probably early to mid-1900s and walled entirely in brick, including its two chimneys jutting from a white roof on either end. I think the barn is farther away. It's too dark to make out much more detail beyond the wraparound porch. The fog's too thick.

I plant my foot on the fence top, carefully positioning my sneakers between spears of iron. *Just remember, Kenzie, this was your idea.* I sling my weight over, never letting go of the fence, and let my grip on the bars slow my descent. My feet hit the ground and sink an inch into the mud as I let my grip on the fence loose. I did it—oh shit! My right foot slips and I stumble backwards. My leg collapses and gravity yanks me toward the earth. I yelp, but I collide with Zachary's chest and his arms wrap around my waist before I can fall. I look up to find his steel eyes inches from mine. His Adam's apple bobs.

"I, uh... Are you okay?" he asks, pushing me up to my feet and quickly pulling his arms away, stepping back.

I nod frantically, eyes stuck on the mud. "Yeah."

"Awkward." Kaity's voice crawls through the fence.

"You're next," I say to Kaitlynn, and whisper "bitch" under my breath.

"I got this." She steps up and bounces over, completely unscathed. "No need to catch me."

I shake my head and don't wait before taking off toward the house. *Just ignore it and move on.* It was nothing and I don't need to see Zachary's reaction.

"That's creepy," Zach says from behind me. I check to see what he's talking about and find his eyes fixated on the house.

"It *is* abandoned, *and* old, *and* falling apart," I remind him. "*And* haunted. At least some say it is."

"Yeah, yeah." He waves me off. "I don't know about that."

"Of course it is!" Kaitlynn says off the cuff. "People died here."

"I'm sorry, what?" Zach catches up with us.

"Yeah," I say. I didn't get to finish the story earlier, and there was more to tell. A lot more. "Several, actually."

"Several... Uh, e-excuse me?" Zachary stutters. "And why are we here again?"

"Because it's cool *and* haunted," I say.

"What the...? I just thought it was abandoned," Zachary complains. "You didn't say anything about it being haunted."

The porch seems to grow as we get closer, and my foot claps against the first step. I was expecting wood and for it to crack and moan, but it's solid, which sort of throws me a bit.

"Should've asked," Kaitlynn says, and part of me wants to high-five her.

"You change your mind?" I stop at the front door once we've all made it up.

"Uh...no." He steps up.

I shrug and continue the house's story. "So, five people died here, and, like, a bunch of animals."

"Animals?" Zachary pouts.

"Yeah, sad, right?" Kaitlynn frowns.

"Really sad," I say, and turn the doorknob. It creaks and scrapes when I pull. At first it doesn't want to budge, but I give it a good yank and the door opens. A swoosh of air floods out with the door, ruffling my hair. It's darker inside. I step in and flick my phone's flashlight on. Without a word, Kaitlynn and Zach become ghosts on my tail.

"They started finding dead cows and chickens around the farm," I retell what I've heard. "At first, they thought it was a coyote or fox, maybe a black bear. But they never caught one."

"Not sure I want to hear the rest of this story," Zach says.

"Squeamish?" Kaitlynn asks.

"No, just not sure I want to know while I'm here," he says.

"You sure?" I ask, looking over the bare walls.

How (Not) to Conjure a Boyfriend

My light exposes a scene of decay. The wallpaper is either peeling or has completely fallen to expose old rotting wood. The space is empty, just a big open square filled with the grays of night, drooping webs, and the occasional ray of moonlight through a cracked window.

"Fine, what happened?"

I smile at his interest. Success. I turn and lean over my flashlight so the beam makes shadows around my eyes.

"Really?" He cocks his head.

"Yes! A year later — the farmer's boy was like fourteen or something — and the story goes that one of the farm hands caught him killing a cow and dis—"

"The kid?" Zach interrupts.

"Yeah, they caught him disemboweling it. The cow. Then when the dude went to run, to tell the kid's dad, the boy ran him down and slit his throat. They found the dead guy in one of the barns after the investigation started."

"After?" Zach steps back.

"Yeah." I nod. "No one realized anything had happened until like a week later. So after that, the kid killed his own sister while she was sleeping. Then he shot his dad in his sleep next to his mom. The mom woke up and tried to get away, but they say he kicked her down the stairs and used the same knife on her that he'd killed the animals with. He ended up disemboweling all of them and arranging them on the floor..."

I pause as the next thing hits me. "In the living room..."

"Here?" Zach's eyes drop to the floor.

My eyes leave Zach, and I shine my phone light around the room. There are stains on the floor, but I don't know what from. I try to imagine it's anything but blood. That's even too freaky for me.

"You're saying he killed them all and brought them here?" Zach asks, and gulps.

"Yep." The word barely leaves my lips. "Then he cut his own stomach open and bled out. They found them a few weeks after, when people realized no one had heard from them lately."

"That's seriously fucked up," Zach says.

"Okay, I didn't know it was that bad," Kaitlynn says, and shifts back a few steps before turning back toward the entrance. "I think I'll just wait out there."

Before I can protest, she leaves me alone with Zach.

"Bitch," I yell after her.

"Damn right," I hear from outside. I adore her.

"I—" Zachary starts, but I stop him.

"*You* are *not* abandoning me too." I point at him and grin even though I've sort of freaked myself out too. "Ten minutes. Then we'll leave."

"How about five?" Zachary negotiates, and I go to lean in and say no, but he speaks up first. "Fine. Ten. But then we're out."

"Deal," I agree.

When I face the room, it suddenly feels a lot smaller and colder. I squeeze my arms around my chest, phone in hand, shining a harsh glow around the room. *Let's just do this. It* was *your idea after all.*

"Here we go." I step forward, and before I get a full two steps, Zach's jacket rubs against mine. I look at him with my nose crinkled.

"What?" he gripes.

"Nothing." I giggle quietly and then start forward again. But it's not nothing. My first thought is, why is he this close? Then, why is my chest pumping so hard? It's just the thought of dead people hanging around here, waiting to haunt us, I'm sure.

Through the next doorway, there's a stove set between scuffed and faded white cabinets and drawers, and a big island in the center. Otherwise, it's empty. I was hoping to find some goodies. Maybe old newspapers or toys from the '90s, something, but nah.

"This doesn't look all that old," Zachary says.

"Well it isn't from the 1800s," I remind him.

"But the '90s were forever ago," he says.

He has a point, but I guess the basics are about the same. Then again, they haven't left much to gauge it by. I step through the kitchen and the floor groans. I wonder, is there a basement? I bet there is, but I don't think ten minutes is enough time to find out. Honestly, I'm not sure I'm that brave anyway. It'd be like going into a dungeon on purpose. You don't do that.

"Let's keep going." I aim at the only door.

A creak spikes through the silence, and without warning, Zachary's hand wraps around my forearm. I look back and his eyes squint from the glare of my flashlight.

"Sorry!" I yelp, and lower the beam.

He grins, but his lips are thin and tight. It's not a smile. "It's fine."

I smile back, trying not to giggle. This is going to be great.

I go to turn back around, and he lets go of my arm but immediately grabs my hand and threads his fingers between mine.

"Nothing weird, just scared shitless." Zach nods.

If I couldn't feel his entire hand shaking, I'd think it was weird, but damn, he's horrified. Now I feel sort of bad. Part of me finds it funny, but I also know I'd hate Kaitlynn if she dragged me into something I didn't want to do. Why the hell did he even come? Oh yeah, that's my fault.

I nod and squeeze his hand. It's the only thing that seems acceptable, and I'm not going to lie, having his hand is easing a little of the tension in my chest, plus they... No. Just less tense. That's it.

"We can stop," I say, looking at the door setting ajar in front of us, with who knows what waiting to be discovered. I'm not expecting much anymore, not after how empty it's been so far, but maybe.

"You said ten minutes," Zach says and taps the face of his smartwatch. "We've got six left."

"You sure?" I skew my lips.

"Don't make me second-guess it." He feigns a smile.

"Okay," I say, and pull open the door.

Behind the door is a long hallway. I can see where photos once hung, at least where the wallpaper is still up, because it's not as dusty in those spots. There is hardwood running up the wall from the floor to about waist height. It's hideous, and even with my light I can't see the end of the hall. Despite the void at the end, I already count two doors, one on each side.

"Right or left." I give our options.

"Does it matter?" Zach asks.

"Left," I say, and guide us around the doorframe.

The first sign of anyone ever living here sets in front of us. It's an old metal bedframe shoved in the corner. No mattress, no box spring, no leftover pillows, just the frame.

"Why'd they leave that?" Zach asks.

"Not like they needed it." I shrug and earn an elbow to my side.

"You know what I mean," he says, tugging me back into the hallway.

I let him lead, trying not to squeeze his hand. It's soft, but I can feel the roughness from his work. Something about it makes me want to hold on. It's…I don't know. It's calming? I like haunted houses, but it's usually because they scare the shit out of me. I like the thrill, but I also like this odd calm in the middle of it all.

"Come on." Zachary tugs again, and I realize I zoned out for a moment.

"Sorry, yeah," I say, and take the lead again.

Why am I feeling like this? In the afterglow of my flashlight, I can just make out Zach's silhouette and a few faint features, but I refuse to look him in the eyes. His jaw is clenched tight, and his lips quiver. Having his hand makes me feel...not safe, but strong, and I never feel strong.

"You go first," Zachary says when we get to the next door.

"So much for my knight in shining armor," I giggle.

"Ha," he huffs. The sarcasm dripping.

I step around the open doorframe and find much of the same. Another bedframe, but this time there's a crinkled-up piece of plastic lying next to the bed. I inch closer to inspect it. An empty pack of crackers.

"Has someone been here lately?" I ask more to myself than Zach.

"I'm sorry, what?" He steps back, unintentionally pulling me back with him.

"Oh nothing, just odd seeing food wrappers around," I tell him. Then again, it makes sense. "Probably others like us coming up here and messing around."

"Messing around?"

"Yeah, you know." I shrug, but he's eyeing me down like he doesn't. I roll my eyes and huff. "You know. They come up here and...yeah. Some people get off on that."

"O-kay." He doesn't seem convinced, and suddenly I feel like I crossed a weird comfort boundary. I just talked about sex...to Zachary...while he's holding my hand...all alone. Dammit. It's everything I can do not to yank my hand away.

"Yeah, but it could be anything," I start to ramble. "Maybe

they came up for a little picnic, or a scary haunted tour. Maybe they were just stopping by. Oh! Maybe it was a homeless person and they stayed here a few nights. You know? And left their trash."

"Stayed a few nights?" Zachary's eyes light up in the dim glow of our phones' flashlights. "Like…like they could still be here?"

"Oh no! That's not what I meant!" I yelp. But oh gods, what if they are? No! That's just a random thing my head said. There is no one else here. Except Kaitlynn, and she's outside waiting on us. "I meant like a while back or something."

"But…" Zachary doesn't complete the sentence, and all I manage is a weak hopeful grin and shrug. He looks down at his watch and then back up at me. "New plan. Let's cut this two minutes short."

"Are you sure?" I say, even though part of me is starting to freak my own self out.

"Yeah, I'm all haunted out." He backs up.

"Okay." I nod. There's no way I'm pushing him to stay if he's scared. Something about the little empty wrapper just threw my mind for a loop anyway. My nerves are on edge now. "Let's go."

I pull him along, back out into the hallway, and start off before realizing I'm headed the wrong way. The door we come to is closed, and our lights paint it in a blaze of gray splinters. I slump and turn around.

"Sorry, wrong way." I smile unconvincingly and crinkle my nose. "My bad."

"Yep, your bad," he says back, and I'm about to giggle when a quiet knock echoes behind me.

I freeze. My eyes widen. What was that?

"What—" Zachary starts, but I shush him. Another knock, and Zachary hears it this time. "What was—"

I shush him again, and flinch around to see the shut door again.

How (Not) to Conjure a Boyfriend

"Stop shushing me," he whispers.

I spring my lids open so he can see my eyes yelling at him to shut up so I can hear. I don't know what the noise is, but it's there. A soft knocking noise, and I swear it's coming from behind the last door. My heart starts to race. What is it? Is someone squatting here? What if they see us? I mean, they're just another person, right? They wouldn't hurt us. Right?

Another bump, and another. But what if it's the Harrels' son's ghost? *Knock, knock!* It's getting louder and quicker. There's no rhythm, no clever tune, just random knocks. *Knock!* It's closer! Then —

The door creaks and moves.

"Uh..." I gulp, stepping back.

With a crash, the wooden door swings out, and screeching squeals burst from the dark. The wood claps against the wall. Chirps echo from the opening and wash over me just as my arm is yanked in the opposite direction. I trip over my own feet but catch my step before I tumble forward. It takes a moment to realize I'm being dragged down the hall by a horrified Zachary, but I'm not resisting. The squalling and squeaking intensifies, but suddenly the sounds start to make sense. My pounding heart settles for a single second at the understanding, and then jumps into overdrive again.

Bats.

Their tiny dark bodies swoop into the hallway. There are so many of them. Maybe hundreds. Vampiric mouths, pointed wings, all swarming at us like a black death. I throw my eyes forward as they wrap around us, flying about as if we're nothing.

"Go, go, go, go!" I yell, ducking as we run.

Their squalls chase us into the kitchen. The only thing louder than the chirps is the beating in my chest as my shoes skid across the splintered floor in time with Zach's to make the next turn. Our feet beat against the old wood. It shakes beneath us, creaking and cracking as we blunder into the next room. I slide to a halt. I don't hear them anymore except for a tiny distant chatter.

"I think we're good," I say, and start to bend over and rest my hands on my knees to get my breath back.

Hands grab my shoulders and I jerk to attention.

"Are you okay?" Zachary's eyes dig into me. He's horrified, but he's asking if I'm all right. "Mack?"

"I'm good, yeah," I huff. My phone is pointed toward the ground, so the light is dim, and I can just make out his long face and sharp jaw, that cute nose, but my eyes land on his lips. I intentionally hadn't noticed them before. They're parted, and he's looking at me. Worried. He seems worried about me. I can't see his eyes in this light, so I let my gaze slump back down to his lips.

Either my eyes are playing tricks on me or his lips are beginning to part. My chest tightens and my heart flutters. I've never been this close to a boy's mouth. I suck my lips in and clamp my jaw. What's happening? He leans in closer, and his eyes close and yes, his lips part. Suddenly the tightness in my chest lifts and my jaw loosens. I lean to meet him. My nose caresses his, and then the most insane thing ever happens. Our lips touch.

Reflexively I take in a deep breath and exhale through my nose as the warmth of his skin meets mine and radiates across my cheeks. My eyes slide shut, like keeping them open would be a sin. I allow my lips to part around his. I can taste him. Oh my gods, I can taste him! It's sweet, like vanilla, maybe a little mint. They're wet and soft. A tiny sliver of doubt tries to wedge its way between us, and I wonder if I deserve the way this feels, but I push it back. I press into him, and a rush shoots from my mouth all the way down to my toes, lifting me off my heels. It's better than I dreamt it could be.

How (Not) to Conjure a Boyfriend

Oh gods! My eyes flutter open and my mouth opens wide as our lips separate and I'm looking at him. Zachary. I'm facing Zachary. His mouth is still open, his eyes gazing softly and longingly back at me. Oh my gods, I just kissed Zachary. My breath stutters. What the hell did I just...but I... Shit. I want to kiss him again, I need to kiss him again, but I can't. He's Hay... But before I can think, he's moving in again. I should stop him, but I can't. I won't! As I lean in, the silence is shattered with a song screaming into existence. I jump back and throw my hands behind me.

"What the—" Zach yelps, and I grasp at my pocket. It's my phone. He stumbles back, and I fumble around my pocket. Everything is happening so fast, but the taste of his lips keeps blossoming on my tongue. Vanilla. Mint.

"Sorry, hold—" I pick it from my pocket and check the screen. It's Kaitlynn.

"Uh...I'm sorry! I didn't...uh...I..." Zachary spews as the nervous grin on my face morphs into an O of realization. His eyes dart to the old dusty floors around my feet while he clears his throat, but he refuses to look at me. "I'm—"

For a second I wonder what he's sorry for. It was amazing. It was an amazing first kiss for me. *Please don't be sorry*, but then a switch flips and I realize why his eyes are filled with guilt.

"Me too." I jump into the cacophony of apologies. "I didn't either. I don't know what...uh...yeah. I, uh, didn't mean to."

But I did mean to. I wanted it. The thought rolls from the back of my brain to the forefront as he finally looks at me again. For a second, I forget I'm not supposed to be into Hayden's brother, but then it rushes back in.

Zach huffs. His smile returns, but there's a nervousness behind it, and a dose of guilt. I'm the one who should feel guilty. *I'm supposed to be dating his brother, but I kissed him too.* And I *wanted* it. I didn't even know I wanted it, but I *did*.

Oh gods! Oh gods! What is my problem?!

"Maybe we should just go," I suggest, and start walking.

"Yeah, that never happened." Zachary nods erratically and follows after me.

"Right. Not a clue what you're talking about," I say.

14

"SERIOUSLY?" KAITLYNN SWATS HER eyes at me. As if I'm the one who just said something senseless, not Zach.

"Yeah." Zach shrugs.

His jacket hangs loose around his shoulders, spread open to show a thick red, black, and white plaid collared shirt. It's cold in the middle of the woods, but the warmth from the flickering firepit has staved off most of the bite for me. I'm still not sure I can sit out here for another half hour.

After the…incident at the Harrel House I had no plans of staying. It didn't seem Zach was keen on exploring anymore either. And I don't think either of us needed a repeat of the incident, even if I might have liked it, because yes, yes I did and that's the problem. We left immediately, once we found a tree close enough to get us back across the fence, hauled Zach's now soggy and muddy project bookcase back to his truck, and got out of there. Kaitlynn, the one who got between me and my first ever kiss, noticed a sign for a nearby campground on our way down, so we stopped.

"You don't know about the demon dog of Valle Crucis?" I lean in, digging into him with an accusing gaze. Fire flicks in his pupils. If I look hard enough, I can even see the pieces of wood in them, little worlds of their own. He grunt-laughs and throws his hands in the air.

"I've never heard of such a thing," Zach says again.

"You grew up around here though, right?" I lean forward even more.

"Yeah. All my life. But I've never heard of it! Sounds made

up to me."

"Excuse me?" I recoil like I'm putting on a Master Class in Shatner Acting 101. A demon-eyed dog chasing all who passed their corridor of Highway 194. Surely not. "Made up? How dare you, sir."

"Uh…" Zach falters, while Kaitlynn covers her mouth. She better be hiding amusement. I can't deal with her not knowing either. And yes, I might be overdoing it a little to avoid anything else coming up.

"It's *very* real, I tell you. A local *legend*," I say, flaring my lips for effect.

"Say that again, slowly this time." Zachary grins.

I don't. Instead, I stare him down, one brow raised, all business. Inside, my lungs are dying to burst out laughing, but I'm taking this as far as I can.

"Slowly," he says again, but even slower this time.

"Fuck you," I blare and let out a few of the giggles I'd held on to.

"Testy." Zachary grins.

Kaitlynn's eyes jump between us. "Flir—"

"It's a cool story!" I shift to my right and about knock her off the log we're sharing. Okay, I kneed her, but she deserved it, and it wasn't too obvious. She'll be okay, because I didn't tell her what happened, nothing, and I'm about ninety-nine percent sure she didn't see us in the house. She was outside. Right? Then again it is Kaity. She could have been spying through the window or happened to be at the door when we kissed. Oh shit. No. Just sidestep it. She said she called because she was getting bored. "Really. Like really cool."

"Oh…" Zachary doesn't seem convinced. "Okay. Tell me about this 'demon' dog then."

The tension in my shoulders lightens, and I allow myself to

How (Not) to Conjure a Boyfriend

lean back so I'm not hovering over the fire, and give Kaity a little room.

"You know where Valle Crucis is, right?" I ask first. It's a crucial part of the story, both in name and location.

"I've an idea. Up above Boone, right?" he asks.

"Depends on how you're looking at the map," Kaitlynn says.

"What?" I side-eye her. How you look at the map?

"Yeah, you know." She shrugs. "Depends on what direction you hold it."

I shake my head and try to forget what she just said before returning my attention to Zach, who seems enormously amused.

"If you hold the map *right*," I stress, glancing at Kaitlynn again for a second, "yeah, sort of, at least. Anyway, it's up there. There's this old white church up there too. Think it's St. John's something. It's an old church with a cemetery next to it."

"Like most," Kaitlynn mutters.

I grunt but otherwise act like she didn't just make a sarcastic comment.

"So according to legend, in like the 1700s, no, wait... No. In the 1800s, a bunch of people kept going missing and some of the townspeople found literal dismembered body parts in the woods." I'm assuming he can stomach this. Probably should have asked first, now that I'm thinking about it, but he'll be okay. "Guess wh—"

"Dismembered?" Zachary interrupts, and swallows. "You mean like severed arms and legs and shit?"

"Yeah, probably some heads and hands too." I shrug and grin.

"And maybe some dicks," Kaitlynn pooches her lips and fake whispers.

I cough, trying not to let her embarrass me. I know that's what she's after. "Yeah, that too probably."

"Definitely dicks." Zachary nods and laughs. "Lots of dicks."

"Okay, back to the story." I pull them back in. Dicks are great and all, but that's not the story. "So yeah, they started finding stuff like that—"

"Dicks," Kaitlynn shouts, but I keep going.

"—and figured… Oh wait! Did I say they found the body parts *behind* the church?"

"Nope," Zachary says matter-of-factly and smacks his lips. "Damn."

"Yeah. Well, so they all thought it was, like, some wild animal. You know, how else are people getting ripped to shreds and left in the woods? But they didn't know what animal or why it was near the church. Eventually someone claimed they'd seen a massive black, smoldering red-eyed dog. It was taller than any normal man. Horrifying and vicious. But it never went past the bridge."

"Wait, it's a demon dog, but it couldn't get past a bridge?" Zach shifts and one of his cheeks draws up toward his ear.

"Yeah," I say like it makes perfect sense and start back. "It—"

"Why?" Zachary isn't done yet.

"If you'll let me finish, I'm going to tell you—it's sort of a big part of the story," I tell him.

Zach puts his hands up in surrender and purses his lips. It's actually cute. I wish he didn't though, because now I'm hyper-focusing on them. The soft texture. The taste of…nope. No. Not going there again. Story. Get back to the story.

"So yeah, the church where they found the bodies, the priest guy picked up on it and started preaching that it was Satan coming to kill the unrepentant, the sinful. Which is funny to me, because I swear Satan isn't the bad guy in the Bible. That's God. Like who else—"

"Demon dog," Kaitlynn spurts. She knows my fascination

with religion, especially the controversial parts that just don't make sense to me. And oh shit, I didn't even think about Zachary probably being Christian. I make a mental note to be more thoughtful.

Thanks, Kaity.

"Right, demon dog," I say. "Supposedly the demon dog still haunts the cemetery and chases down the sinful when they pass by. Until they get to the bridge, of course."

"Ah," Zach sighs. "Interesting. I was thinking something way more scary, like them being stuck there forever, never to leave."

"How would they tell the story if they were stuck there forever?" I ask.

"Not everyone would get stuck, right?" Zach argues. I guess that could happen. "Anyway, you didn't explain why the dog couldn't cross the bridge. Like, it's a bridge. Dogs can cross bridges, and even if it couldn't for some reason, they can swim. And it's also a demon dog."

"Oh, right!" I say, remembering what I'd forgotten to tell him. "Valle Crucis."

"Uh..." Zachary squints at me. I can feel Kaitlynn staring at me.

"Valley of the Cross. Sorry, Valle Crucis. It literally means Valley of the Cross." I fill in the main blank.

"Ah, okay." Zachary nods. "And?"

I drop my head and sigh. I'm going to have to spell it out for him.

"Like holy place. And it's a devil dog. So the devil can't go to holy... You know what? Let me start over. The town gets its name from three rivers that intersect with each other, making a type of cross. So it's like, supposedly holy water or something." I think it's called an archbishop's cross. One of those with an extra line across it, but I personally have never seen it. Like, I've looked on the map and still don't see it. "The main river runs under the bridge.

So the idea is that it's like a wall for the dog because it's possessed, demonic, and the cross is all holy. So it can't cross."

"Now that's a little cooler." Zach nods. "Definitely would make for a crazy escape. Trying to get to the bridge before it gets you."

"Yeah, and people say it's so fast, it can keep up with cars too," Kaitlynn chimes in.

I nod. She's right. That's what they say. "Of course, it's all dog shit. See what I did there?"

Kaitlynn rolls her eyes, but I get a smile and laugh from Zachary. Take that, Kaity.

"Lame," Zachary says, but I don't care because he's still laughing.

He's adorable when he laughs. He gets dimples in his cheeks and they bunch up under his eyes and make him squint.

"You laughed though," I clap back. "Guess you're lame too, then."

"Someone's brave." Kaitlynn side-eyes me as if Zachary isn't sitting right in front of me, *and* I hadn't kissed him just an hour ago, *and* I'm supposed to be dating his brother. Gods. I'm screwed.

"Maybe I am." Zach grins coyly at me, ignoring Kaitlynn entirely.

It's everything I can do not to let my eyes blast open wide, and I don't think there is anything I could do that would stop my cheeks from blooming red. I can feel them already. It's not what he said. It's the way he said it, the way he looked at me. That head wobble and smooth cadence.

I'm so absolutely screwed.

"Did you hear that?" Kaitlynn interrupts my self-destruction.

"Hear what?" I ask. Don't be trying to spook me now. I've had enough of that tonight.

The only thing I've heard the past half hour has been her and Zach, the crackling of the fire, the wind whistling through bare branches and pine needles. The occasional chirp and caw, and the growl of my stomach. I forgot to eat before we came up here. I should have known to bring a snack.

"Listen," she says, and angles her head down, eyes bouncing from side to side.

"Okay now." I push her arm playfully.

"I hear it," Zachary says.

Huh? He hears it. I still don't know what they're... Oh. There it is. The tiny echo of a thousand raindrops falling from the sky and pelting the forest below, somewhere out there. It's gentle at first, in the distance, but it's getting louder, growing. It begins to crescendo. One second it's just a faint noise, the next the first drop splats on my nose, and then another. I twitch as if I hadn't expected it.

"Rain," Kaity says the obvious.

"Maybe we should —" Zach ducks when the entire forest lights up in an explosion of white. I fling my hand up. In a second, my eyes take in a hundred trees that were just moments ago veiled in endless black. Then comes the booming clap. The entire earth quakes, and I scream.

"Shit!" I shout, and then as if on command, the clouds unleash a deluge. "Wet! Wet! Wet!"

"Let's go," Kaitlynn yells.

I don't have to think. I'm on my feet immediately.

"Come on!" Zachary yells at me. His voice sounds distant, drowned out by the sudden clamor of the rain.

It's no longer a single drop here or there. It's everywhere, like the floor of Valhalla dropped away and let loose all its oceans. Again the entirety of night disappears into bright white, and for a brief moment, everything is frozen in time, flashed in brilliant light.

Zachary stands in front of me, hand outstretched while Kaitlynn fades out of sight down the trail. For the tiniest of seconds, I debate it. It's a moment that drags on like the booming echo of thunder from far away. His fingers are appealing to me. His mouth moving with words I'm not hearing. My teeth clamp tight and my arms jump forward before my mind can make a call. Okay, guess I'm doing this. His fingers wrap around my palm and he pulls as darkness takes over again.

Surprisingly, I don't trip.

All that should be going through my mind is getting to Zachary's truck and getting out of this rain to somewhere dry. That's all, but my mind is split between the way my pants are starting to cling to my knees and how warm his hand still is. It jumps from the chill of icy water pelting my hair and slithering through my curls to the warmth from his lips. Between glimpses of the deluge around us to smoky gray eyes that belong to the wrong person each time lightning strikes.

In another flash, we're back to the truck, flinging the doors open and practically throwing ourselves inside. When I open my eyes and actual thoughts start to overtake the adrenaline, my first is that his seats are leather.

"Your seats!" I yell, and lift my soaked rear.

"Who cares," Zach says, letting his head fall against the headrest and blowing out a big breath. His cheeks expand and his lips flap. It's actually sort of funny, but I look away.

"You sure?" I ask.

"He's sure." Kaitlynn leans forward.

"I—" I'm about to say I wasn't asking her. It's his truck, not hers, but he interrupts.

"It's okay. I seriously don't care," he says. "I can just let it air out later. As long as we're not stuck in that."

He points out the windshield. I can't see a thing. It's not just dark, the window is blurred by sheets of water. Yeah, definitely don't want to be in that anymore. Zachary's hand lies on the center console next to me. My attention snags between it and Kaitlynn. She's eyeing me down, grinning. I think she *did* see that.

"Ready to have a hot ass?" Zachary asks, and I twitch at the statement.

"Uh…excuse me?" I ask.

"Your seat, doofus." Kaitlynn leans back and crosses her arms, fully content with herself.

"Oh, sweet," I save, sort of. "Nothing like toasty buns."

"I agree." Zachary grins at me and laughs.

What was that supposed to mean?

"All right, let's get back."

THE HEAT FROM THE truck vents feels like heaven. It dries my face and has already started in on my damp clothes, but the downpour isn't done with me yet. It's waiting for me to get out, just like the weird silence broken only by the rain pelting the roof.

It's just Zach and me sitting — uncomfortably mushy on his leather seats, I might add — in my driveway with his engine rumbling. We dropped Kaitlynn off at her house down our little gravel road. I got a real quick reminder how much she talks the moment she closed the door behind her and Zach started to my place. It got so uncomfortably quiet.

If one of us doesn't say something soon I'm going to jump into the freezing rain — it's literally sleet — before I can't handle it anymore. And I'm too cold for that. I can anticipate the chill, the way it makes me shiver. I only got the feeling back to my fingers like ten minutes ago, but I think we are both stuck on the same thing. The kiss. The kiss that didn't happen, but for sure did too. I don't want to bring it up though.

"The campsite was nice." Zachary glances at me, but he's quick to look away. His eyes set on the window where all you can see is rain and the distorted glow of my porch light.

"Yeah," I whisper.

"Huh?"

"Yeah," I say like a normal person.

My yard is lit up by a flash of white, followed almost immediately by a boom of thunder. I can feel its rumble through the truck. *Calm it down, Thor. I'll say something.*

"Oh, okay. Yeah." He nods and swallows, smacking his lips quietly.

With Kaitlynn in the back seat, it was easier. I didn't have the opportunity to say much with her craning over the center console, talking about the *Keeping Up with the Kardashians* reruns from this week, how her miniature Schnoodle won't stop peeing when he gets excited, and something her science club friends—which she's only part of because she heard they might go to the Alcatraz Museum for a trip this year—said about Henry Cavill not being gorgeous. Zach and I both gave her shocked looks on that last bit. It was enough to distract from the thing running through my head the entire time that felt like it would make me explode inside.

Now, though, it's quiet. Unbearably, suffocatingly quiet. And why does his truck's center console have to be small? He's so close, too close. In one night I've managed to cheat on my make-believe boyfriend with his brother twice. Kissing and holding hands are cheating, right? Of course they are. Obviously. Shit, I want to kiss him again...but I shouldn't. I shouldn't want to. I like Hayden. I know Hayden, or well, I know him better. Okay, maybe I don't anymore, but that's not the point. His family thinks I do. But does this boy sitting across from me still think that? One moment he acts like he believes me, and the next he's eyeing me with suspicion or leaning in for a kiss. This is so frustrating and confusing.

I close my eyes and focus on the notes playing on the truck's rooftop from the raindrops. It usually calms me, so I listen and grasp my necklace. There's a moment it works, so I put my hand on the door handle, but I can't get myself to pull it. The rain. The cold. Wet. I don't want all of that again. The taut cord lacing from my chest to Zach's. The need to look at him. It's all in my head. *That's right, Kenzie. It's just my head.*

"Uh…" I mumble, trying to break the silence and get myself to move. I shift toward the door and Zach finally speaks up.

"You can sit awhile." His voice is small, almost a coo, and I hate him for it. Be abrupt. Tell me to get out. Please! "Maybe the rain will pass soon."

The rain never passes soon when you want it to. If I stay put until it's over, I could be here until four in the morning, and I won't be able to keep my sanity if I have to sit in here with him for hours. Also, I have to open at work tomorrow. That means I have to be up by seven o'clock. I've really got to get going.

Then again, it could stop before the minute is over. Who knows? Maybe Odin or Freyja, but not me. Actually, Freyja, please don't get involved here. I need Odin's wisdom right now.

"Maybe," I agree, and make a popping noise with my mouth. Why? I don't know. It just felt like it made more sense than the weirdness right now. "Actually, I think I'm just going to go."

"Mack!" he nearly shouts, his entire body twisting to face me.

The truck shakes and I scream. My hand flings from the door handle and slaps the seat.

"Going to kill me doing that!" I say.

"Sorry, sorry. Uh…I…" Zachary apologizes, but starts laughing while I'm getting myself back together. "You are so jittery."

"And?" I tilt my head.

"Nothing. You just are. You hiding something?" he asks.

Gods, if you only knew. It helps though. My chest isn't as tight now. I still feel like I'm wearing a corset, but it's better. I glance at him, unable to do much more than that. He's looking my way confidently. How?

"No!" I bite.

"Sure." He drags it out suggestively, and I let my mouth drop into a big O and finally face him. Zach's hands go up. "My bad!"

A laugh jumps from my lips and I can't stop a smile from spreading. His eyes look like a puppy dog's, but there he goes giggling again. You are making this so difficult! Be stupid. Make me want to leave!

"Obvi," I grumble, but I know what I need to do. I put my hand on the door handle. "I have to work in the morning. I need to go."

"Oh, okay." Zachary nods, his head low. "Don't get too wet."

"Sure." I shrug and go to shove the door open. Gods, I don't want to get wet and cold again!

"Thanks for showing me that scary house," Zachary spouts before I can get out.

"Yeah," I say, not letting go of the handle. "Sure. It's cool."

"Yeah. Cool." Zachary grins and grunt-laughs, but he doesn't break eye contact.

"Cool," I repeat. This is so awkward. Here we are, *cooling* it away. Just the two of us. "I gotta go."

"Yeah, no, it's late," Zachary says a little too quickly.

I delay. Him leaning in to kiss me in the dark plays in slow motion behind my eyes. He's so close I can feel his heat, then my eyes close and it happens. I know that's what's going through his head right now, it has to be, but I'm not going to be the one who brings *it* back up. I can't. I won't. I can't decide whether I'd rather let it disappear into a faint bygone memory or if selfishly I want to keep it untainted in my head.

"Bye," I say, hoping he'll tell me to stop and reel me around in his arms to kiss me again. But no! I can't let him, and he doesn't.

"Bye," he says.

I swallow the knot of nothingness in my throat and shove the door open. The gurgling and rat-a-tat of the downpour rushes inside with a gust of wind as I slide out and my feet plop onto the wet rocks. Before I can second-guess myself, I take off into the freezing pellets. They smack my face, melting on impact and pouring over my shoulders as I rush across the yard and up the front porch steps.

At the landing I stop under the small overhang and look back. His headlights are shining harshly, seeming to wobble under the falling sleet. I can barely see his truck until a brilliant streak of lightning illuminates everything. I duck as thunder claps over the mountains and Zachary's truck starts to back up. I swear I can feel him moving farther away from me, like a piece of me is rolling away. And why? Because I gave in to whatever it was brewing inside my chest back there, and I kissed him.

What have I done?

WHAT TYPE OF SCHOOL *takes that many kids on a trip with only one chaperone? Maybe they should have thought about that first.*

That's what I want to type, but I don't think that Mr. Nelson would give me good marks for it. I'm only on page two. I keep checking the bottom of the screen, hoping the number will magically tick up a few so I can ditch my desk for my bed and that new Japanese BL drama I started last week. It's been so cute. The more I think about how absolutely clueless the main character is about Taichi being into him, the longer this five-page paper feels. Also, five pages is so freaking much to write about kids getting dumped on an island and deciding the best option is to start hunting each other down. So naturally, I text Kaity about it.

MACKENZIE: WTF is up with this title? Lord of the Flies?!?!

I get that the story is supposed to be about how easily society, left to its own devices and without order and structure, can devolve into savagery — it's what a review on Goodreads said anyway — but I'm still struggling to figure out the title. I swear it has nothing to do with this book.

KAITLYNN: Something weird.

She had to read it too, and so far we agree on one thing easily. It was boring. Old. Musty maybe. Seriously, how often do a bunch of teens get stuck on a deserted island nowadays? Is this even relevant?

MACKENZIE: Obvi, but... What?

The little bubbles move at the bottom of my screen while Siyun and Kyrell serenade me through my AirPods. I think I've added three sentences today, and this paper is due on Friday. *This* Friday! How am I supposed to analyze the literary significance of this? Like it's significant, I guess. That's what my teachers say, but why couldn't it have been, like...you know, a book written *after* 2000.

My phone dings and lights up with *Zach* in bold letters. He's been texting like last night never happened, and I've been more than willing to oblige in that delusion. Even if I have thought about it a thousand times.

ZACHARY: Arty just ran into the wall. He really wants the laser.

I'm jealous. I want my own familiar. While I type a reply another message pops up.

ZACHARY: And again.

Wow.

MACKENZIE: OMG! He needs to chill!

My phone buzzes again. It's Kaitlynn this time. Why am I even trying to write this now? It's a Sunday anyway. Aren't I supposed to be relaxing? I could do it tonight, when I'm not intentionally allowing Zach and Kaitlynn to distract me.

KAITLYNN: Dunno... 🧚 Killer flies?

Yeah, no. I don't think that's in there. Killer kids, check. But I don't remember any flies killing anyone. Zach's name flashes on the screen again, and the urge to tell Kaitlynn everything about last night spills into my gut. We don't keep anything from each other, even gross stuff we both wish we hadn't heard. So why change that now that it's about a guy?

Shit. *Just tell her.* I start to type, but stop. Maybe I shouldn't. She's just going to nag me about it, and for what? It's nothing. It has to be nothing. I can't like him.

I throw my phone onto the desk. It thwacks against the old wooden surface, and without delay I'm scooping it back up and checking the screen. Please don't have cracked. Please! My lamp light reflects off the glass with not a single defect. I let out a relieved sigh and catch my own reflection. I growl. My eyes have dark circles under them.

I bring my phone to life and open my thread with Kaity.
MACKENZIE: Zach kissed me at the Harrel House...
I hit send before I can delete it.
KAITLYNN: YOU KISSED HIM!?!?!?! That explains so much!
"*No!* He kissed me!" I scream at my phone while she's still typing.
MACKENZIE: NO!! HE! HE kissed me! Not the other way!
MACKENZIE: Explains what?!?!
Oh my gods! What does it explain? Everything was normal after that!

My phone dings and I scramble to open the text.
KAITLYNN: Why y'all were both so awkward when we left. And the hand holding at the campsite... 😱
We didn't hol—
Ugh. Okay, yeah, we did. But it wasn't romantic. He was making sure I got out of the rain. That's it! We weren't cuddling and blowing kisses at each other across the fire.

I try to type *No we didn't!* but I can't really say that. It just wasn't like *that*, but she's never going to believe that.
MACKENZIE: 👌👌 **It wasn't like THAT!**
Less than a second later, I get a new text, but I ignore it and open my thread with Zachary. There's a video of Artemis. His soft blue coat shifts and ruffles as he pounces on a red laser dot. In the background I hear Zachary laughing. It's the cat that's making me smile though.
ZACHARY: He's so stupid, but I love him!
I shake my head and giggle.

How (Not) to Conjure a Boyfriend

MACKENZIE: *Just don't knock over the spider cagey thing. PLEASE!*

ZACHARY: *Teo is fine.*

As long as he stays away from me. I let the video play again and there's his laugh again. It's quiet, joyful. Sweet.

I breathe hard and put my fingers on the screen and start typing a new message, ignoring how many times my phone keeps buzzing. Suddenly Kaity's face appears on my screen. It's the photo I took of her looking like a soaked dog at an amusement park last summer. She's a persistent one, that's for sure. I giggle and deny the call. She wants answers, and she'll get them. Later. Right now I'm trying to figure out how to bring it up with Zach.

We need to talk about last night. You know, in the Harrel House...right after we got chased by bats... I didn't mean to kiss you back. I shouldn't have... I mean I wanted to, but I...

Ugh! I can't say that! I can't say any of it. What if he goes to court and his phone gets subpoenaed and they read them aloud, or worse, Holly finds them. *I mean I wanted to.* Hell no. I backspace the last sentence and try again a few times, until I get it right. Then it just sits there. I stare at it as if that'll make it sound any better. *We need to talk.* Do we though? Can't this just wait, or even better, just be forgotten? *I didn't mean to kiss you back.* I don't know. The more I think about it, the more I think I did. I definitely didn't stop him.

The bubbles start moving at the bottom of the screen. I have to do this. We have to confront it! I hover my finger above the send button, but I can't get myself to press it.

Ding!

ZACHARY: *OMG! He learned he can jump on top of Teo's cage from my bed! I'm going to need a lid now.*

Below it is a video of Artemis literally cat-walking along the open edges of the spider cage. My stomach sinks. No, Artemis! Don't do it! Oh wait... No! Do it! Eat the spider!

ZACHARY: *What were you typing?*

Good question. What *was* I typing? A big mistake. That's what. I hold down the backspace and watch it all disappear. I exhale and start again.

MACKENZIE: *It was nothing. Artemis! Eat Teo!*

ZACHARY: *No! Not Teo!*

I grumble but drop my phone next to my laptop. This sucks so much.

16

"**I WILL NOT FALL** for Zachary Marcus." I say it a fourth time and pencil a line through his name again.

The sentence is written on a small piece of parchment paper — the cool type with the uneven edges and old dingy look — five times. I've now marked off all but one of them. I keep thinking about him, and I shouldn't. He's a bad idea, but he haunts my mind. Okay, *he's* not bad, but for me, *now*, he is.

It's not just the kiss anymore. That pops into my head a lot, but it's more than that. It's the things I've started noticing, even without being around him, and the more he comes to mind, the more I notice. The strength in his steel-gray eyes, but a warmth I hadn't noticed before. The timbre of his voice. This gentle music in his laugh, and maybe I'm imagining it, but I swear there's something in the way he looks at me. I hadn't thought much about that until today, but it's different than when he looks at other people. It's like he either lingers a second longer or he can't look away quick enough.

That's why I have to do this. I take a deep breath and say the words again as I guide my pencil through the letters one last time.

"I will *not* fall for Zachary Marcus." I release all the oxygen from my lungs in one slow breath. I close my eyes and nod, like I need permission to continue.

I squeeze the grill lighter in my hand and open my eyes. A little flame flickers to life and I hold it over the candle. Then there's his family. Hayden's family. I know they're not mine, and it's probably stupid to think they could be, but what if? They freaking radiate love. They're a real family, the type that has each other's back. A *whole* family. I know it's not mine, but I don't want to lose them.

Finally the flame catches, throwing the tall slender black candle in ghoulish shadows next to the paper. *Positive thoughts. Think positive thoughts.*

I stare at the parchment. Now to complete this. I pick it up and tear it into three pieces, trying to focus only on ridding myself of the flutter in my chest when I think of Zachary. Not Hayden. Not what Mom would think. Not their family. Just him. With the last piece ripped, I hold it over the candle and watch the paper curl over the flame until it's overtaken and tendrils of smoke ascend. I drop the remaining fragments into my ash dish as the hues of brown blacken and disintegrate.

I will not fall for Zachary Marcus. I repeat the phrase in my head to keep focus. That's what most witchcraft is — focus, determination, vibes, and a little psychology. Not spooky weird shit.

The last piece falls from my fingertips and crumbles into ashes. I put out the candle with my little snuffing tool and waft the smoke trails away from my face. My eyes are locked on the ashes. Charred black remnants of the thoughts in my head, of the outrageous feelings prodding my chest.

"Come on." I close my eyes only to see gray eyes — Zachary's eyes, not Hayden's. I huff and get up. "I'll do it again tomorrow."

17

"**MR. FRANZ.**" I hand my favorite customer his usual. "Flat white with an extra shot of espresso."

He takes it, depositing it on the wooden tabletop next to his cane. How he handles *that* much espresso without having a heart attack is beyond me. He has to be in his seventies. I don't want it to be my coffee that sends him to the hospital. I've had enough of that.

"Thank you, Mackenzie." He smiles, and before I can start back to the kitchen, he asks a question. "You excited for Christmas?"

Christmas? Is Christmas soon? Oh my gods, it's mid-December. I completely forgot!

"I honestly hadn't thought about it," I admit. I've been a little preoccupied lately, but I leave that part out as another thought hits. "I haven't even bought gifts yet."

"That's not all that matters," he tells me, nodding and snuggling his ceramic cup between old worn hands. "It's presence, not presents. That's what matters. But…what are you getting me?"

"I…uh…" I hesitate. It was wise, almost poetic, and then boom. My eyes have to be so wide right now.

"No, no." Mr. Franz waves his hand and laughs slowly. "I'm just joshing you."

"Oh." I smile nervously. Am I supposed to? No, right? I barely get Kaity anything. "You had me for a second. Enjoy your drink."

Mr. Franz nods and I walk back to the front counter. It's been a quiet evening. We've had a few people float in and out the past hour, but it's mostly been to-go except for my old friend. Yeah, that's what he is.

"You want to start mopping?" Kaitlynn says when I get behind the counter and prop against the door.

"No." I drop a little truth. Why would I want to?

"Obviously, bitch." She rolls her eyes, which is exactly what I was going for. She's too easy sometimes.

"I'll do it once Mr. Franz leaves." I laugh and walk into the kitchen to get the mop water ready. "I'm not having another incident."

"You going to profess your undying love for him too?" She grins and laughs at her own joke.

"No!" I bite back as quietly as I can. I make one mistake, and this is what I get. Sure, that mistake has snowballed into an abominable snowman, but still. "I didn't do that with *him* either."

"Sure you didn't." She grins even more.

"We have time anyway." I'm not acknowledging that last bit. We also don't really have a lot of time. We close in twenty minutes, but I'm not chancing it. Especially with Mr. Franz on a cane. I'd die if he got hurt. "And don't worry. I'm getting ready."

"Guess we're staying—" The doorbell dings and Kaity seems to lose her voice. "Uh…he's here."

"He? Who?" I stand up straight. Why am I even asking? There's only one person who would get that reaction.

"The only person whose name you said I'm not allowed to say." She gives me a skewed grin. "He came in for once!"

I might have threatened to put a curse on *Siesta Key* so they don't renew it for a seventh season if she mentioned Zachary's name again.

"Shit," I exhale.

"Hey." *His* voice slips around the corner. I freeze. I'm not turning. Kaitlynn can handle this.

"Hiya," Kaitlynn greets him in her least *inconspicuous* voice. I

How (Not) to Conjure a Boyfriend 159

slump and switch off the water faucet. I lean around the corner. There he is. Mr. Perfect Hair in an unfortunately stylish leather jacket.

"Is Mack here?" He stops at the counter.

"Uh…"

For once Kaitlynn doesn't know what to say. Why now though? Just lie! Say I'm not working tonight. Forget that my car is sitting on the road out front. That could be explained away. Maybe it stopped working and Mom picked me up, or Landon took me home.

"You good?" Zachary leans forward.

"Yeah, yeah." She laughs. "Of course. I'm great. We're… I'm great."

"O-kay." Zachary squints and looks around the store. "Umm… So are they here?"

"I—"

"Hey." I rush out of the kitchen to save her. Fine. I'll sacrifice myself. I put on my best smile and wave, kicking Kaitlynn in the shin under the counter.

"Mack! I haven't heard from you lately." He starts off strong. He's not wrong. I haven't responded much lately. Not at all today.

"I've just been sort of off," I say. It's a massive understatement. I don't have a clue what to do. I'm in over my head.

"It's okay." He shrugs. "What are you doing after work?"

I freeze. Kaitlynn's eyes burst into horrified saucers. Not helping, Kaity!

Technically the plan was to go home and do another spell. A spell specifically about you, Zachary. The *Want You No More* variety. Maybe some XG or ENHYPEN beforehand to amp me up. I doubt that's what he wants to hear. Not to mention, it's arguable that my spell track record isn't too great at the moment.

"Don't know yet," I say instead.

"Wanna hang out at the pub when you get off?" he suggests, then looks at Kaitlynn. "You too."

"But they won't let us. It'll be after nine," I remind them.

It's their curfew, unless you're with an adult—well, a twenty-one-year-old or older adult.

"Outside," Zachary says. "They'll let us sit out front. The owner knows Dad. He'd tell if I asked for alcohol anyway."

"That sucks." Kaitlynn puts on a show. As if she's ever had alcohol.

I know better. If she ever had, I would have been there to join her, *or* she would have called me right after to tell me, probably totally shit-faced.

"Outside?" I ask again. He nods. "Tonight? In December?"

Zachary squints and nods uncomfortably. "Yeah." His shoulders slouch.

"I'll freeze," I say. I do have limits.

"You can borrow my coat," he tries.

Kaitlynn sucks her lips in, visibly restraining a squeal. Me too. Internally, big time. I clench my teeth together and a gush of something warm and scary runs up my chest. I need to say *no*, that's the only right answer, but he offered me his coat. Like how freaking adorable is that? He has to stop with the sweet shit! *Okay, compose yourself!*

I so don't have this under control. My smile breaks free and instead of saying no, I nod. Oh my gods, what is my problem?

"So, yeah?" Zachary leans across the counter and the smile on his lips grows.

"No!" I yelp. It's louder than I'd intended, but I'm saving this. "No, I mean. Sorry. I meant you're right. About them letting us sit outside."

What? What am I saying? *You are so fucked.*

How (Not) to Conjure a Boyfriend

"Oh, okay. So you *don't* want to go?" he asks again.

"Uh..." I mumble, trying to figure out how best to turn this back around without being the pathetic enby who can't say no to the handsome gray-eyed man. I could just say no, or no thank you, but I need a reason, an excuse. Right? And it has to feel important. I can't just say no. It's mean.

"I can't," Kaitlynn says. "Gotta work on this paper for school."

My paper! I... Wait. I see you, Kaitlynn. Very good.

"Me too. It's due Friday." The save I needed. I *am* technically behind. I "finished" it, but it still needs another page. More fluff.

"Oh, okay. Maybe I can just wait for you to get off and talk a little after, walk you to your car?" he tries again.

"I..." He's going to find a way regardless, isn't he? What would it hurt to let him walk me to my car? It's only like a skip and a jump down the street. We'd be there in no time, and I can use my paper as an excuse not to stick around long. "Sure."

"Awesome, I'll be back at close then," Zachary says, walking backward toward the entrance all smiles.

"Wait!" I yell. Stop walking backward! Flashes of Hayden spring into my head.

"Huh?" Zachary stops.

"Please watch where you're going." I nod toward the floor. There's nothing there, but in my head, I remember it was wet and dangerous. "That's how Hayden, you know..."

"Ah."

Realization lights up behind his pretty eyes and then he smiles. Ugh. Stop it! You're making me smile, and I shouldn't be. Not for any of this! It's a *real* problem!

"That your boyfriend?" Mr. Franz speaks up from the corner. I'd forgotten he was here. "Or partner?"

I love how much he tries to be considerate of labels. They're not that important to me if I know you're a truly kind person, but it's really nice, even if his question is sending the blood rushing to my face. I can feel the heat in my cheeks. I'm blushing something major. When I dare a glance at Zachary, he's looking at me wide-eyed, face as red as Pennywise's balloon.

"No!" I yelp, and it's less than a second later that Zachary is blurting the same thing.

"No! We're just friends," he says quickly, hands up, waving at Mr. Franz like it's urgent.

"Friends," Kaitlynn mutters under her breath and grunts comically.

I side-eye her, and speak again. "Yeah, just friends. He's Hayden's brother."

"I knew he looked familiar. That's the one you've been fancying, isn't he?" Mr. Franz continues. He noticed that? I want to cover my face and die. End me right here, right now. "He's got the same eyes."

Zachary's gaze springs back and forth between Mr. Franz and me like it's being slapped around in a ping-pong machine. His mouth hangs half open.

"Yeah," I admit sheepishly. He's much more observant than I realized.

"They're my brother's enbyfriend," Zach springs in.

Mr. Franz angles his brow at the word, but he doesn't question it.

"Well that's nice of you to watch after them," he says to Zachary and gets up and walks out the door after his goodbyes. "Night, you two."

Kaitlynn and I say goodbye at the same time, and Zachary's still frozen halfway between us and the exit. He sighs, looks at me once, and nods.

"I'll see you in a little," and then practically runs out the door.

How (Not) to Conjure a Boyfriend

"**HOW BAD WOULD IT** be for me to sneak off with you before he can catch us?" I whisper after Kaitlynn and twist the deadbolt to lock up the shop.

"Coward," Kaitlynn blurts back. Her eyes never leave her phone.

"You got a partner's brother crushing on you?" I ask. It sounded better in my head.

"So Hayden *is* your partner now? Or is it Zach?" Kaitlynn's focus zooms in on me, and she puts a hand on her hip.

"No!" I cut back.

"Not what you just said."

"But…" I roll my eyes.

"You're crushing *so* hard, it's adorable." She elbows me.

"No I'm not!" I pull my coat tight. It's not that cold tonight, but enough so that I wish I'd brought a thicker jacket. "Let's go."

"Too late." Kaitlynn grins.

Shit.

"Almost missed you!" Zachary calls from behind.

"Almost," I mutter, then put on a smile. "Oops. Wondered where you were."

A lie.

"Y'all closed up quick tonight," Zachary says, which makes me wonder how he knows that, or if he's just blowing smoke.

"It wasn't bad tonight," I say.

"This is fun and all, but I'm off." Kaitlynn smiles at Zachary, then me. Her grin turns mischievous when she meets my eyes, and then she fast walks down the sidewalk and disappears inside her car.

Fine. Just leave me.

"You look cold." Zachary gets my attention back.

His gray eyes are squinting at me, considering me. I don't know what is going on behind them, but I feel like I don't want to know, or well, I do, but I don't.

"I'm good," I say snappily. Was he going to give me his jacket? Maybe I should have said yes.

"Okay." He nods and starts walking toward my car.

I follow at his side like some freaking couple down the sidewalk. Does he not realize this is a bad idea? We shouldn't be hanging out. Not after the other night. Not after he, or we, you know… kissed.

"It's cold, isn't it?" he says more than asks.

"Yeah," I say. Just get it over with, Zach. What do you want?

"Yeah," he echoes me.

I nod, waiting for him to say more, but he doesn't. Instead I focus on the dull buzz of the streetlights and the distant hum of muffled engines. The moon is bright tonight against a pristine sky. Each star is like a little diamond, some steady and calm, others sparkling through our atmosphere. It puts me at ease, sort of, and reminds me that the moon will be full on Sunday. I'll be able to recharge my crystals again. But the quiet is still annoying. What am I supposed to say? I'm not the one who asked to *walk me* to my car. It's mad awkward.

Finally, we stop next to my car, and I shove my hands in my pockets. The door handle is so close. All I'd have to do is move my hand a few inches, but I'm tugged in two directions. I'm really trying not to be, but I am.

"So." Zachary's mouth skews to the left and he looks down. "This is awkward."

You think? I squint and look up at him.

"I'm just going to ask. Did, uh…" Zachary huffs and stutters his next few words. It's actually cute. "Did…you, uh…d-did you not like it? You know, when…"

"When?" I scrunch my brow like I'm super confused. He's nervous. I can even see it in his eyes and hear it between each hesitation. "When what?"

"You know...when we..." Zachary sucks his lips in and takes in a deep breath through his nostrils. His lips bunch up tight. It's so effing cute! No, not cute. It's funny! Not cute. Definitely not cute.

"What are you talking about?" I ask. I'm not going to be the one who says it. Not now that he's bringing it up.

"Uh..." he tries but clamps his jaw shut.

"So much for just asking," I joke. Immediately I feel bad for it.

"Okay, fine." He rolls his eyes and licks his lips, then the words spill out at a hundred miles per hour. "Did you not like it when we kissed?"

"You mean when *you* kissed me?" I reframe it. I'm not ready to admit that I did enjoy it. Not yet, and I'm definitely not letting him pin it on me. He *did* initiate.

"Huh? When I kissed you?" Zachary's eyes become wide moons. "We kissed each other."

"But you initiated," I remind him.

"That's not how I remember it." He grins.

"I..." But my mind runs back to the scene, doused in blackness with the receding chirp of bats. The first time I really saw him. The gentleness in his eyes. The way he looked at *me*, like he truly saw me. The sharpness of his jaw. How the cold in my bones seemed to disappear the closer he came. His lips. Parted. And yes, I moved closer. I went in for their soft sweetness, not knowing I'd find exactly what I wanted to know so bad. I'm just as much to blame, but he did start it. "Maybe it wasn't just you. But we shouldn't have."

Zachary starts to say something but stops. In the dark his face is half-lit by the dim orange of a sodium streetlamp. His eyes wander everywhere but toward me. There's conflict in them, and I think I understand it.

"Yeah...maybe we shouldn't have." He nods again. "But..."

He clamps his lips tight. I don't think that's what he wanted to hear, or what he expected, and now I feel horrible. I want to run, to dive into my car and speed off. To make for the hills and hide so he never finds me, so I never have to look at those eyes again, but he speaks out of nowhere.

"I just..." Zachary pauses to grit his teeth. "I...I just thought you and Hayden, you know...that it wasn't real. I thought it was a joke or something. It doesn't make sense in my head."

"Make sense?" I reel back. I've been thinking the same thing. How could anyone ever believe Hayden would want me? The perfect high school jock who isn't a complete douche wanting to date the little unknown enby. But to say it!

"I didn't mean that in a bad way," Zachary backtracks. "I just—"

"How else am I supposed to take it?" I ask.

"Just that I know my brother," he sighs. Zachary's eyes slide closed before he looks at me again. "At least, I thought I did. Maybe he's been hiding from me. I just can't believe I wouldn't see it. I mean, I know his type. I've known him my entire life. He's my brother."

"So it's too much to believe that he could love me?" I ask.

"No! That's not what I'm saying. Not at all. Mack, I'm just trying to understand," he says. The sincerity in his voice is almost too much. He sounds...broken. "Hayden tells me everything, or at least he did. I mean, we were closer before he got big on the team, but still."

Before he got big on the team. Hmm. It starts to sink in. Their dynamic must have been changing, and this feels like another loss to him. Not understanding what's happening. Not being in the loop like he once was. And now I'm feeling like crap because he's feeling this way all because of a lie. All because I'm trying to keep up a ruse, and even worse, I like him too.

I hide the need to decompress all of that by pumping my fist inside my pockets and clearing my throat. I can't tell him all of that, but I've got to do something.

"I'm sorry," I say.

"Huh? For what?" Zachary asks.

"For everything. For how things are with you and Hayden. For being snappy. For Hayden not telling you about us." The last one stings. Another lie. Another foot down in the dirt and knot in my noose, but I can't tell him the truth. Not now. If I did, how would he look at me? Would he even? I don't know that I could bear that. Maybe the lie is better than the truth. "And yeah, I liked it. But I shouldn't."

"Yeah." He nods quickly. "Sorry about that."

"It's not just your fault," I remind him, finally admitting it out loud. It actually feels good, even if it is still a little terrifying.

"It's okay." He says quickly, then gulps. "We can still talk though, right? We have a lot in common."

"Yeah, sure," I say a little too quickly. Now it's all weird.

"Good." Zach gives me a weak grin and we drop into an awkward quiet for a few moments before he saves us. "So, uh, what are you planning to do after high school?"

After high school? What? We're going from admitting we royally screwed up to what my plans are after high school? That's a big switch.

"I..." My eyes twitch as I rebound from the topic whiplash. "I don't really know for sure. I mean college. I'm going to college.

Just not entirely sure what I want to major in yet. Probably nursing or maybe psychology though."

"Oooh! Really?" Zachary's face starts to glow, which is so much better than the doom and gloom he was giving a few seconds ago. It's so obvious that he's trying really hard not to think about it though. Gods, I feel awful.

"Yeah," I say, contemplating whether or not to tell him why. I don't want him to think badly of my mom. "I want to be able to help people. You know, people who deal with things in their head they have a hard time handling. Get what I mean?" It sounds sort of foolish when I say it aloud to him. To think I could really help people. I can't even do this right. "Probably sounds weird to you."

"What? Why would that sound weird?" Zachary asks.

"Dunno," I admit. "Just thought it would."

"It doesn't. I promise. It's actually really cool." He's smiling and it seems genuine. Maybe it is.

"I like to cook too, but I don't think I'm going to make a living as a cook," I tell him.

He laughs. "You never know."

There's a pause because I don't know what to say, and he must not either.

"Have I told you about my greenhouse?" Zachary breaks the silence.

"You have a greenhouse?" I ask. My first thought is that I could get all my herbs for my spells from him, but that's selfish.

"Yeah, I have a little one out behind the basketball court at home." Zachary grins. "It's nothing major, but yeah. And I love woodworking! You saw my project. I could help you and Hayden build your house and then grow your food — you know, since you'll probably be my person-in-law by then anyway."

"Oh really? Person-in-law?" I smile jokingly. "You mean

sibling-in-law? And isn't that assuming an awful lot?"

"Maybe, maybe not." Zachary shrugs. "It'd cost you less than hiring a carpenter."

I laugh and nod. "Family discount?"

"Of course." Zachary shakes his head, and his hand goes to his pocket and pulls out his phone. It's lit up and buzzing. "Speaking of family, Mom's calling. Hey, Mom."

I'm still laughing when his brow scrunches and all the excitement drains from his eyes into a pale gray. What's going on? Finally he looks up at me, still on the phone.

"We'll be there ASAP!" he tells her.

"What's going on?" I ask.

"It's Hayden. He just woke up."

18

"MACKENZIE?"

My eyes go wide. My name isn't the first word I expect out of Hayden's mouth when I walk into the room. I bite my lip, then put on a grin and pop my head over Mr. Marcus's shoulder. Zachary nudges up against me. I don't know if he's trying to remind me he's here or just being clumsy.

"Hey." I make barely a whisper above Kiki going on about how he already looks so much better and lively.

I shouldn't have come. I shouldn't have followed Zach, but how was I going to explain that? *Your brother just woke up from his coma, and oh yeah, of course I'm his enbyfriend, but I'm not coming?* That would be a disaster, almost as bad as showing up. I ran through every scenario on the drive here. I even texted Kaitlynn—sorry, Mom—to help me get out of this. She was halfway home by then, but like the amazing friend she is, she immediately turned around. Still, she was literally *no* help. The best I could conjure up was: A, ditch and run at the next stoplight—there aren't many around here; B, say I need to get a drink before we see Hayden and get "lost" in the hospital and just leave—but that's not very believable after interning here, plus a weird thing to do on the way to see my supposed boyfriend; C, somehow beat Zachary into Hayden's room and start yelling I'm not Hayden's enbyfriend and it was all a lie and then run off; or D, play sick.

I almost went with D, but I couldn't do it.

I can't tell if the wince in Hayden's confused grin is from pain or confusion. He looks from me to Zachary and then back again

How (Not) to Conjure a Boyfriend

just as Kaitlynn stumbles in behind me, gasping air like she just ran a marathon.

"Sorry, did I ruin a moment?" Kaity squints.

"Who is—" Mr. Marcus turns on the balls of his feet.

"Kaitlynn." I bolt to her side and grab her arm up in mine, turning enough so the rest can't see my face and give her a nervous glare. "She's my bestie."

"Oh, uh...okay." Mr. Marcus doesn't seem sure what to do with the information.

I knee Kaity and whisper just loud enough for her to hear without moving my lips, "Don't be weird."

The looks bounce between us but quickly recenter on Hayden. Right. Hayden's up! And he said my name! And apparently no one fixed his hair. It's...everywhere. I pull Kaity with me a few steps to stand with Zachary. It's better than standing with his dad, who still sort of scares me.

"You take my barista while I was out?" Hayden grumbles at Zach.

Immediately heads turn and all eyes are on us. All of them. Even Dr. Kline with a clipboard clasped between her hands and her coat. She smiles. It helps a little.

"Huh? I don't like coffee." Zachary playfully punches Hayden's shoulder. He doesn't grimace, so I guess he's not in pain. "They—"

"You two dating? Wait, is that why you were so determined to go to the shop with me all the time?" Hayden shakes his head with a giggle.

I'm sorry, what? *Is that why you were so determined to go to the shop with me all the time?* Every muscle in my body wants to sling my face toward Zach, but I refuse.

"No! It wasn't that! I, uh...I just..." Zachary stumbles all over his words as other voices jump into the mix.

"You're dating Mackenzie?" Holly looks up at Zachary. "But—"

Wait. Did Zachary come to the shop to see *me*?

"Zachary! How dare you…" Mrs. Marcus starts into him.

"What?" Zachary goes on the defense. "You—"

"Are y'all a throuple?" Super Old Gran's eyes go big and excited, followed immediately by my own.

No! No! It's too much at once. Too many voices. And no, we're not a throuple! But did he?

"Hey now!" Eliza throws her hands in the air to get everyone's attention off us and on her. It's exaggerated, but I don't care. It's a distraction and hopefully this means she's going to save me. I didn't want to be here when she finally did, but right now anything is better than this. Once the voices dim to a whisper between Mr. and Mrs. Marcus, Eliza coughs and continues. "Well, isn't this exciting. How about we—"

"Dating? Us two?" Zachary interrupts Eliza, laughing and looking back at me. His façade is thin, but it might just do to cover the fidget in his eyes and sudden disdain when he looks at me. It's a drastic change from the want in them earlier. A crowd of laughs explode behind us. They think it's a joke. "Why would we be dating?"

I fight my impulse to bore my gaze into Zach.

He's not wrong though, and suddenly the thought makes my shoulders slump. We're not, but like, that was way too quick and forceful. Especially after tonight. Ouch. What the hell is happening?

"I-I…" Eliza stutters and tries, but it's no use.

"He's your type," Hayden blurts.

I suck in my lips and feel the blush rising in my cheeks. Why me?

"Uh…but he, I mean, they're dating you," Zach argues.

"What?" Hayden's eyes bloom. He goes to sit up, but a wince traces his cheek, so he stops and lies back down. "Me? Mackenzie and me?"

"Yeah, they're your enbyfriend."

"*My* enbyfriend?" Hayden is so confused, and I can't blame him.

"It's okay, Hayden," Mary-Anne says. "They told us all about it after your accident. It's okay, you don't have to hide it."

"You should know that, Hayden," Mr. Marcus follows it up. "We love you no matter who you—"

"But we're not..." Hayden's eyes scrunch together and his tiny pupils race around his bedsheets. The gray in his eyes is smoky with confusion. "Why? I don't understand. I never... I'm not dating anyone. *Am I?*"

Hayden locks on to Zach's eyes like he should know the answer.

"I...mean I...Mackenzie." Zach looks at me, but I wrench my eyes away. Something in his puppy eyes hurts deep in my soul.

"I think I'd remember that," Hayden says back. "Last dude I dated was Dalton."

All eyes, including mine, blossom into bright orbs and lock onto Hayden. Even Zachary's. What did he just say? *The last dude I dated.* He's... Wait. This is too trippy. I can see the questions brewing behind everyone's eyes, none more than Zachary's, whose mouth is practically on the floor. *So much for telling each other everything, bitch.* Nope. Wrong time for that one.

"Oh yeah, I'm bi. Surprise." Hayden smiles awkwardly and does his best jazz hands.

"Hold up, Dalton?" Zachary tilts his head. "I can see the gears behind his eyes turning extra hard. "Dalton on the soccer team?"

Hayden nods with a surprising grin.

"No wonder he wouldn't talk to me last year."

Everyone else's silence is deafening. For me it's the realization I might have had a chance after all, mixed with a little bit of wanting to know who this Dalton is. The thought trickling in that all those days he came by the shop, maybe he was looking at me like I was at him. It's like a moon lights itself over my head with a morsel of hope, even if it's only a sliver like before all this mess started.

I think the others are absolutely stunned. It's sinking in that he'd been queer long enough to date at least two non-females. Part of me revels in the thought, but I keep my cool.

"If I may." Dr. Kline's smooth voice cuts through the tension. She nods at Hayden and smiles at the rest of us as she settles next to his bedside. "It is possible, Hayden, that you're experiencing some sort of memory loss."

"But I remember them." Hayden points around the room and starts naming off his family. "Mom, Dad. My brother and sister, Zach and Holly. That's my Super Old Gran, and that's Kiki and Gramps." He looks at the doctor like it should be enough, but decides she isn't listening and starts rattling off about anything that might help. "Okay, fine. That's my Uncle Jeffrey and Aunt Eliza, Catina. My name is Hayden Dean Marcus. I'm seventeen. I play varsity basketball at Mitchell. Dad's a lawyer. Mom's a financial consultant. Gramps does A/C stuff. Kiki used to… I actually don't know what you used to do, sorry. But I even know that *they* work at the Woodsy Café."

He points at me. I resist the involuntary urge to step back. It's like I've been pointed out in a police lineup, or worse, been outed a second time around, but this time surrounded by the guy's family instead of an entire classroom of eighth graders. I'm not sure which is worse.

"I—" I'm about to spill the truth in a moment of terror. I can't hold it in any longer with him like this, but Eliza interrupts.

"He could have just lost recent memories, right?"

"True." Dr. Kline nods and smiles disarmingly. I'm not sure if I'm glad or infuriated Eliza stopped me. "Short-term memory is most often affected during traumatic events, such as your fall. You took a nasty hit to the head, Hayden. Remembering big events from your past, or your family, name, etcetera is common. It's the more recent events, even big ones, that tend to go missing. Sometimes specific events go missing. But they usually come back. Do you remember what happened the night you fell at the shop?"

He didn't forget anything. Not about me, but...

"Yeah, I went to get a frappe," Hayden says, but his face is more flushed and white than a few seconds ago.

Maybe he forgot just a little bit, something pointless, and it can make the blow of *not* technically forgetting *me* not so big.

"Good." Dr. Kline nods approvingly. "Now do you remember anything else, anything after that?"

It feels like a distraction at the moment while I'm stuck between Hayden and his family, an imposter. It's keeping me out of hot water for the moment, but it's also digging me a deeper grave to shovel out.

"Uh..." He squints, focusing hard on his knees under the plain white blankets. "I remember saying hey to hi—I mean *them*, uh, Mackenzie"—he points at me—"and Landon."

He looks at me again as if I'm supposed to verify, so I nod dramatically. He knows Landon's name too?

"I ordered my usual, and then left— Wait, no... I...dammit." He grunts. "That's it."

"It's okay, Hayden." Dr. Kline pats the bed next to his arm. Mary-Anne mumbles something. Probably a comforting word, but I can't tell what it is. *It must be nice having all these people here just for you, Hayden.* "It's not uncommon. Your injury put you out for thirteen days. You had a bad fall in the shop and hit your head. Your body reacted by putting you in a short coma. Mackenzie here brought you to the hospital."

She moves aside like she's unveiling me to him. Dr. Kline, no! "Oh," Hayden whispers, his eyes stuck on me now.

No! Don't look at me. Don't think about me. I shouldn't be here. Maybe he did lose some memories, but he didn't lose "our" memories. Those never happened. They never had a start, there is no story there for him to rediscover, except that I'm a major asshole. I look at his scared gray eyes and a new guilt sets in. It's worse than before, but I also see the guy I remember. The one who smiled so brightly when he'd walk into the shop and very predictably order an iced caramel latte with cinnamon. And he's bi.

"But…" He stops and considers me a moment. Then a smile creeps up his cheek. "I mean, you *are* cute."

It's everything I can do not to react. I hold in the well in my gut and give him a coy grin. What the hell is happening right now?

"There you go," Kiki cheers. "See, that's a start. It'll come back."

Did Hayden Marcus just tell me, Mackenzie Nicholas Jackson, that I am cute? Did he seriously just say to my face that I, the tiny enby witch who stands nearly a foot below him, am cute? He thinks I'm cute? I can't stop hearing his words echoing through my head. *You are cute.* I've dreamt of them coming from his mouth, and there they were. *You are cute.*

"I can't believe you didn't tell me, man!" Zachary blurts.

"Huh?" Hayden jumps.

"That you're fu—freaking bi! What did you think I'd say?" Zachary sounds genuinely hurt. "I came out to you first, man!"

"I know, sorry!" Hayden wiggles under the blanket.

It looks super uncomfortable. One of those stiff cheap-looking things that I'm sure would never be found at the Marcus's estate.

"Fine," Zachary huffs. "You always did say you'd go for Ryan Reynolds and Pedro Pascal. I just thought you were joking."

Hayden giggles. "That's what you get for thinking, bro."

"Fu—ugh…you." Zach grins but doesn't finish it. Mr. Marcus is already staring him down from the other side of the bed, where we've all gathered again. "No more secrets."

"Fine." Hayden lifts his arms in defeat, and it actually makes me giggle at the two of them. "I still don't remember…us dating."

"You just need a little time." Mary-Anne smiles at her son, then looks toward the doctor, who gives her an assuring nod. "You said his memories should come back, right?"

"They should." Dr. Kline shifts from her left to right foot. "We can't say for sure, but usually they do."

"How long?" Kiki steps forward, which gives me a glimpse of Eliza. She's eyeing me from behind Kiki, but I ignore her. We can talk later.

"It could be days. It could be weeks, months." The doctor shrugs with a smile that tries to belay the indefiniteness of the answer. "It's hard to say."

"Months…" The word barely exits Hayden's mouth, which I'm suddenly mesmerized by again.

"It's no matter," Super Old Gran practically yells from the lone chair in the corner. I don't remember her sitting down. "Sometimes not remembering shit is great."

"Gran!" Mary-Anne admonishes her.

A giggle threatens to breach my mouth, but I hold it back. I need her to be *my* grandma. Like, I really need that woman to be my grandma.

"What? It is!" Gran doubles down on it.

"Language," Mary-Anne clarifies.

"Oh dammit, right." Super Old Gran looks at me and winks.

I have to look away so I don't break. Gods, I love her.

"Hayden, it's good to have you back, regardless of all of that." Mary-Anne ignores Super Old Gran and wraps her son, the boy of my dreams, in her arms.

He grins and the rest of the family moves in to give him careful little hugs. When I get to the side of the bed, I'm not sure what to do, and I can tell by the hitch in his smile that he doesn't either. Everyone is staring at us though, even Zachary. I see him from the corner of my eye, off to the right, and suddenly I'm back at the Harrell House. In the dark. Surrounded by the dust swirling in phone light, with Zach's face less than a finger's width in front of me. His pupils wide, mouth parting.

I blink it away and I'm back at the hospital. I swallow. *Act normal.*

"I'm so glad you're back, Hayden." I say it as enbyfriend-ish as I can imagine.

I don't wait for a response. I'm horrified right now, so I lean in quick and give him the tiniest, most careful hug anyone's ever been given, and he lightly hugs back before I scoot away. But his touch... Where was the euphoria I expected, the electricity when my hand simply brushed Zachary's hand?

I let myself sink behind Mary-Anne where I can think, as Kaitlyn gives Hayden a hug. It's weird. It's not what I thought it would be. Where I thought excitement would be, I felt dirty, guilty.

19

THE FRONT DOOR SLAMS shut behind me and I fall against it. Warm air heats my goose-bumped skin, and I thank the gods Mom keeps it warmer at home than at the hospital.

"Was work that hard?" Mom's voice reaches me seemingly out of nowhere.

Then I catch the changing colors spilling out of the living room into the hallway. I breathe in the warm air and reluctantly make my way over. When I hang around the doorframe, I find her in the pajama set I got her for Christmas last year—soft pink top and bottoms with Hello Kitty all over them—lying on the couch with her hair a mess around her face. At least she hasn't been drinking.

"Huh?" I ask.

"You sound like you just got home from the coal mines." Mom taps the remote to pause whatever she's watching. Looks like one of those crime dramas.

"Just tired," I say. I haven't told her Hayden woke up yet or that it's got me on edge.

"You sure?" she prods. She sounds more alert today, even better in a way.

Her brown eyes appear nearly black, interrupted only by a single little star from the TV's reflection. She looks tired, but not like usual; her cheeks and the heavy bags cradling her eyes don't seem to droop as much tonight. She seems more herself, and here I am with everything falling apart.

I want to go to my room. Talking about my problem—well, problems—isn't high on my to-do list. Explaining it all again seems like a daunting undertaking after Kaitlynn's barrage after we left the hospital. Yes, I heard. He's actually bi! I just don't want to get into it right now. Then there's the other thing. Mom already carries so much on her shoulders. She doesn't need another worry. Not from me. Not more than I've already put on her.

"It's just the Hayden stuff," I mumble, and start down the hall.

"Hayden? Your boyfriend?" She sits up, and I stop and twist to face her.

Her arms seem frailer, but that's probably just in my head. She fumbles with the blanket next to her, finally pulling it away and patting the newly empty space for me to sit. Internally, I sigh. Here we go. The way her brow creases makes me feel bad. I don't want to worry her, but I do need a mom.

"Yeah." I resign to the inevitable.

"What happened?" she asks.

The real question is what didn't happen. I feel like the whole world opened up and devoured me. Is this the end? Is it all falling apart? In the car things felt surreal, almost like that feeling you get when you're speeding on a roller coaster and anything is possible, except without the assurance of a harness to keep me safe. Maybe Hayden and I *could* be a thing, but now… Now my mind is racing with the lies I have to sort out but refuse to deal with.

When I don't answer, she pushes, "Is he awake?"

"Yeah. Few hours ago." I fake a smile.

I fasten my gaze on the glass jar of winter iris and snowdrop blooms I put together last week. They're thriving, growing. Even the single white Christmas rose in the middle is going strong. How lovely it must be to simply exist without worry. Not to be aware there is so much to worry about. To simply be. To grow and blossom. To be beautiful without effort. Somehow *that* is living under the same roof as I am. I, however, I'm not blooming.

I feel like I'm withering away instead.

"That's great!" Mom's face brightens a little, but I ruin it with the fake grin I give her. It's like my face just can't hold in what I'm feeling. "And..."

I shrug. It's not the amazing feelings I thought I'd be feeling when he woke up. Is that my fault too?

"Uh..." I briefly make eye contact before drifting off into the corner, where a tall brown and red vase sits atop a little table. It's always made me think of the desert, the way the red waves between bands of deep sandy browns. I wouldn't call it beautiful, maybe different? I can't remember how many times Mom had to threaten to ground me for a whole year if I touched it. It's from Germany, some potter in her hometown. "Yeah. It's awesome."

She's asked about him a few times. Wanted to know how we met, how long we'd been "dating." All of the basics. Most of it I made up on the spot.

Mom's looking at me as if I'm an alien. "Did you get to talk to him?"

I nod. "A little."

"That's nice. I bet his family is happy," Mom says, but all I can think about is how dirty I feel. How am I going to make this work?

"Yeah," I say again. I say it too much.

This junk is too much. It isn't life or death, at least I don't think it is. Gods, what if it is? No. Of course it isn't, that's silly. Still, this isn't what I should be dealing with. I should be worrying about finishing my English paper, passing my math exams next week, finding an *actual* boyfriend. Not building a story around how I'm dating a hot jock I've barely carried a single full conversation with who's been in a coma for two weeks, who only now woke up and thinks he's experiencing amnesia—*all* because of me.

"Night, Mom," I say before I can break into tears.

My emotions are welling up behind my cheeks. It's a confused mess of feelings, all culminating into this weird nauseating feeling in the pit of my stomach. There's worry for sure. A little jealousy floating alongside it. Then terror. Lots of terror surrounding what's going to happen when people find out. And shame. Shame is the centerpiece. It's what has my stomach churning.

"Nacht, mein Schatz." She grins.

She doesn't use her familial language often since I only know a few phrases. All my relatives on her side speak English, so it was never important for me. Sometimes I'll overhear Mom FaceTiming my aunt back in Böblingen and have to remind myself they're not mad at each other. German's weird like that, but this one is sweet. It's one she's said since before I can remember. *Night, my little treasure.*

"Gute Nacht," I say good night back.

I start down the hallway, but my chest is stiff and every step and breath seems harder than the last. Since when do I lie to my mom? It's become too easy and I don't like it. I huff and turn around. She's standing there, watching me. Was she waiting for me to turn around?

"What's going on, Mackenzie?" Mom smiles caringly.

It's not often I hear my full name from her. Usually it's Kenzie, that's it. But my full first name—that's usually only from people who don't really know me, or from Mom when she's worried.

I huff, letting all the air drain from my lungs, and take in one long breath. Am I actually going to do this? Am I really going to unload this all on her? Yeah. I am. I force my lips to curve and push up my dimples in one of those sad smiles. Please don't think less of me for this, Mom.

"Hayden's not exactly my boyfriend," I admit. Oh shit, I did it! She's the first person—okay, second person—I've actively admitted it to. Well, maybe Kaitlynn, but that's different. She doesn't count.

Mom's head tilts and her eyes squint. The massive weight bearing down on me doesn't lift. I don't feel airy or free. None of those things happen, but maybe a single little ounce falls off. I'll take it.

"What do you mean?" Mom asks slowly. "You said…"

"I made it up," I blurt. It sounds a thousand times more pathetic when the words blare from my lips and are immediately absorbed by our little suffocating hallway. "I don't even really know him."

"But…how? Why would you make up something like that? Kenzie…" Her words cut, and each question stings as her voice rises an octave and comes at me quicker. "Doesn't his family think you two are a couple? His brother was even here."

"They do," I admit. And Zachary…why do you have to bring him up? I was trying so hard to block him out. "And yeah. Zachary thinks so too."

"But you're not?" Mom asks again.

"No." I bow my head.

"Why would you lie about that?" she asks again. The subtle accusation in her tone is painful.

I don't want to answer. The more I think about it, the worse I feel and the more frustrating it all seems. How did it ever seem like a good idea, like somehow it would all work out in the end and I'd be happily in love with Hayden Marcus? Who was I trying to impress? Myself?

"It j-just sort of happened," I stutter. Oddly enough, it's not entirely a lie. It did just sort of happen. I hadn't planned any of it. I mean I had thought of a few scenarios to get him to date me before any of this ever happened, but none of them included lying to a nurse and his family to convince them I was dating him after he fell, hit his head, and went into a coma at the shop. Even then, I didn't go into the hospital scheming, concocting a way to make him think I was his enbyfriend. No! I just went because I was worried. He fell and passed out *at* my work. Right in front of me! The boy I was...*am*—I think—head over heels for. I just had to follow the ambulance. Why did I do that? But the worst was that foolish sentence. Those outlandish words I muttered to Regina. I sealed the deal with that first lie. Or maybe it was the spell, I don't know anymore.

"It just happened?" She leans against the doorframe like the question is exhausting. The disbelief is building in her eyes, the disappointment, and I hate it so much. "How does something like that just happen, Mackenzie? Wie? People don't just assume your Freunde. And if they do? Du sagst ihnen, dass es nicht wahr ist."

She stops herself and breathes. It's not common to hear her become angry and revert back to German, but when it happens I know I've crossed a line, as if I didn't already know that.

"You tell them you're not!" she says in English this time.

I'm not used to her getting riled up. It's so rare that I don't know what to do, so I do nothing. I just stand in place, trying to blink away the tears slipping over my cheeks. I know I should have told them I'm not Hayden's enbyfriend. I know! But I couldn't! I didn't. I messed up. I know.

"I'm sorry, Schatzi," Mom says, sinking her lips in and back out before gulping. "I don't mean to be angry. I just don't understand."

"I know. Me too," I huff. But I think I do now. If I hadn't told Regina he was my boyfriend, I could have avoided it all. But I did, and when it bit me in the ass, I didn't know which was worse: to break the trust of my friend or a little white lie. A white lie. Gods, it's not a white lie. It's horrible. It was the most absurd thing I could have said. If not for one choice, I wouldn't be here right now, but here I am. "It's pointless, but I'm stuck."

"Why are you stuck?" she asks.

I think about it. There is only one explanation. Me. It all comes back to me, but it's still not easy. Nothing about it is easy.

"I just am," is what I say though.

"Kenzie," she finally says my name the way I'm accustomed. "It never *just is*. There's always a reason, Schatzi. What happened?"

I dip my head. Can't it just be this time? I don't want to answer. I've already ruined the night enough, but how can I not? I roll my head back and sigh.

"You remember the night Hayden fell at the shop? And I went to the hospital with him, right?" I start.

"Yes." Mom nods.

"When I got there, I might have done something foolish." I wince.

"What did you do?" she asks.

"Well, first, I sort of cast a love spell. A few, actually. I know I can't make him love me, but I wanted to give it a push, you know? Put my intent out into the universe." She grins when I tell her, and I'm not sure why, but right now I'll take it. "I think maybe I did something wrong. I don't know what, but I must have. Maybe my vibe was just off."

"Schatzi." Mom closes the distance between us and cups my face, but before she can say anything else I ramble on.

"But yeah, when I got to the hospital, I sort of told Regina that I was dating him just to try to see him. Then when…uh…when his…" I stumble over myself and take a quick breather. "When his family got there, she sort of…uh…told them I was…you know…"

I squint, hoping Mom will fill in the rest, but she seems determined to hear it from me.

"Like…I was…" I try again and finally just blurt it out in one big word vomit. "That I was his enbyfriend, and I didn't say no."

"And you what?" She leans in and cups her ears. I know her hearing isn't bad, so it's theatrics. I huff.

"I didn't say no," I repeat slower.

"Oh." Mom's lips pooch under an understanding glint in her eye.

"Yeah." I grin stupidly. "I couldn't get myself to. So I sort of *became* his enbyfriend, and well, that's it."

"And you've never told them?" Mom asks.

"It's only been two weeks." I bounce my shoulders, hoping it'll make the horrible seem a little less horrible. It doesn't.

She stares me down a moment, patting my shoulder. Seconds pass and her serious gaze transforms into something softer and more understanding.

"Mein Schatz, you *have* to tell them the truth. You do know that, right?" Mom says expectantly, but with a heaping of understanding in her voice. "Especially now that he's awake."

Her head twitches in realization, and I see a bulb light up.

"Hold on, if he woke up, how do they not know yet?" Mom asks.

I smile. It's one of those big shit-eating grins. I hate me for it, but you know how they say things can't get worse? Well, they do.

"Mackenzie?" Mom says again.

"I was going to tell them! I swear!" I tell her. "But the doctor said he could be experiencing amnesia."

"How does that change anything?" Mom asks.

"It doesn't...but she told his family he might not recall recent memories. That he probably lost those memories of us. And now he thinks he just doesn't remember us dating," I say, chewing on my sucked-in lips when I stop talking.

Mom dips her head again and sighs. "Kenzie, you can't keep this up. You shouldn't. It's not right."

"I know." I dip my head too.

Who knew the shame already overflowing in my gut could somehow intensify in a matter of minutes.

"You have to tell them the truth," Mom says.

"I will, but…" I'm about to confess more, but I stop.

"But what?" Mom asks. "You *need* to tell them the truth. It's not going to be easy, but you can't go on trying to hold up a lie, especially like this. Hayden is a person too."

I nod and remember what Eliza had said.

"His aunt knows!" I blurt.

"But they haven't said anything?" Mom asks.

"No. She said she'd break the news to them though, she just hasn't yet," I explain. I know I shouldn't, but it's nice not to feel like all the blame is on me.

"You should still make it right, Schatzi." Mom smiles sadly at me, then steps up and puts her arms around me. "You're a good one. Stubborn and strong-willed for such a little package, but you have a good heart. I know you do."

She ruffles my hair like I'm ten, and I roll my eyes so she can see.

Do I though? My heart, that is. Do I have a good one? If I'm honest, it feels shrunken and wrinkly. It feels foreign.

"You're growing up, becoming a ma—" She stops herself and grins at me. "A great *person*. Things are changing. It's how growing up works. But you *do* have a good heart. I know you do."

"Are you sure?" I can't look at her.

"Yes. Yes, I am." She pats my cheek. "You're figuring things out. You're learning, adjusting, growing. I *definitely* don't want to imagine what all goes through that head of yours, but it doesn't make you bad. Only what you do with those feelings and thoughts can do that. But even that can be made right." Mom pauses and looks me hard in the eyes. "It's not too late to do what you should have done. And I know you will."

I smile and nod. It must be enough because she squeezes me and tells me good night again. When she turns around, I say, "Gute Nacht," and make off down the hall to my bedroom. I shut the door behind me and fall face-first on my bed's thick gray weighted comforter.

"Ahhhh!" I scream into the blanket to muffle the sound.

Semi-satisfied with the release, I flip over and throw my arms out like limp wings. "Why?"

I scan the motionless brown blades of my ceiling fan like they're filled with sigils and unknown mythologies to be decrypted. I try to focus on them, looking for an easy way out of all this, if for no other reason than for Mom. She's right. I need to say something. I *have* to. I can't let Hayden think he's just forgotten me. It's wrong, on so many levels.

But how?

I know how I'm going to start, at least. I get up and head over to my altar, where I write on a new slip of parchment.

May I have the strength to tell Hayden and his family the truth.

I'm about to write it a second time below the first sentence, but instead I continue it with one more statement.

I will not fall for Zachary Marcus.

I can't do all this. I can't tell them the truth and expect Zachary to want anything to do with me. How could he? I have to be ready for that. I have to accept it.

After writing it down another two times, and ripping the paper into three pieces, I fold them each three times. I pull the tall slender black candle closer and light it.

"You can do this," I say, but underneath the words and flicker of flame and smell of smoke, there are things running through my head that I can't seem to stop. A feeling. An idea.

Maybe I can fix this. Maybe.

I drop the parchment before finishing the second repetition. Making a spell with mixed intentions, with a conflicted heart, is dangerous. Instead, I kill the flame with a quick breath and move my ocean-blue pillar candle front and center before lighting it. I don't bother writing my intention down. I simply watch the flame flicker and beg Freyja for clearness of mind and peace, because I can't imagine that even being possible on my own. I feel it deep in my gut. A deep hole, sloshing over the edges with guilt and greed. It's a version of me I didn't know I could be, something foreign and burdensome. Oh gods, please don't let this be me.

20

"HOW DID WE MEET again?" Hayden asks.

I snap back to reality, wrenching my eyes away from the rhythmic jump and fall of Hayden's heartbeat on the monitor. It's hypnotic. What did he ask? Right, how did we meet? Well…okay, so what did I tell Mom last night when I promised I'd be honest. Right!

"At Woodsy," I tell him without any further explanation.

I know he's searching for more. He's looking for the moment one of us made a move and asked the other out, what possessed him to date a curly haired runt of a they, what made him choose me. Sorry, Hayden, but what you're looking for never happened.

"Yeah, but like, you know…" His words drift off for a second as he considers how to say it. I focus on his carefully constructed messy hair. He looks more like the Hayden I remember today. "How'd we start dating? Did I ask you out? I feel like I would have asked you out."

"I…" I start, not sure whether I'm about to admit it all and tear down this façade, but he keeps talking when I pause too long and saves me from it—for now.

"Yeah, I bet I asked you out," he says. "I'm always the one to ask girls out, and you're…you know…uh…"

"Girly?" I squint. It wouldn't be the first time someone said it, not like it bothers me. I like my feminine side. Oh my gods, but on the other hand, please don't tell me he's one of those hyper-masculine dudes who think girls and femmes are helpless and have to be led. You can be queer and still think that unfortunately. Puke, nasty!

"Yeah." He shrugs nervously.

I think *he* thinks he hit a nerve, which is sort of funny. He swallows and starts talking again immediately.

"I don't mean you're too girly or anything, or that a girl couldn't ask me out. But you're a guy, I mean…fuck…a non-binary person and more feminine, and I figure I'd be…" He stops and huffs. His eyes are rolled up, looking at the ceiling for a full second before he looks at me again. It's all I can do not to giggle. "I'm not doing this well, am I?"

"No." I shake my head and laugh. It's sort of cute seeing him like this. Endearing, even. Him being the nervous one and not me, finally, is refreshing.

"So how *did* we start dating?"

He is persistent though.

The correct answer is, *We didn't. I made it up because of a stupid spell I did and then my nurse friend told your family we were dating. I did sort of tell her that, so that's not her fault, and I* really *wanted it at the time* — oh wow, *at the time*, I never thought I'd say that — *and your entire family was staring me down. I wasn't thinking, and agreed. I was being absurd and I shouldn't have done it. I should have told the truth. I'm so sorry!*

"You asked me out at the shop." I punch myself mentally. What am I doing? Am I *trying* to be an asshole now? "But our first date wasn't until like a week later. I was too scared, and you had to ask twice."

"Oh." He grins.

I was too scared? Ugh, no. And *you had to ask twice?* What's with that? What am I doing? Trying to make a cute romance story out of it? Sure, he used to make my knees go weak and I didn't know what to say when he'd come in for his coffee, but I'm better than that. Why would I say that?

"Yeah. You took me to dinner. Uh...we went to, uh..." Gods, where would we have gone? Quick, what did I tell Mom? Shit! I don't remember. "Taco Bell."

Shit! That wasn't it!

"Taco Bell?" Hayden angles his head and scrunches his nose. "I took you to Taco Bell on our first date?"

"Yeah, it's my favorite restaurant." It's actually the truth, for once, even if it's not my stomach's favorite. I keep my head upright and focused on him despite the urge to drop it in shame.

"O-kay. Guess that makes sense. I don't like Taco Bell. I mean I guess you already knew that," he says.

"Yeah." I fake laugh. Oh my gods! "It was super sweet of you though. Not liking it and all, but taking me there anyway. And then we went to the Harrel House and we got spooked, and you thought I was horrified, and you kissed me."

I hate myself with every single word that comes out of my mouth. That's not his memory. It's not our memory. It isn't his to have or to think. It's mine. Mine and Zachary's. Mine and his brother's. I fight back the urge to close my eyes and sigh in defeat. Why can't I just stop talking? Get out of my head, Zachary!

"So we had a *good* first date," he says, but I bet the thought of kissing me sort of makes him ill. "Wish I could remember it. I don't even remember thinking about asking you out, or liking you before this."

Oh wow. That was very honest. I didn't need to know that. I mean I guess I did know it, but like, I didn't need to hear it directly from him. That's how he really feels, how he feels about me. I'm nothing. He's bi and I was still never an option.

The thought spears through my mind, clashing with my heart and fracturing it into tiny pieces. Still, my mind conjures images of Hayden kissing me in the Harrel House, his face superimposed

How (Not) to Conjure a Boyfriend

over Zach's. It's uncomfortable and off-putting, but I'm not sure if it's because of what he just said or because of how it really happened. It's the kiss I'd always dreamt of, the moment I'd wanted, but it feels more like a nightmare. Why would I want that from someone who thinks of me that way, even if they don't see it?

"Yeah," I grunt. I don't want to say anything else. It's become too unpleasant. I don't feel like trying right now. Not anymore.

"I'll have to take you to Taco Bell." He makes a puking face, laughs, and continues, "When I get out of here. It shouldn't be long either. The doc said maybe a few days."

"Oh really?" I refuse to respond to the date comment, even if I do giggle as genuinely as I can manage at his "funny" face.

"I don't want to be rude, but…" He trails off, and all I can think is *you don't want to be rude, but what? You're going to be anyway?* "My friends are coming by soon, and uh… I'm assuming they don't… you know… know… about us? I'm assuming we hadn't told anyone."

From the look on his face, I'm not holding back the boiling feeling of betrayal and astonishment as well as I think. Everything is brewing together into a heaping mess, and it's literally all I can do to force a grin and nod.

"Maybe they do. And sorry for breaking the news to your family," I blurt.

"No, I didn't mean it like—"

I throw my hand up and stretch my neck.

"Don't. I'll be okay," I say. It's like we're genuinely having a couples fight in the middle of the hospital, even though we're not a couple. Not a real one, at least.

How do you just assume we've not told anyone? I mean we hadn't. There's no *we* did *anything*, but that's not the point. That was brazen.

"I'm sorry, baby," Hayden says as I get up and start toward the door.

Weeks ago I would have melted to the floor in a heap of hot, embarrassed putty had he called me baby. I would have literally let him do or say whatever the hell he wanted. He could have gotten away with murder in front of my very eyes, and I would have said nothing. But now, with his clear distaste for me? Hearing it now, my stomach drops like a massive weight into my bowels and twists my insides in nauseating knots while I fight the reflex to gag. I'm so glad I'm facing away from him so he can't see the disgust on my face.

"It's okay," I say without turning, and march into the hallway.

I don't think my timing could have been better. The moment I pass the nurse's station, a group of unruly, ugly, tall, acne-covered boys in letter jackets stampede past me. I know where they're going without even looking.

Why did I think he would be different? Was it his pretty face? That disarming smile? The kindness that seemed to seep from his eyes when he entered the store? Or was it some fake idea of him I had in my mind? Or was it because I thought it could only ever be a fantasy?

I press the elevator button and fidget with my fingers while I watch the numbers tick off closer and closer to the fifth floor. I notice my foot is jumping, so I slap it to the ground and blow out a deep breath. The familiar arrival ding sounds. I just want to get home and—

The elevator doors slide open and Zach steps out. He freezes when he finally notices me, his feet like a statue on the threshold.

"Hi." Zach grins.

"Hey," I practically growl despite the surprise, and push past him into the confines of the little box.

"You okay?" He moves out of my way and away from the elevator, giving me some space.

"I'm perfectly fine," I spit back as the doors slide together.

His eyes don't leave me until the doors have closed, and that's when I let it all sink in — the enormous mistake I made, not just in the lie that started everything, but in thinking I knew anything about Hayden. I imagined his whole personality. It was a fiction of my own making. An illusion I couldn't unsee until now.

I swallow the lump in my throat, let a tear form in the corner of my eye, and let the tremors loose.

21

I THINK ONE OF the school administrators is trying to save money. The cafeteria is so frigid, I have my hood up *inside* to keep my ears warm. It's not even forty outside today, why would you skimp on the heat?

"They're fake." Julieta feigns embarrassment.

"They look good," Kaitlynn says.

If she hadn't said it, I wouldn't have known her nails weren't real. They're long and translucent with pretty blue tips. I almost did that same look this summer, but I ended up with stars on midnight blue polish instead.

"I love that," I tell her.

"Next time I'm going to get acrylics—like, you know, from the nail salon downtown," Julieta says. She's always so animated, throwing her hands around, or wiggling her fingers like right now, or making grand gestures and sighing every other sentence.

"Maybe we can all go!" Kaitlynn suggests.

It's not a bad idea. I haven't been in a month at least, and my nails are looking ratty. All the polish is gone, and my cuticles are in dire need of some attention.

"I'm game," I say.

"Period," Julieta says. Her eyes are big and brown, dark fawny things that complement her brown complexion. "Maybe we can do it before Christmas?"

"The sooner the better," I say half-mindedly. I'm still not entirely here.

"You really need it." Kaitlynn nudges me. "Have you been

How (Not) to Conjure a Boyfriend

biting your nails again?"

"What?" I snap at her. "Have not!"

I throw my hands up like I'm trying to show off my nails to the entire school. Okay, they're bad, but they're not that bad.

"Uh-huh," Kaitlynn huffs.

"I swear!" I tell her, which earns me a laugh from Julieta. "I've done so much better since I've been getting them done!"

I really have. I used to chew them to the quick, and then I'd have them bleeding when I went too far, or they didn't rip right, but I've done better. I just haven't had a manicure in a while.

"They're not that bad," Julieta comes to my aid.

I nod appreciatively at her, then grunt at Kaity. See, they're not that bad. Even if I did maybe chew on my thumbnail this morning. It was just a little though, and I've been so nervous! Hayden's coming home from the hospital today—much earlier than expected—and I feel like this is about to open a whole new level of wild that I'm not ready for. I've not talked to him since yesterday.

"Maybe next week, then?" Kaitlynn suggests.

Julieta makes a big show of checking her phone to see if she's free. How busy could a fourteen-year-old freshman be? I'm not even busy enough to have to check my schedule, and I work.

"I can do it. We'll still have to go again before the Winter Formal," Julieta reminds us. "Have to look good for Kadin."

Ah yes, Kadin. The two of them have been going steady for a month now, I think. Which is awesome, and besides, he looks like my K-pop crush, Hyunjin, from Stray Kids. I swear he could be the singer's doppelganger, and my, is he gorgeous. He's one of my many unattainable straight crushes.

"Can't be seen next to that piece of perfection looking like trash," Kaitlynn echoes her.

"We all look like trash next to him," Julieta sighs lustfully.

If I didn't agree, I'd be rolling my eyes.

"Agreed!" I laugh.

"You want to look good for your man too," Julieta says, looking straight at me.

My man?

What is she talking about?

"Huh?" I quirk an eyebrow. Kaitlynn's eyes widen and she shakes her head at me as if to say, *I didn't say a damn thing*.

"Hayden Marcus." Julieta says *his* name.

"What? No," I laugh, trying to play it off. As if he doesn't actually think he's my boyfriend right now, which while I'm thinking about it, seems beyond insane. I mean, it is insane, and after yesterday there is no way. "He's just a crush. He'd never."

"But." Julieta's eyes fly wide, her dark black eyeshadow becoming barely a line above long lashes. "You two are dating. That's what they're saying, at least."

"Dat...dating?" I blurt. "They?"

"Yeah, *everyone's* talking about it." Julieta grins. You'd think it was the biggest thing to happen at Mount Laurel High in ages the way she's bouncing her shoulders and stressed *everyone's*. Except *everyone* doesn't seem to include *anyone* who's talking to me. "I heard you two have been dating for a while but keeping it quiet. So selfish."

Shit! That's what I want to scream. I want to yell it loud and clear and profound across the cafeteria. Instead I duck and swipe my eyes across the room, scanning my classmates. People I know, don't know, don't want to know. Do they all really think I'm dating Hayden? They're probably stunned beyond belief. Especially my bullies. Yeah, I've bullies. This is the mountains.

"Uh..." I make a noise that's sort of a groan.

Kaitlynn's eyes are as wide as I've ever seen them. Mine too probably, but I blink it away and try to start up the damage control. I can't deny it. Did he say something? Did he tell one of his friends? Were his parents or grandparents too talkative about us? Oh my gods, there are so many possibilities. I don't know, and I'm one hundred percent not about to text him to find out.

"Yeah, we are." I surprise even myself. No point in stopping it now. Gods. Freyja is never going to let me into Fòlkvangr after all this. "Surprise!" I do jazz hands and breathe heavily. I didn't think things could get worse than they already were, but here we are.

Julieta squeals and shakes her shoulders. I wish I was that excited. "That's so awesome! He's dreamy."

"Yeah, he is." I grin.

The bell rings, so I say a quick bye before using it to get away. I waste no time snatching Kaitlynn's arm and pulling her along. I need her with me. Hell, now that I think about it, maybe I wasn't being unreal to feel like people were watching me. *Freyja, please make them stay away.*

"Slow down!" Kaitlynn yelps as I tug her between the tables and chairs and down the main hall. I need somewhere we can talk, but privately!

"Kenz—" she starts again.

"Hold on!" I interrupt, finally seeing an option. I dive right between some tall dude I know I've seen a hundred times but haven't a clue his name, and someone else. Then it's another hard right, fingers gripping a long metal handle, yanking it open and shoving Kaitlynn inside before she can protest, and shutting the door behind us.

"Why are we in the janitor's closet?" Kaitlynn bops her head and winces. "I'm not making out with you."

"Make out? What? No!" I grimace at the thought and make an exaggerated puking noise.

"Well you don't have to make it that obvious," Kaitlynn says.

"What am I going to do about all this?" I wave my hand toward the door while she rolls her eyes.

"Do about it?" she asks.

"Yeah! Now everyone knows. Everyone isn't supposed to know!" I tell her. "Now everyone is going to know I lied!"

"I mean they don't have to know." Kaitlynn bumps her shoulders with this very innocent look that says *I'm guilty as hell*.

"Kaity, darling," I start off, as calmly as I can, "do you really think Hayden is going to keep thinking he chose to date me?"

"May—"

"No!" I practically yell, but still keep it quiet. She doesn't know yet that I had my argument with Hayden. I've been keeping it close to my chest.

"Ugh, you're going to make us late for class," Kaitlynn complains.

"Forget class, this is more important!" I tell her. "This is terrible. I'm ruined! No one will ever see me as a decent person again once word gets out."

"Little dramatic, but…" Kaitlynn drags it out. "Maybe you just need to not think about him—"

"Or Zach," I interject.

"—for, and yeah, Zach too, for a little." Kaitlynn's amusement morphs into what seems sincere, but that's anyone's guess. "You need to clear your head and do something that makes you happy. Get away from them so you can think clearly."

"But it's *all* I think about," I complain, cupping my face in my hands for dramatic effect. Wait!

"Or you could fuck both of them and see which you—"
What?

"Uh, no!" I yelp. "I feel bad enough I kissed Zach. But may—"

"So you admit it now! It *was* you. I knew it!" Kaity is raving in her own world.

"—be, what? No! I mean, yeah, but that's not what we're talking about right now."

"Maybe not you," Kaity laughs.

"Focus, Kaity!"

"Sorry." She pouts.

"What I was trying to say is that maybe you're right." I pause to clarify. "About the getting my mind off them part."

"Duh. I don't know why that always seems like such a surprise to you." Kaitlynn raises a brow at me.

"But how?" I ask.

I ignore her and start listing the things I could do to get *them* off my mind. First, stop saying or thinking *their* names. Second, something fun. I could go to a movie. Hmm... What's playing? I could bake a cake for Kaitlynn's mom. She loves my layered lemon and lime cake. Go for a drive? No. That's just more empty time to think.

"The park?" Kaitlynn suggests.

"Hell no! It's too cold for that," I say just as the bell rings again.

"Yep, we're late," she complains and then lists another idea. "Go on a drive?"

"Nope, already crossed that one off the list," I tell her.

Maybe do some light trespassing somewhere abandoned. Nope, I don't need Mom even more upset with me.

"Well, I can't read your mind. Ouija board?"

Ooh! I could have a Sandra Bullock movie marathon tonight and make Mom join me. That actress is amazing. She also happens to star in my all-time favorite movie, *Practical Magic*. Or maybe...

Oh! I have it! I throw my hand up, pointer finger extended.

"We can have one of our baking nights!" I'm pretty sure anyone in the hall who's late for class like us could have heard that.

"Oh yay," Kaitlynn deadpans. "I can't wait."

"And a movie! Come on! It'll be fun! And you get to help me!" I tell her.

"Yeah, yeah, whatever." She rolls her eyes. "What are we watching?"

I give her one of my big cheesy grins, the type she hates. She huffs and I let out the tiniest little giggle.

"*Practical Magic*," she sighs. "I get to pick the music."

I nod, and you know what? I think I'm already feeling better.

22

"I HAVE THE STRAWBERRIES and blossom water!"

There's no time to hear the door swing open before Kaitlynn yells her presence.

"Orange blossom, right?" I yell from the kitchen. The last time she went to the store without me for ingredients, she came back with yellow cake mix instead of the powdered sugar in my text, plus a ton of candy.

"Of course, of course!" Kaitlynn lumbers around the corner with not one but three reusable grocery bags in tow.

I stop and huff. "What did you get?"

"The necessities." She shrugs, dropping them on the kitchen table behind me. Her hands dip inside the first bag and she starts pulling things out. "The strawberries. Can't make our margs without them. *Orange* blossom water."

I squint, examining the clear bottle while she lowers it to the table. Okay, good. She got the right thing.

"Chips. Your favorite." Kaitlynn lifts a bag of Cool Ranch Doritos, then an orange bag. "Cheetos for me. And of course, candy."

Kaitlynn tips the third bag over and heaps of individually wrapped candies scatter the table. So much sugar.

"What the…?" I gasp. She always does this. "Why?"

"The better question is why not?" Kaitlynn shrugs, picking up a plastic sleeve of Smarties and dumping the entire packet in her mouth.

"Isn't *that* sort of why not?" I squint.

"Nah," she says, crunching down on the chalky bits.

The day our metabolisms slow down, we're both screwed. Enjoy it while I'm young, right? I pick out a Twix and unwrap it as I go back to the kitchen counter.

"You going to make the margaritas first?" I ask.

"Yep." Kaitlynn breaks open the strawberries. "You're *really* going to forget those boys tonight!"

"Oh my gods, Kaity!" I huff. I'd managed not to think of either of them for the past hour, but now their gray eyes are plastered in my mind again. "Not helping! And the drinks are virgin, not alcoholic!"

"Duh." She rolls her eyes. "Doesn't mean we can't act like it!"

"The blender's in—"

"I know where it's at." Kaitlynn grins at me.

I close my eyes for a brief moment, letting the music sink in, hoping it'll fill up some of those areas where their faces are still trying to pop into view. I need a calm night. Not more stress. Especially since I'm going to have to listen to death metal in a bit. Kaity's been into it lately. A whole lot. Like it's scary, but she loves it, and like a good friend I let her make the list.

Tonight's goal is simple. Bake one cake each, make frozen virgin margaritas, blare music, then watch *Practical Magic* while we devour our creations. I'm also going to send half of mine home with Kaitlynn for her mom. And no boys. No talk of them. No thinking about them. Just us and our food.

"Your mom around?" Kaitlynn asks.

"Yeah," I say. "She's in her room."

"Ah," Kaitlynn says, switching off the blender and setting it in the freezer. She comes over and settles to my right in front of her ingredients, picks up her directions, and starts rearranging her bowls.

How (Not) to Conjure a Boyfriend

"Of course," I groan, gesturing at the bowls. I swear she only does it because she knows I like them a certain way.

"Duh," she says, and we both laugh.

"Fine, let's get to baking," I tell her. "First you'll—"

Kaitlynn puts a finger up, a spoon in her other hand.

"Tsk, tsk," she utters. "I know what I'm doing."

I shrug doubtfully as she picks up the jar of peanut butter and dunks the spoon inside. It comes out with a huge gooey dollop. She looks at me with the happiest grin and licks the spoon clean.

"That's how you start." She nods affirmatively.

"Chef's privilege." I shake my head, but I'm smiling anyway. "Just do your thing and try not to burn my house down. And clean that spoon before you start."

"YOU REALIZE THIS MOVIE is ten years older than we are, right?" Kaitlynn slouches on the sofa next to me.

"And?" I shrug. Sure, it's not new, but it's aged like a fine wine. At least that's what I hear Mom say.

Why else would the opening credits be playing on my television right now? Maybe most of my generation hasn't seen it, but it's one of Mom's favorites, so we used to watch it together. It's also one of the things that sparked my interest in witchcraft. It wasn't the main thing, I think that was my civics project freshman year. It sort of soured my take on religion and put me on the path to spirituality and witchcraft.

"It's old!" Kaitlynn complains. She'd never been fond of it, but I still make her watch it when I get the chance. "Like *sooo* old."

"We're watching it! I'm not turning it off."

She should be glad. She can't keep her mouth shut during movies, and usually that drives me up a wall. Lucky for her, since

I've watched it so many times, I don't mind for this one.

"Fine," Kaitlynn huffs while an early American scene unveils on the screen. It's time for a witch hanging, or at least that's what they think.

Sort of like I thought I'd get through this night without thinking of the Marcus boys. Yeah, that didn't happen. Why is it so hard not to think of them? I just need this movie to start so I can let the dopamine from one of my favorite stories fill my brain and crowd out the junk I don't want to think about, especially Zach.

He sent a text after school today. So that didn't help. It's the first from him since Wednesday, but it's like it came at just the wrong time. It isn't anything problematic, or sappy, or about us, or even Hayden. I don't know, maybe that's worse though.

I unlock my phone and let his last text sit on the screen.

ZACHARY: How r u?

I haven't opened it yet. It's just the preview, so he can't see I've read it. That's all it is though. *How r u?*

Well, I'm sort of losing my mind, Zach. I've managed to unintentionally convince your whole family, and now both our high schools, that your older brother and I are dating when we're definitely not. Now even Hayden thinks we are. How does this shit even happen? Oh, and to make things even worse, I think I like you!

I'm one hundred percent not replying. Oh gods, I did it again! Stop thinking about them!

"You remember the forts we used to make at my house?" Kaitlynn interrupts the movie, and thankfully my thoughts.

"The blanket forts? In your playroom?" I ask.

"Yep." She grins big.

Her parents converted their finished basement into this massive playroom when we were around five. It's the whole length of their

How (Not) to Conjure a Boyfriend

house and filled with toys, and a lot of spare chairs. It was always cold down there in the winter, so Kaity's mom always left us a big stack of blankets. We'd suspend them between the walls and chairs, or chairs and tables, or with whatever we could find that was heavy enough to keep them in place. They were elaborate for blanket forts. Whole rooms, halls, and entrance. We'd play in them for hours.

"Those were so much fun!" I tell her. "Except that one time it collapsed on me, and I thought I was going to die."

"Yeah, that one wasn't so good. It had been up a couple days though," Kaitlynn reasons.

Try being the one suffocating under four comforters at like seven years old with a big chair tipped over on top. I can't say safety had been one of our biggest concerns in our building codes. It never was. They were fun, that's what we were worried about.

"It's been forever. This might sound sort of silly, but why don't we do that anymore?" she asks.

We grew out of it? I don't know. It's weird now that she brings it up. It's like one day we were spreading blankets between chairs and navigating tiny phone-lit multicolored halls, and then boom, we're doing makeup and talking about boys and college.

"Guess we just grew up." I shrug. I was about to suggest we try it again soon, but we're sixteen. Isn't that too old for that type of thing? A part of me recoils in embarrassment even thinking about blanket forts. "We're older now."

"Sounds lame if you ask me," Kaitlynn says.

"Well, I didn't say..." I shoot her a grin.

"So rude," she says.

"The worst." I roll my eyes and smile back.

"You so are," she laughs.

"That's not what I meant, bitch!" I laugh.

"Yeah, yeah," she giggles, and we settle down into a quiet contemplation.

"And we didn't have boy problems then. I still can't get Za—"

"No! Don't say his name! It's not allowed tonight!" Kaity jumps across the couch and shoves her pointer finger against my lips to shush me. WOW! Aggressive much? I wasn't going to start spilling my guts about him. "Tonight is a boy drama-free night, except for what's her name's drama."

She's pointing at the television, and honestly I'm surprised she doesn't know Sandra Bullock's character's name by now. Sandra's an icon. A literal treasure! There is no way she doesn't know Sandra's name, or her character's name, not after watching this one with me at least five or six times before. Hell, I know I've made her watch *The Lake House* and *Two Weeks Notice* too!

"Sandra Bullock. She's Sally in this," I say, exasperated. "Sally and Gary. The detective."

"Yeah, Sally. Hers can stay, but you aren't allowed to think about it tonight," she says. That *was* sort of the point.

"Yeah." I give her a muffled sigh.

It gets quiet for a little after that, and I manage to let myself be drawn back into the movie. Sally's at her apothecary stocking, and a crashing noise echoes in the shop. This is where it gets sad.

"You decided where you want to go to college yet?" Kaitlynn asks, pulling me back away before I can get too invested.

It's so far off topic. But, to answer her question, no, not really. Part of me doesn't want to think about it. I don't really want to get away from here like everyone else, I want to stick around. I'm not entirely sure I want to leave Mom all by herself either.

"Not really," I admit.

"Same," she huffs.

"But you know what you want to do, right?" I ask. I know the answer, but I thought she was more excited about going off to college.

"Yeah." She sinks further into the couch. "But who's going to take care of you if I go off somewhere?"

"Oh my! Don't even start with that." I roll my eyes and playfully kick her shin. "I'm not a child—"

"You sort of ar—"

"I won't be." I come back quick. "But you know what I mean. I don't need to be taken care of."

"I know, but it seems like so much. You know...*college*."

Now I get her tone. She's more worried about college as a whole, not me, and I can sympathize with that. Especially if it's far away. Maybe she'll go somewhere close, or maybe an hour or so away. There are a few good places in that radius.

"Yeah, it does."

"You still thinking nursing?" she asks.

Thinking, yes. Wanting though? I don't really *want* to, but it seems like my most sensible option. Who *wants* to work?

"I'd rather open an apothecary here, but yeah, nursing," I tell her. I can start that at the local community college too, so I'd get to stay close by. "What about you?"

"Yeah," Kaitlynn sighs. She's heard about my newish dream of owning my own shop. She also knows it's a wild pipe dream at best. "Still thinking veterinarian. Maybe go to UT or State."

I sigh. University of Texas. An out-of-state school.

"It's not like we can't visit each other."

I think that's what bums her the most. It's what scares me about graduating. Going off to different schools and not getting to hang out. Growing distant. We've not been apart for more than maybe two weeks for years. I'm going to be so lost without her.

I swear I won't let it happen.

"Yeah," she says.

"How about we promise each other right now that we'll always be friends, no matter what?" I suggest. Her eyes lighten up even in the dark. "I'll even promise on my amethyst."

"Are you sure? Are you supposed to do that?" Kaitlynn sits up and asks.

The honest answer to that question is *I don't know*. I'm just going to hope right now that it isn't like bad juju or something. It sure isn't what the stone was meant for, but that's the beauty of witchcraft. It's malleable and easily conformed to need; it is what it's needed to be.

"Sure," I say, and grab my necklace in my hand and squeeze it. Kaitlynn grabs my other hand and I start. "Repeat with me three times. No matter how far apart we may be, I will always be your friend."

"No matter how far apart we may be, I will always be your friend." She smiles and says it again.

I tighten my grip around the tiny bottle on my necklace, imagining the amethyst inside as I say the last recitation. I need this to work. We might bug the shit out of each other sometimes, but she's my forever person.

"No matter how far apart we may be, I will always be your friend."

23

"WHY HAVEN'T YOU SAID anything yet?" I ask Eliza.

She's by a display of necklaces and earrings, hanging up a few more pieces. An anxious grin bounces on her face and disappears as quickly as it came, and her hands reach for her cute black mid-thigh skirt dappled with orange crescent moons and tiny starlets, fidgeting with the hem.

"Timing?" she asks me.

I almost pounce with my words, but I stop myself. *Timing?* A question? To me?

"Why are you asking me?"

"I...just haven't found the right time, Kenzie." Eliza smiles again and her eyes grow smaller above her dimples. Why does she have to be pretty even when I need to be mad at her? "I'm trying."

"Hayden is awake! He's on his way here. Right now," I tell her. "He's about to take me, his fake '*enbyfriend*,' on a date."

This isn't what's supposed to be happening. Gods, I would have died for him to come walking in the shop to ask me on a date weeks ago. I even cast spells for it...which might have just gotten me into this mess in the first place.

"Maybe you are." She shrugs. For a moment I think she's saying I *am* maybe *that good a witch*, but that's silly, that was in my head. Wasn't it? Of course it was. "Maybe the date's a good idea. You do like him after all. Or..."

My reaction might be a little too heavy to that one. Probably my pinched lips and squinting makes her second-guess it.

"...not."

Maybe not. I don't know. It's all so complicated now and I don't know exactly what I feel. That's sort of why I'm here in the first place. When Hayden asked me out tonight, I didn't want to be stuck in a car with him for too long, so I suggested we meet at his aunt's shop. As far as he's aware, it's because I felt bad making him drive so far to pick me up so soon after getting out of the hospital. That part was only half true, maybe less. Meeting here, I could grill Eliza on why his family doesn't know the truth already. She was supposed to tell them! Even if the thought still makes me sick.

"I don't know. He's not really like I thought," I tell her. "I just think…"

I stop. Nope. I'm not going there.

"What? You think what?" Eliza asks, her interest piqued.

Oh no. That thought is staying in my head. She doesn't need to hear the ending: *I might like Zachary*.

"I'm just worried he's going to remember and then I'm going to be this horrible person," I tell her instead.

I'm really beginning to wish I'd gone with my first excuse to get out of tonight. I was going to say my aunt had unexpectedly flown in from Germany for a visit, and I couldn't skip on her since it doesn't happen often. It's not like she'd care if I lied about her; she's halfway across the globe. Plus, the last bit isn't a lie. I can count the number of times I've seen her in person on one hand. Even if I lost half my fingers. In the end, it would have only delayed the inevitable.

"You're not a horrible person, Mackenzie, don't do that to yourself. You — we all — made a mistake." Eliza pats my shoulder and says a quiet intention I can't hear. For me? "We just have to figure out how to fix it while hurting the least amount of people."

"That's it, huh?" I grimace at her.

Sounds horrible to me. I stare blankly at her.

"What el—" Eliza stops when the door chime rings and in walks Hayden.

He's dressed to impress. His shirt is white with a paisley blue vest draped over it. The collar is open a button lower than normal, but it suits him. So do the black slacks and matching cowboy boots.

"Uh…" I don't know what to say.

"Your mouth." Eliza nudges me, and I snap my teeth together.

"Hey," Hayden says the first word.

"Hayden," I say, or maybe gasp, finally dropping out of my weird little trance. Something about that first glance took me back to all the times he walked into the coffee shop, and I'd go into a frenzied competition with my nerves not to be an idiot. It passes quickly this time though.

"Hey, Aunt Eliza." He looks beside me and nods.

Eliza steps up and gives him a hug, "How was school?"

"It was okay. The Duke scout was at practice today. Fingers crossed he liked what he saw." Hayden crosses his fingers and looks to the ceiling with his eyes closed like he's praying. I can think of a number of better things to pray for, but I keep my mouth shut.

"A scholarship would be great." Eliza is rooting him on.

"And to be a Blue Devil starter!" Hayden purses his lips.

"Let's take things one at a time." Eliza slaps him on the shoulder. "And right now, you two lovebirds need to get out of my shop so I can lock up. Y'all have a date."

"Fine," Hayden moans way too over the top.

I'm still trying to process the feeling I had when he walked inside. It was like old times, before the coma, before I let everyone think the most perplexing lie, before Zachary. Simultaneously, I'm super annoyed I don't get to grill Eliza more and that I'm actually going on this date.

"Y'all have a good one," Eliza coos with a little extra New

Orleans in her drawl, and shoos us toward the exit.

"*Night*, Eliza," I say, scooting out the door behind Hayden and giving her an annoyed grin when he turns away.

We pass dimly lit storefronts, each door decorated with bland *Closed* signs, on our way to one of the very few restaurants left in downtown that isn't a brewery. It's mostly little local shops, cobweb-filled abandoned windowpanes, and like three breweries. They keep popping up.

"So how was school?" Hayden asks after an excruciatingly long minute goes by with nothing but the buzz of the streetlamps.

It's such a freshman question to ask your date. Right? Or am I being too critical? I don't *try* to hate this, but had the Kenzie from three weeks ago gotten that question from *the* Hayden Marcus, they'd have lost their freaking mind, maybe even had a heart attack and fallen dead on the spot, and I would have been happy about it. Now…

"Good. It w-was good." I bounce my head and try to think of something else to say.

The scholarship! I throw my foot forward, kicking it through a shallow puddle. "So you got a scholarship? For Duke?"

My right thigh vibrates. My phone. It's probably Kaitlynn checking in. I told her to text me with an "emergency" if I sent her *the text*. Basically "HELP," which I'd promptly delete from my phone, but I'm sure she's going to bombard my phone all evening for updates.

"No." He smiles and shakes his head. There's an attractive confidence in that grin that rushes my head with dopamine again. I cough and look away before he starts again. "I'm *hoping* to get one. We just had one of the scouts at practice today, so I'm hoping he liked what he saw and that'll work for me. I really want to play ball for Duke!"

"You *are* Mitchell's star player," I say, but it's also a question. I've always heard he was, but with my bias, I would have assumed he was the best at anything he did.

My phone vibrates again. *Stop it, Kaity!* I need to check it. Well, I guess I don't *need* to, but I want to. Is that rude on a date? This is my first, so I don't know.

"I wouldn't say star." He grunts and shakes his head.

Okay, there's some humility. I thought the other day in the hospital I'd discovered a new version of him that wasn't so humble. Not the idyllic vision I'd built of him from innumerable visits to the coffee shop, religiously ordering the same iced latte with cinnamon to sip between the most swoon-worthy lips.

"But," he says, dragging out the word and swaying his head from side to side. "I do have the most points and field goals this season so far. And coach says I should have no problem getting a scholarship somewhere. Duke's just harder, but I can do it."

And there it is again. Or maybe I'm just in a bad mood because I can't decide what I want and I shouldn't even be here. To mask my annoyance, I pull out my phone. "Kaitlynn's texting me."

"That your friend?"

"Yep." I unlock my phone, but it's not what I thought.

ZACHARY: He late?
ZACHARY: Oh right! 🤦 Prob not looking at your phone.
ZACHARY: Has he effed it up yet?

I suck in my lips and laugh. My heart does a little jump, and I shake to calm myself while I type back. "It's your brother, actually."

MACKENZIE: Not yet.

"Zachary?" Hayden asks, and I can hear the surprise in his voice.

"Do you have another I don't know about?" I ask while the bubbles are still going.

ZACHARY: *Just wait.*

I laugh and pocket my phone.

"No," Hayden laughs with me. "What's he want texting you?"

"Asking if you messed up yet," I say truthfully, but spin a little toothy grin into it to hopefully make it seem like a joke.

"That checks out," Hayden huffs.

Maybe it'll also blow up in my face and give me an angry Hayden.

"So Duke is no problem, huh?" I ask instead to get us back on track. It comes out more condescending than I'd intended, but too late to take it back.

"Basketball is my thing. It's what I thrive on. It's what I'm good at," he says. "And if I don't get a scholarship, I'm sure Dad or Gramps will help me out."

Something tickles my hand, and suddenly there are fingers wiggling between mine. *Don't pull away, Kenzie. Don't do it.* I should be excited. This should be thrilling. Hayden Marcus, *the* Hayden Marcus, just chose, of his own free will, to hold my hand. Hayden Marcus, that tall athletic man of my dreams, the man that I practically drooled over for months and dreamt some pretty unspeakable things about is holding my hand... but it doesn't feel right.

I remember another instead. The one who just texted.

Okay, so he's Zach's brother. Shouldn't it be similar? Shouldn't his hand have the same soft heat to it? Shouldn't it send a thrill up my arm? Because it doesn't. It's more like an icky creepy tingle. What the hell am I doing? I put on a sweet but fake grin and bear it while we approach the restaurant in silence. Maybe he'll be scared and let go before we get there.

I reach up and grab my amethyst bottle coyly to make it look like I find the hand-holding cute. Hopefully he doesn't sense my intention being sent up to Freyja.

Please get me out of this, Freyja. I'm literally begging you.

This is getting too awkward. I don't know what to say, and I'm getting the idea he doesn't either.

We're only a car length from our destination when he finally makes conversation again. I guess I could do it, I tend to talk enough, but I don't really want to.

"You play any sports?" Hayden asks.

"Not really." I shrug.

"Ah." He looks at me with this weird grin. "I guess I already knew that, didn't I?"

"Huh? How?" I ask before thinking.

"From before." Hayden steps ahead of me to get the door and waves for me to go in first. At least he's a gentleman. "I'm sure I've asked you that before. It's so weird."

It's warm in here, thank the gods. The lights are a little dim, but it's a nice glow, and the fluorescent signs dotting the wall give it a more roadhouse feel. The hostess is waiting at a wooden podium when we shut the door. She's tall — well, taller than me, which isn't saying much — and standing with her hands set on the podium just out of sight. There's a petite and ritzy look about her.

"Will it be two tonight?" She smiles at me, then Hayden, but the left side of her lips jumps when she finds Hayden.

"Uh, yes," Hayden grumbles and swallows.

Is he nervous? Does she know him?

"Follow me," she says, and we wind through mostly empty tables, past the bar.

"It's not weird. Promise." I pick our conversation back up as I slide into the booth the hostess stops at. "What's weird is that you were in a coma."

"You two have a good night. Your server will be here in a moment." The hostess nods at Hayden and steps away.

He grins as she leaves, the nerves blossoming all over his face. Jealousy? No. Of course not. It can't be. I wait until she's out of earshot before talking again.

"How many people can say that?" I ask.

"What?" Hayden jerks back to reality.

"How many people can say they were in a coma?" I repeat, realizing on the second mention it doesn't sound as great a point as I'd previously thought.

"How many people want to?" He leans over the table, eyes wider than a second ago.

"True." I bow my head.

"It's okay," he laughs. "I didn't mean to make you feel bad. I still can barely believe I was asleep for thirteen days. For me, it was like I fell asleep and then I was awake. It's ridiculous."

"Seriously. So ridiculous," I breathe.

"And woke up not remembering you." He blows out his lips like an explosion. "That's a lot."

"Yeah," I whisper.

"Okay, so you don't play sports." He settles back, returning to his previous line of questions. "At all? None?"

I giggle. I don't want to, but it just feels like the thing to do. "Not really. It's not like I've never. It's just not something I do for fun. I did play basketball with Zach like a week or two ago."

And there I go bringing Zachary into the conversation again. *Stop it, Kenzie.*

"I like to watch more. It's exciting. Especially basketball and baseball," I tell him. "Oh, and soccer. I do like watching soccer. And I'll go to football for the late-night post-game Cook Out tailgating."

"You and Zach played? Where?" he asks after waiting patiently for me to finish rattling off my viewing habits.

"Yeah, up at your house," I tell him. "Your mom thought he needed someone to play with since you were asleep."

"Hey now, not my fault," he comes back.

"Not mine either, for the record." I put up a finger.

"Of course not." He grins. "Landon's fault, right? He's the one I get to sue?"

"Please don't sue him," I laugh. "He's still horrified."

"I couldn't do that," Hayden says. "You only watch sports? You don't play. Wow!"

"I like *Apex*. I love watching their videos and the tournaments," I say.

"*Apex*? Like the video game?" The derision in his tone is easy to catch. "That's not a sport. I can't believe people actually get paid to play that shit."

"Oh," I say, stunned. I wasn't expecting that type of negative talk. I mean, the way I see it, if it's a game, it can be a sport. Chess is a sport after all—a sport of the mind. "I... It's fun to watch."

Usually I'd have said more. I would have chided him for thinking he can decide what others can do for sport. Such a 1990s mentality. But with him, right now, knowing that he's nervous as it is and that this is supposedly a date, I can't.

"So you were up at my house?" Hayden looks down at the table like it's unthinkable.

"Yeah." I shrug, taking the distraction.

"Oh," he grunts. He nods and looks around the table like it'll make sense down there. "So we were close to telling people at least, right?" His gray eyes find me again.

"Uh..."

What do I say? There's only one truth, and none of the ways I can answer end without me admitting my shitty lie unless I lie again. And oh shit. I guess he didn't start the rumors at school then. I bet it was Holly. I keep getting stopped in the hallways by people who'd never talk to me in the past asking me about it. It's been excruciating.

"Sort of." I try to ease us into the idea as I weave another fantasy on the fly. "We'd talked about it a little last month. You know, if you were ready."

"Was I?" Hayden shuffles in his seat. Unease is written all over his face and body language.

"Uh, well, you…yeah," I stumble.

"Oh," he says and takes a breath.

He's definitely not ready, and I've made him do it anyway, and it's not even the truth. He's just determined he can't remember. I'm honestly surprised he wasn't more headstrong and antagonistic of the very idea that he would be dating me.

"Well, we're public now." He nods and swallows.

I want to crawl under the table and cry because this is all my fault. I can see the fear in his eyes. Fear that I caused. Fear that shouldn't be there, that has no reason to be there, except because of my selfishness.

I can't do this anymore!

"Hayden," I blurt.

"Yeah." His head raises.

"I'm not what you think I am." I string the words together in one big note. I go to open my mouth again, to scream to him and the whole world that I'm a fraud, that I let one little moment get way out of hand, but the syllables catch at the back of my throat. "I…I…"

"You okay, Kenzie?" Hayden leans across the table.

Okay, maybe he is a little full of himself, but he's still a lot of what I thought he was. The kindness and worry in his eyes right now. The way he genuinely seems concerned about me. Hell, the way he's trying to "date" me despite it all being made up. Freyja, am I the worst person in the world? I can't be the Loki of my own story, my own life.

"I just..." I stumble again. "I..."

"What do you mean you're not who I think you are?" Hayden's practically pleading with me now.

The lights that were dim and calming moments ago feel like spotlights now. Their beams focus on me, illuminating every part of my mind, screaming out all of my secrets and revealing to everyone the disgusting person I am. I clamp my fist under the table atop my lap, pushing my skirt forward.

"I... We're not..." *Dammit, Kenzie, just say it and get it over with!* "We—"

"Hey, y'all, I'm Meredith. I'll be your server to—" She stops. Surprise is painted across her face while I try to hold back the frustration wanting to burst from behind my eyes. Meredith swipes at a layer of short bobbed blonde hair and apologizes furiously. "I'm so sorry, I didn't mean to interrupt. I...I can come back, if that's okay."

"It's okay, Meredith. We do need another moment though." Hayden nods at her.

Does he know her too?

"Be back in a few minutes, then." Meredith dips backward and disappears.

"Now, what were you saying?" Hayden locks on me again.

"I was, uh... I was saying that we're..." *Breathe, Kenzie. Remember to breathe. Give me strength.* I grasp my necklace and think it again. *Give me strength.* "I was saying that we actually weren't ready yet. I'm sorry. I didn't mean for your family to find out! It just sort of happened. I was selfish and didn't deny it. I'm sorry, Hayden."

Fudge nuggets, Kenzie! What are you doing? You were supposed to tell him the truth, not ninety-nine percent the truth minus the one percent that actually matters!

"Oh." He dips his head and swallows again. "It's okay. I guess that's why it all still feels so weird and off to me. I just don't remember any of this."

Me too, I think. *Me too.*

24

"DO YOU HAVE TO do that in here? You're going to make it smell weird," Mom complains.

I grimace, fanning my palm over a handful of smoldering sage. I'm not letting any bad vibes or negative thoughts stay stuck around tonight, even in the living room. I need a clear head.

"Yes, I have to," I say matter-of-factly.

I discreetly put my biggest amethyst on the center of the kitchen table before Mom woke up. A few black obsidian stones in the corners of the kitchen and living room with clear crystals to amplify their wards against negativity. Oh, and the spire of selenite on the coffee table in the living room. Mom protested that, too, when I replaced the pretty vase of multicolored flowers I set up just last week, but it actually looks good there. Maybe I can convince her to let me keep it.

"Surely your stones are enough, Kenzie," Mom says.

She's dressed up nicely with her hair hanging in long waves over her shoulders. I helped her pick out a moss-green knee-length dress and matching sash-like belt. She looks pretty in it, even if she is annoyed with me.

"I'm not sure anything is going to be enough." I huff, moving on to the hallway and then the tiny guest bathroom.

I told her that I almost told Hayden the truth, so she demanded that I invite him over for dinner. She wanted to "meet the boy who's causing all this turmoil in her child's life." Her words, not mine. It was either this or I call him right then and come clean. Just the thought of doing that was too much—it was overwhelming to the point I almost fainted. So naturally, I took option B, although now it seems like it might have been the worse of the two. Plus, why does Mom want to meet him, knowing what she does? She isn't going to say something, is she? No! Please don't! The idea immobilizes me for a good ten seconds before I can regain control again. I have to finish purifying the house. He's supposed to be here in — I check my watch — five minutes.

"Why are you so worried about me meeting him?" Mom asks.

"I don't know." I shrug. There's no way in hell I'm admitting I think she might betray me like some Judas. Maybe she's right. Maybe I'm overreacting. It wouldn't be the first time.

"Well you're stressing too much, mein Schatz. He's just a boy. You're young, and you're even stressing me out." She follows me down the hall into the kitchen as I put out the remaining smolders. "If you can't admit you lied to him, maybe tell him you need a break. Or do you actually like him? *And* does *he* like you too?"

She says *and* before I can speak, but I think I do know the answer to both questions, or well, sort of. After last night I might be a little more conflicted. He's still drop-dead gorgeous, but he's not exactly what I had thought. A little more into himself than I admittedly care for, but he's not a total ass. He's neither of the extremes I'd seen before last night. He's somewhere in the middle with maybe a few extra tethers to the confident end.

But does *he* like me? I think I know the answer to that. Sure, he's into guys and girls and theys, and yeah, he's even making an effort to like me, but it's still no.

"I mean, yeah, I do," I say.

"That wasn't the most convincing from you," Mom says.

I roll my eyes and check the lasagna baking in the oven. The cheese is melting nicely, and the garlic and tomato aroma wafts through the tiny opening.

"I-I don't know."

She looks at me with this expression that says *ah I'm sorry*, so I look away and snatch the dishes from the cabinet. I drop each to the table with a high-pitched clink. They're not the *nice* plates, but they're some of my favorites. Pure black, square with rounded edges. They appear to be made from obsidian, but they're not.

The truth is I don't know what I want anymore. Weeks ago I wanted Hayden. Now I "have" him, and I'm horrified because it's all a house of cards built on an ignorant mistake. I think part of me still does like him. Maybe, but there's Zach now. I didn't know him before. I didn't even know he existed, and he managed to make me feel more important and seen in a week than anyone I know has in my entire life. But he's Hayden's brother. It's like some bad porn skit, except my clothes are staying on and I'm not getting caught with either of them because both of them are going to hate me when they realize the truth.

A knock comes at the door and I freeze. My eyes lock on Mom and she simply grins. It's a smile that says so much. *I love you. It's going to be okay. Don't worry.* Oh, but I'm going to worry—a lot.

"I'll get it," she says, and I rush to take the lasagna out of the oven so the breadsticks can get going.

"Ouch," I yelp as my finger slips and touches the bottom of the pan. I pull my finger to my lips and kiss it like it's going to make it stop burning. "Just get the bread," I tell myself, and place the individual breadsticks I prepared earlier on a new pan and slide them into the oven. If nothing else, there will be bread.

The door creaks from around the corner, and I listen as Mom says hey.

"Hello, Mrs. Jackson," comes Hayden's voice. I take a deep breath. "It's great to finally meet you. Oh, and I hope you don't mind, but..."

"Hey, Mrs. Jackson!" Another familiar voice rings around the corner.

"I brought Zach with me, he sort of begged."

"That's okay," Mom says.

Excuse me?

My eyes bloom into the widest circles as I hone in on the entrance to the kitchen. First around the corner is Mom, then Hayden looking sober and nervous with a small bouquet of the sweetest little pink camellias, and then Zachary with a massive grin on his face.

"Hey, Mackenzie," Hayden says, and comes straight up to me with his arms out like he's going to hug me.

I freeze. "Hayden, thanks for coming."

His arms wrap over my shoulder and side, and he gives me a tug while I pat his back, making sure my arms don't touch him. Oh my gods, this is freaking awkward. Finally he lets go and turns back to Mom.

"And these are for you." Hayden hands her the camellias.

Uh...okay. Not going to lie, I thought those were for me.

"How kind, Hayden." Mom takes them and places them on the counter. "It's been years since a man's brought me flowers."

Why is Zach here? And Hayden's giving my favorite flower to my mom. What's next? I tell the truth?

"Hope you don't mind that I brought Zachary along." Hayden's looking directly at me.

"It's...uh...it's okay," I stutter. Why the hell would you bring your little brother to dinner with your enbyfriend and their mom? It's not like my mom needs a date! And oh no, Zach's about to say something, so I open my mouth first. "Food's about ready. Y'all can sit."

I spin around and check on the bread. It's got a minute more to go, but I'm not turning back around. What was Hayden thinking? I don't even want *him* here! I definitely don't want Zach around to make things even more weird. Could things get better just for once? I really need this bread spell to work and make Hayden decide he's just not into me and want to "break up." Then maybe I won't ever have to admit it was all an awful mistake.

Just don't look at Zachary. Act like he isn't there. It's just you, Hayden, and Mom. That's it. He's only in my imagination playing tricks on me. That's it.

"Your home is adorable, Mrs. Jackson," Hayden says, and I want to vomit.

Neither one of them could ever think my home is adorable. It's small, and old, and simple. Yes, it smells good, my touch. Lavender and rosemary dot the house. There's some on the hall table. A vase of them on the kitchen counter. A few in my bedroom, and a candle with their scent in the living room. So yes, it smells good, but that's it. Otherwise it sometimes seems almost claustrophobically small after seeing their house.

"Thank you," Mom says. "So who's the oldest?"

While Mom distracts them with random questions, I take another look inside the oven. There's only ten seconds to go, so I don my black mitten that says *Don't Make Me Poison Your Food* and take them out of the oven. The heat jumps out at me, and the intrusive thoughts in my head say to jump inside, it'd be so warm in there, but I refrain.

Once I've gotten them on the counter, I bunch them all into a little woven basket and take them to the table. I try not to look at either of the boys. If there was a way I could get through this without interacting, I'd do it so quick.

"How was work?" Hayden asks the moment I sit down directly across from him.

It's immediately awkward. It was going to be bad enough having him here with Mom, but now there's Zachary. It's like they're both locked on me, waiting for some exciting answer.

"It was good. The rush was shorter than usual, so that was nice." I nudge the bread basket an inch to the right, looking at Hayden but trying not to focus on him. "The dude that tripped you worked today. Landon."

It makes me laugh. Mom's nonplussed, but it gets a snicker out of both Zachary and Hayden. It wasn't Landon's fault, I know, not really. He didn't physically make him trip, but it hasn't stopped me from telling Landon he was the cause.

"It's not his fault!" Hayden shakes his head, but his laughing betrays him. "I've already told you. It was my fault for not paying attention. Bet I was distracted by you. That's probably what it was."

My eyes grow. Did he just compliment me? Is he saying what I think he is? Nah! But, actually, yeah, I think he might. Gods, he's really trying. A heated blush rises in my cheeks, and suddenly I'm back at the shop before all of this, watching Hayden walk inside in near drool mode, except it's Zach that my mind conjures up instead.

No! Snap out of it.

"Nah!" I swipe my hand at him playfully, but I'm still taken aback by it. "Don't be blaming it on me now."

"Oh no, not like that," he tries to rebound. "I meant—"

"What he meant is it *was* your fault." Zachary leans in, all grins.

With that, Mom starts loading her plate with lasagna from the pan in the center of the table, then passes it to Hayden.

"Shut up," Hayden claps back at Zachary at the same time as taking the tray and smiling at my mom. "I meant, like, you know."

I think I'd like to hear him spell it out for me.

How (Not) to Conjure a Boyfriend

"Do I?" I put my elbow on the table and prop my fist under my chin.

Mom falls back in her chair. I don't know if that means she approves or if she's annoyed, to be honest. Zachary's got the pan now. He's shoveling a big helping onto his plate.

"Of course." Hayden shrugs.

"Maybe they're a little, you know…" Zachary looks at Hayden. "A few crystals short of a set."

My mouth drops open, and I gasp. Did he seriously just say that? It was sort of clever, but still.

"Really?" I gasp.

"He's not." Hayden rolls his eyes. Zachary shrugs, all smiles and contained giggles, then passes me the lasagna pan.

"You mean *they're* not?"

I take it and scoop a piece onto my plate before putting it back in the center of the table. Thankfully no one had to be prodded to grab bread. I'm the last to take from the basket.

"Oh yeah, sorry," Hayden apologizes, and right now I'm not sure whether to hate or appreciate Zach.

"It's really okay. It's not a big deal. I know what you meant," I assure him.

Still though, the fact that Zachary thought it important enough to correct his brother is sort of admirable, and a certain kiss in the dark floods back into memory. Okay, it's never left. It actually is rather omnipresent, I just try to push it to the back of my mind and shut it inside a dark closet and hold the door closed for dear life.

"Now I've forgotten what we were talking about," Hayden says. A few looks around the table confirm we all seem to have forgotten. "Well, then. Zachary mentioned you like haunted houses."

"I do!" I nod excitedly but refuse to acknowledge Zachary.

"You might have to do that stuff on your own. We weren't

built for that type of thing," Hayden points between himself and Zachary.

"Speak for yourself," Zach corrects him. "I enjoyed it. Every *single* bit of it."

My face floods with heat and I clamp my jaw. *Every* single *bit of it?* I may not catch everything all the time, but unless I'm just paranoid right now, I think he was saying a lot more than that he liked going to the haunted house. I take a deep breath and open my mouth to let it all out again, trying my hardest to look natural.

"Really? You?" Hayden seems taken aback by it. "The dude that nearly peed himself when the power went off at home last winter?"

"I did not pee myself," Zachary bites back.

"Nearly." Hayden looks at me proudly.

I smile, but part of me doesn't like it. I'm not sure if it's that he's being sort of mean to Zach, even though it is his brother and that's normal from what I hear — I mean it's sort of like how Kaitlynn and I are with each other — or if it's just because it's Zachary he's throwing under the bus. I don't know.

"Yeah, yeah," Zachary huffs. "That was over a year ago, and I was just scared. I'm not a big fan of the dark. Mack knows that, but I did all right. It was fun."

"Yeah, he did all right. He didn't want to stay too long, but he did good," I say, chancing a quick glance at Zach. He smiles back, and I yank my eyes away.

"Surprised he went in at all," Hayden says. "And *Mack*?"

Zachary shrugs, so I do the same. It seems to be enough for Hayden.

"If it weren't for the bats, I would have stayed longer," Zachary says.

"Ugh, bats," Mom comments. "I keep telling Kenzie they

should stay out of those houses. You never know what the creatures in there are carrying. It could be dangerous."

"We didn't get bit," I tell her.

"But you could have." Mom shakes her head and sighs.

"I wouldn't have let them get hurt, Mrs. Jackson. Promise." Zachary leans over his plate and takes a bite. "Oh my God, this is good."

"Thank you, Zachary, but still." Mom nods.

"Whoa, this *is* good," Hayden echoes Zach's sentiment, looking at me until I catch his eyes. "Like don't tell my mom, but it's better than hers."

"Our mom's lasagna comes from the freezer aisle. That's why." Zachary squints at Hayden. "Mack here is a cook. The real deal. Wish you could have had their pecan pie brownies at Thanksgiving. God, they were good."

I look down nervously, both loving the compliment and at the same time unsure what exactly to do with it.

"Sounds like I've missed a lot," Hayden says.

"You can say that again," I whisper.

25

THE DINOSAURS THOUGHT THEY HAD TIME TOO.

That's what's plastered in big green letters on the bumper sticker of Kaity's white Chevy. It stares me down as I follow her to the nail salon and park on the nearest side street. I've been thinking of getting one too, because in fact, they did not have time. Sort of like us if we aren't careful. Plus, my car is a heap of trash. "I love that—" I start when her door opens, but she's already talking. I shouldn't be surprised.

"I should do something Christmassy, right?" Kaitlynn asks again. She's been super indecisive since lunch. It was one of those last-minute decisions. Getting Julieta on the same schedule wasn't working after all, so we just said never mind and came right after classes let out.

"Yes!" I say. I've known what I'm getting since she brought it up early, but like always it's a huge ordeal for her to make up her mind. Inside, we wait half an hour before they call us back. Apparently, Monday is a more popular manicure day than I thought.

"Have you decided finally?" I ask.

Kaitlynn takes the seat next to me and puts her hands out, fingers spread wide, and wiggles them.

"I think. Yeah, I know," she says, and then turns her attention to the dark-haired nail tech. "I want a mix. I want these to be bright Christmas red. These the same color but with a white dot at the top. And the others like candy canes."

Candy canes? That's going to be intense.

"And you?" my nail tech asks.

"Can I get a steel gray on my pinky, thumb, and pointer fingers? And then dark *dark* gray on my middle finger," I say, pointing to each finger. "And the same color on this one, but with a big snowflake surrounded by small ones?"

"Ah, that's going to be cute," Kaitlynn whines.

"No copying!" I tell her.

I don't mind matching, but if we're going to do that, I want it to be planned and for a reason. She's done it a few times after I came out, and it's just weird.

"Fine," Kaitlynn grumbles.

The nail techs start filing and I do my usual: look awkwardly in any direction other than at them while they're holding my hand and cutting my cuticles back. It's the only reason I would do my own nails if I had the coordination. It feels odd, sitting here with some random person holding my hand. Like, I know they're doing their job, they're making art of my nails, and that's it, but still. I asked Kaitlynn if she felt the same after my first manicure and she thought I was insane.

I try to focus on the TV in the corner. Some old show is playing silently with the black and white letterbox captions at the bottom. My eyes aren't that good, even if I were wearing the glasses I almost never wear, to read them this far away though. It doesn't work anyway. My head can't let go of the awkwardness.

It's no different now after tons of them. The woman carves away at my nail. Her fingers are wrapped around mine, moving them about where she needs, and all I can do is cringe that I'm holding someone's hand. There's only one hand that hasn't given me the heebie-jeebies. Zachary's. The one hand I shouldn't want but for some reason I do, even though he pulled a douche move and showed up to dinner last night with Hayden. Like who does that?

My phone vibrates, but I'm stuck with one hand dunked inside a bag of questionable-looking liquid while the other's in this woman's firm grasp with clippers traveling from finger to finger. It's just one vibration. A text. Why do I want to see it now more than normal? Just because I can't. It's always that way. It's what I can't have that I want the most. Like Hayden was.

"What you doing after this?" Kaitlynn asks.

"I don't know," I say. My paper was done and handed in on Friday, so I don't have that to stress me out anymore, just everything else. I'd thought about going home and making Mom watch more *Evil Lives Here* with me. It's this show I found about families of murderers and serial killers and growing up with them. It's intense sometimes. "Probably just watching some TV."

"Lucky," she huffs.

"Poor Kaity," I jest. "Gotta work a little."

"If my hands were free, I'd show you a finger right now," Kaitlynn says, then lowers her voice to a whisper, "*bitch*."

I laugh, which I don't think makes my nail tech the happiest because it causes my fingers to shake.

"Dry," my nail tech says, and motions to the UV lamp machine in front of me.

I put my hand in while she starts the next layer on my other hand. I watch the number tick away, counting down to when my hand is free long enough to check my phone. It blinks down to zero and I pull my hand out and steal my phone from my pocket. The name accompanying the single text on the screen sends a flurry of mixed emotions through my head.

ZACHARY: You work tonight?

Huh? Why do you want to know?

MACKENZIE: No. Why?

MACKENZIE: I'll be there a little later though.

My second text is sort of like the *I'm sorry, that wasn't meant to sound short and mean* message after feeling too snippy about it. I really do need to stop talking to him, but how do I get that across?

ZACHARY: Just wondering.

ZACHARY: Oh, you're there now?

Where did he get that?

MACKENZIE: No. I'm getting my nails done now. LATER.

ZACHARY: OH! Gotcha. The nail place in downtown?

To confirm or not. I stare at the text a few seconds, but the nail tech nudges me.

"You ready for the next layer?" they ask.

"Yeah, sorry!" I say, and quickly type out a response. "Got distracted."

MACKENZIE: Yes.

I hit send and lay my phone on the counter next to me.

"Who was that?" Kaitlynn asks.

"Zach." I roll my eyes.

Kaitlynn's lifted brows and kissy lips say it all.

"Stop it!" I tell her again. It's never-ending lately.

"What'd he want?" she asks.

"He..." I drift off. What did he want? "I don't know. He didn't actually say."

"I bet I know what he wants." She sticks out her tongue and wiggles it around suggestively. "He's hungry."

"Oh my gods, Kaity! Stop!" I yelp.

Not in public! And no! That's not what he wants. I mean I don't think so. Sometimes I do think she lives to embarrass me publicly.

She grunts, happy with herself. "You know you want it."

"I mean..." I shrug. There's no use in denying that. "Generally speaking, not from him."

That's my story and I'm sticking to it.

I try to ignore her until my nails are done. She's getting new acrylics, which take way longer than mine. So as usual, I'm waiting while she's got her hands under the dryer.

"This takes forever," I complain.

"Calm down." Kaitlynn thoughtlessly yanks her hand out from under the light and brushes me off.

"Get that hand back under there," I chide her, and she shoves her hands under the machine. "You close tonight?"

"I get off at eight. Landon and Dawn close," she says, and pulls her hands back, checking them. "And we're dry."

"Finally!" I gasp. "If you want to come over and watch TV when you get off, you can."

"Maybe," she says, and we get up and head for the door. "I'll have to see how tired I am."

"You work at a coffee shop. How tired could you get?" I ask.

"Eh," Kaitlynn says, and follows me outside. She stops and laughs, but she's not looking at me.

I turn around and Zachary's getting out of his car. Seriously? What is that important?

"Well..." Kaitlynn smacks her lips. "I would stay and see what's about to happen, but I have to work."

"Of course you do," I say, and before I can complain more, she's at her car, swinging around, and waving.

"See you tonight, maybe," she yells and then slings her voice toward Zachary. "Hey, Zach. Bye, Zach."

"Bye, Kaitlynn," Zach yells over the car roofs, and steps onto the curb a foot or two in front of me. "And hello, Mack."

"Hey." I try a fake grin, but I'm smiling before I can do anything about it.

"So. I just needed to talk to you. Text didn't seem best," he says.

"Okay." I string out the O sound. That seems suspicious.

Zachary twists from side to side, twiddling his fingers together.

How (Not) to Conjure a Boyfriend   237

He doesn't seem able to look me in the eye. Oh no! No, Zach! Don't bring the haunted house back up. I do *not* need to talk about the kiss. I can't. We can't! I'm about to blurt it when he finally smiles, all nerves, and speaks.

"I don't know how exactly to say this, but I think you should know," Zachary says. My nerves prick at the edge of my skin, sending my invisible arm hairs into high alert. *Just stop.* "Hayden's having a hard time with...this."

"This?" My head bounces back reflexively. What?

"You and him. Uh... Apparently there was, uh...someone else he remembers. He didn't give me details, but...i-it's another guy, but he can't remember you two..." He stops and scratches the back of his neck, and his mouth twitches. "You know...dating."

My teeth grind together harder with each word coming from Zachary's mouth. *Someone else.* I'm in so much trouble.

"He's trying to trust the doctor and you, and us, but he's confused. He really doesn't want to hurt you."

Hurt me? But I...I'm the one who...

My mind sputters out of control like some car on its last makeshift trip. He doesn't want to hurt me? I'm the one who needs to come clean, but he's worrying that he might hurt *me*? But he knows it's not real, or at least he's catching on. Wait! Or is he? Gods, this just feels worse and worse every single day.

"I, uh..." I don't know what to say, but why? My eyes fix on Zachary. "Why are *you* telling me this?"

"Because you should know, right?" he says.

"Isn't that Hayden's decision to make?" I angle my chin up at him. "Did he tell you to talk to me?"

"No..." Zachary swallows. "But if you're not—"

"If I'm not what?" I interrupt with a bite in my words.

"Uh...I don't want to press, but if you weren't really dating him before, you can tell me." He bows his head, and I swear his body flinches.

Does he really think that again, or is it something else? *I'm not* sits at the tip of my tongue. It's ready to spew out, but I hold it back. I want this to be done, but if it's done, how does it all end? Hayden. Zachary. Mr. and Mrs. Marcus. Holly. Eliza and Catina. Gramps and Kiki. Super Old Gran. Surely they'll hate me. I know what I should do, but I can't do it. Instead, I lock my knees in place and go on the offensive.

"This is about us, isn't it? We kissed. Yeah! I know. It doesn't mean I like you, Zachary!" I lie, and part of me somewhere deep inside shatters with each word. I hurts, but how can I be honest with him right now? "It didn't mean anything. You don't have to go trying to ruin what Hayden and I have!"

My heart is breaking. I can feel what's left of it throbbing like it's about to rise up my throat and scream for him to hold me. But I can't allow that because I've gone too far. Instead I'm left clamping my jaw tightly to hold back the sob building in my lungs.

"But...that's not it!" Zachary's eyes morph from realization to fear.

"Is it not? You want us to break up!" I raise my voice. I blame him. All to keep myself from breaking in front of him, but my voice still starts to shake. "You think that's going to win me over?"

"I..." he whispers. "No! I didn't mean—"

He stops as I stare back, my face stricken in faux anger while my heart breaks into a thousand pieces over and over again. It's like a hammer crashing against a spike, impaling my hardened heart again and again, but still I hold the truth inside.

"I j-just... I thought you should know. He doesn't want to hurt you, but he doesn't know how to tell you. I'm... He's scared, Mack," Zachary tries. "And I don't want you getting hurt either."

"Stop calling me that!" I yell. "No one calls me Mack."

His eyes are full of confusion, entrenched in sadness. And is that…a tear? No, Zach. Don't do this to me. I clamp my jaw. I want to wipe it away, but I'm the cause. It's my words that have put him in this place. My arms start to tremble. It's just a name. Why did I have to react like that?

"I'm sorry. I didn't mean to…" Zachary's eyes drop away with his words, drifting somewhere along the sidewalk.

I break my gaze as well. I can't continue.

"Yeah, I-I'm sorry," he says again and turns around.

"Zach," I call after him. I want him to stop. I want to confess everything to him and tell him not to leave. To stay here with me, but I can't.

"Yeah?" He stops.

"I… Nothing," I snap.

What the hell is wrong with me? My body starts to quake. If I don't get out of here soon, he's going to see me break down, and I'm not letting that happen. I refuse. Without another word, I sprint down the sidewalk and jump in my car without looking back.

My head drops to the steering wheel, and I fall apart. Floods burst from my eyes, dripping on the wheel while my hands squeeze it tight. I try to shake it, but it's me that gets yanked around as I scream and strangle the steering wheel.

"Why?!" I yell between sobs and the flashes of Zachary's face.

The dim glow of my flashlight on his cheek in an empty and abandoned home. The campfire reflecting in his eyes. The way his dimples moved when he smiled during my story. Sweaty, playing basketball. The way his steel eyes fluttered shut as he moved in to kiss me in the near pitch dark. The burst of life that he gave me. The flame I just dumped a barrel of water on.

"What the hell is wrong with me?"

26

THE LAST TIME I was here, Hayden sat across from me, not Kaitlynn. That was probably the final time too.

"I finally got Lola and Moira to tie the knot!" Kaitlynn blurts excitedly.

"Who?" I ask.

I know those names. I don't know why I know them, but I do. Who was she trying to get married off?

"Lola and Moira, my Sims," she says.

"Oh! I had no idea who you were talking about," I tell her as it clicks. She's had them going since last year, when I got her hooked on the game. I haven't played in weeks, due to other stressful events.

"I've been trying to get them to get married for months, but they never would!" Kaitlynn complains. "They've been living in the same house for like half a year. They even upgraded to a bigger one."

In my defense, I'm tired and distracted. We closed the store down half an hour ago and came to Hammy's Diner for a quick snack. AKA Kaitlynn is trying to keep me from thinking about the Marcus brothers. It's sort of helped. I haven't spoken to Zachary since Monday at the nail salon. Still, my mind keeps flipping between how any of that was his business and why did I have to lie to him…again?

I've only texted Hayden a few times since, and he's said nothing about it. Not a thing. I'm also discovering he's a real shitty texter. The more I overthink it, the more I think Zachary was telling the truth. The more I think it wasn't just about us, even if part of me also hopes it was. Zachary might not be able to see it, but this is eating me alive too. I didn't mean for any of this to be, it just is. Right? Gods. Maybe not. I mean it's not that simple. I made choices. It's not like someone pushed me into it. I was just too weak to make the right ones. I shouldn't be mad at Zach. Shit. It's not his fault.

"That's cool." I zone back into reality. "I need to get back to mine. It's been forever. Chase is probably still being a hoe as always."

"No better life." Kaitlynn grins.

"Eh." I shrug. "Maybe."

"Have you been doing something I don't know about?" Kaitlynn asks.

"No! Of course not!" I sit back against the cushy bench and snatch a fried cheese stick from the basket in the center of the table. I take a bite and give her a naughty smile. "Not that lucky."

"Bad enby," Kaitlynn laughs.

"If you only knew what goes through my head," I say. It's more trying to distract myself than anything, but it's not a lie for once, I guess. She'd be all types of embarrassed, maybe worried.

"Oh, I don't want to know. No, no," Kaitlynn says.

"You really don't," I tell her.

"You have any exams tomorrow?" Kaitlynn asks. It's a total topic switch. Unfortunately, the answer is yes. A few. Maybe I should practice putting a spell on myself not to think of Zachary. And a hex on...

"Yeah, math and English. And art. Yeah, I literally have an art exam. It's so frustrating," I say.

"Really?" Kaitlynn asks. "That's lame."

"Pssh. So lame." I grunt and let the intrusive thoughts win. "I ought to put a hex on Regina."

Kaitlynn's expression morphs into confusion and there's a pause.

"What? And why?" Kaitlynn asks slowly.

"She started all of this," I grumble, eyes lost beyond her on the glass bottles hanging above the bar. I imagine Regina's bright green eyes and curly brown hair.

"Oh…" she sighs. "But wouldn't that actually be you?"

"I mean…but—" I try to find a way to spin it.

"No, no, Kenzie. I might be your friend, but that's ridiculous. It's not her fault," Kaitlynn reminds me.

"But it's Regina who told them." I try to justify my moment of anger. She's right though. There is no justifying it.

"Again, not on her. You shouldn't have lied to her in the first place. Just because she told them," she slows to emphasize her words, "*what you told her* isn't her fault. Then you didn't even deny it and correct her. That's so much worse, Kenzie."

"B-but… Shit," I blurt. Why does she have to be so right?

"Yeah," she says, letting the word string out for a few seconds like she's waiting for it to settle into my thick skull.

I don't know what to think. I didn't mean to. I wasn't prepared for any of that. But…I don't know what to say. That doesn't make it okay.

"Well, I need to hex Zach, then," I blurt without thinking.

Kaitlynn's entire head twitches and freezes. She stares at me with this searing gaze. I rarely get that look. It only comes out when she really thinks I'm full of shit or delusional.

"What?"

"Zach is not the problem either," Kaitlynn says plainly.

"But—"

"No buts. We're not doing that. You're head over heels for him, Kenzie. It's *so* easy to see." She stops and looks away with this amused grin. "You get so giddy when he's around. I love you, Kenzie, but he's not the problem. The problem is you can't figure out how to have him while fixing the shit you started, and it's eating you alive. That's the problem. It's so clear."

"What? No! That's *so* not it." I lean over the table, trying to keep my voice quiet. There is only one other table occupied besides us, but I'm not having this overheard.

"Yeah, it is!" Kaitlynn laughs confidently. "Every time he shows up, you become this ball of nerves. You talk about him more than you ever did Hayden, and let me tell you, bitch, you talked about Hayden a lot. And why else would you get so defensive about him?"

"I-I…" I grumble to a stop. Is it really that obvious? I thought I hid it so well. "I…yeah. I do like him."

"I know," Kaitlynn says, but the accusation in her voice is gone. "It's beyond obvious."

I grunt, defeated, with my eyes drooping to the ugly red plaid tablecloth. There's only one cheese stick left, so I steal it from the basket and shove it in my mouth. I try to focus on it instead of the uneasy feeling in my chest that's swinging hazardously between nausea and fuzzy warm patches.

"They do say being in love is like being drunk." Kaity slaps my cheek to get me to look back up at her. "You do weird things."

"Not in love!" I wave my hand frantically. Let's get one thing straight here. I don't even know what it means to be in love for sure, so that's not on the table yet. I refuse. "Definitely not in love."

Kaity shrugs and grunts. "Maybe we should talk about how you're going to fix all this, then. You can't keep this up. Even if you don't do it for them, you have to for you, at least."

I huff. That might have been the wisest thing I've ever heard come out of Kaitlynn's lips, but I so didn't want to hear it. Can I just not think about it? Can it just stop being this black cloud looming over my head day and night? I want to act like it's not on my mind. Go on living like things are normal, like they used to be when I was just lusting after a boy, and that's it. Can't I just be delusional?

"Come on, Kenzie." Kaitlynn leans across the table.

Our faces are close, and she's got this look that says *listen to me or else* in the kindest way a threat can be conveyed. I lean back and let out another huff.

"Fine. How do I fix it?" I ask.

"Tell the truth?" she suggests. "Isn't that the most obvious solution?"

"And the hardest," I counter.

"And the only way." She brushes her hand in the air dismissively. "Do you really think Freyja and Odin want to keep saving your tail?"

"They're gods, they're good for it." I shrug.

Kaity laughs and then cups my hands in hers. "Joking aside, Kenz, you need to tell them the truth."

"But I don't want to hurt anyone," I say.

I wish I could say that's the only reason it's hard, that it's the only reason I haven't done it yet, but I can't. Besides Kaity's unfortunately accurate point, it's pride mostly. I don't want to be seen as *that* guy. The liar. The asshole. The screwup. That's what I think holds me back the most. It's selfish, I know, but it's also about them. I swear. I truly don't want to hurt them. And I don't want to lose them. They're everything I always wished I had. And then there's the whole school knowing I'm "dating" Hayden... That doesn't help anything.

"Someone is going to get hurt, Kenzie." She gives me the news I didn't want to hear. "I'm sorry, but it's true."

"Yeah. You're right. Maybe Hayden will be relieved though." I try to laugh.

"Maybe." Kaitlynn giggles with me. "Or maybe he'll be disappointed he doesn't get you."

"I doubt that. But what about Super Old Gran?" I pose the question.

"Who?" Kaitlynn looks confused, eyes twitching back and forth going through the Marcus family roster in her head probably. "Oh—"

"His great-grandma," I say before she can.

"Still can't believe they call their great-grandma Super Old Gran." She smiles.

"Same," I say.

"My nana would freak if I called her that," she laughs.

"Oh gods, she would for sure!" I agree. Her grandmother is great, but she doesn't like it when people bring up her age.

"Yeah." Kaitlynn nods.

"But yeah, I'm just worried, you know. She's old and Eliza said she might have a heart attack from the shock. Well, she didn't say that exactly, but still." That's even worse than hurting someone's feelings. They'd all be hurting if I killed Granny. "Can't do that."

"You're not going to off Super Old Gran by telling the truth. And wait." Kaitlynn frowns. "Eliza knows?"

"Yeah," I say with the same surprise. "I told you this! She said she was going to do it for me! But she still hasn't."

"Sorry!" Kaitlynn huffs. "That's right. You did. My bad. But she still hasn't? You sure that's best anyway?"

"Maybe! She knows them best. It makes sense, right?" I reason.

"See how that's worked out?" Kaitlynn stares me down.

"Fine. You're not wrong," I admit. "Gods, I wish I'd never met Hayden. Like why did he have to come to the shop all the time?

And be so dreamy?"

"You don't mean that," Kaitlynn says.

"I do! I mean it." I'm not backing down from this. Had he not, I wouldn't have followed them to the hospital, and then the nurse wouldn't have repeated what I told her. If not for all that, I'd simply be happily single Mackenzie again. Okay, maybe not happily single, but better than whatever junk this is.

"But then you'd never have met Zachary." Kaitlynn shrugs. "And don't tell me you would prefer that. Don't!"

"If I'd never met him, then I wouldn't know what I'm missing," I remind her.

"Yeah, but you have," she says.

"Stop being wise, Kaity! I like crazy Kaity better." I roll my eyes.

"So wise." Kaitlynn poses with her hand under her chin all smiles. "So now what are you going to do about it?"

I slouch back and allow my shoulders to slump. If I do what she's saying, I'll have to face everything that's happened the past month. But I have to do something. I can't keep this up. It's not getting better, it's getting harder.

"Hmm... Text him? Hayden, that is," I ask more than tell.

"No. Hell no." Kaitlynn jumps. "You're not breaking *this* through text."

"No! That's not what I meant," I say. It really isn't. "I meant like text him, you know, to tell him I need to talk to him, to tell him something. Then I can admit it all in person."

"Okay, now that's better." Kaitlynn calms. "I can get behind that."

"So I'll do that," I tell her.

"Now." She tilts her head expectantly.

"What?" I rebound. Now? Why now? Let me dwell on it and

make myself sick first.

"Now!" she says again, pointing at my phone lying next to my arm.

"But..."

"*Now!*" she says again, all command this time.

"Fine." I roll my eyes and pick up my phone. The text box has never looked this menacing. Hayden's name sets at the top of the screen under a photo of him I stole off Instagram. I breathe.

"You got this, Kenzie." Kaitlynn tries pumping me up. "You the man. No, wrong. You're not the man. You're the one! Oh shit, you're Neo! You're freaking Neo! You're The One!"

I stop and look at her like she's an idiot. Part of me wants to break character and laugh with her, because I one hundred percent got the reference and that's so epic, but I refuse. I need her to think I can't stand her right now.

"See! You're the freaking one, you..." She stops, all grins. "Too much? Okay. Just fix this shit. Okay?"

"Not helping," I say, even though it sort of is. Sure, my insides feel like they're churning all I ate today into a massive mush they want to expel from my mouth, but it's not as bad as it was a minute ago.

I focus on my phone and start typing. After three different renditions, I get it.

I show the screen to Kaity so she can see I'm doing what she told me to.

"Now send it," she says.

I hover my pointer finger over the little send icon and cough. Oh my gods! Once this goes out, I have to tell him something important regardless, and honestly this is the only thing that would warrant the message, so I'll be stuck. Ugh! This is so not fun! I'm not having a good time, and I want off this ride!

I close my eyes and let my finger drop. The little whooshing noise confirms it sent, and immediately I want to puke everywhere.

MACKENZIE: Hey, I need to tell you something sort of important, but in person.

"Done," I say between gritted teeth.

"You just started," Kaitlynn corrects me.

"And I already hate—" I stop when the bubbles start jumping at the bottom of the screen, and my stomach starts to churn quicker. "I'm going to be sick."

"*So* dramatic," Kaitlynn says in time with my phone vibrating from the new text.

HAYDEN: Same! Come to my house for dinner tomorrow and we can talk.

Uh… That's not how I want to do this.

"What did he say?" Kaitlynn's bouncing impatiently.

"Well, uh…he wants me to come to his house for dinner tomorrow. He says he has something important to tell me too," I say, stopping with my lips pooched awkwardly.

"Oh." Kaitlynn sits back. "Baby steps?"

"I hate you so much." I roll my eyes at her, then send a response.

MACKENZIE: OK

27

BY THE TIME I pull in I'm going to have every pine needle on this damn tree memorized. I've been sitting on the side of the road next to the Marcuses' mailbox for the past ten minutes, contemplating my every life choice and possibly even my very existence. I'm trying to find the mistake that led me here, as if it's not obvious. Maybe it was when I decided Hinduism wasn't for me, or when I decided not to go on the eighth grade field trip to D.C. Maybe it was none of that, or maybe it was when Dad died.

It would just sound so much better if I could say it wasn't just me being totally and completely pathetic. I'm not going to lie this time. I'm not. It's a lie that got me into this. It's a lie that compounded into more lies and made things even worse, so it's not going to be another lie that gets me out of it all. I promise myself and Freyja.

I really hope they don't have cameras out here. They strike me as the type that would have little hidden cameras spread around the property, and it'd be my luck that I'm staring one down right now. They're probably watching me on their phones, wondering what I'm doing out by their mailbox.

I slouch and put my car in gear. *Just get this over with. It's not going to get any easier just because you wait another minute.* I barely press the pedal and my tires start crunching down the driveway. I still take my time, letting the now familiar canopy of pine needles and bare branches guide me to my doom. It's fitting. It's dark under the branches. My headlights sweep the pavement but fade to nothing at the edges of the trees, into the unknown. It's sort of scary until it opens up and the stoic black columns and hard geometric lines of the Marcus residence slide into view.

I come to a stop and sit with myself a moment, fingers gripped around the amethyst hanging from my necklace. *Please Freyja, Odin, Thor. Please give me strength.* Somewhere in my chest I find the will to open the door and practically ooze out onto the pavement. At least, that's how it feels. I'm upright, on my own two feet, but it feels like my legs are coated knee-high in some thick, heavy, sticky goo pulling me back, tethering me to the ground. Each step is a labor of sheer willpower, and it only gets harder when I mount the steps, fear crashing through me, and without me so much as reaching for it, the front door swings open.

"Mack!" Zachary steps outside and shuts the door behind himself. "I need to say I'm sorry. I shouldn't have—"

"No, Zach, don't." I cough against the cold to uncrimp my nerves.

He freezes, eyes confused and hurt. I brace myself against those beautiful gray eyes so they don't bring me to my knees. *Why do you have to make it so hard to be strong?*

I look at him. Gods, it's so hard to hold back the feelings roiling through my chest. The need. I steel myself. I can't show him the struggle behind my eyes. I know the truth about my feelings for him. What I want. *I want him.* I don't know if I love him, but I don't think I really know what that means yet. *I like Zachary. I want Zachary, not Hayden.* I want the boy standing right in front of me. He's kind and thoughtful, even if he gets a little carried away. Funny. Confident but not full of himself. A bit of a nerd, and a lover of this big ball we call home. Someone who sees *me* and still wants me.

And I ruined it all.

"Gods, I'm sorry," I blurt when I realize I zoned out for a moment.

"No, you're okay," Zachary says, fiddling with his fingers. It's the only thing that betrays the calm in his eyes.

I want to reach out to him and wrap my arms around his waist and kiss him. I want to tell him how I feel and run away with him—go anywhere but here, but that's another life. Another time.

"Can we just act like we're okay?" I ask and start forward, trying my best to ignore the chill in the air.

He doesn't answer. Instead, he dips his head and gives me the saddest smile I think I've ever seen. Eyes on the floor, he pushes the door open and holds it open for me to go in. Torture isn't harsh enough a word to describe walking past him. He's not even making eye contact, yet I can feel the hurt I've put him through in his downward gaze. I finally breathe again when I cross the threshold and smiling faces turn to greet me. It breaks me all over again knowing how I'm about to ruin everyone's idea of me.

"Kenzie!"

It's a chorus of voices. Everyone but Gramps and Kiki are here. I hone in on Eliza. She's smiling uncomfortably, like me.

"Hey, y'all," I say back, and then Hayden comes around the corner.

"Kenz, you're here!" He sounds excited, but it's off. His tone is almost like an act, or maybe it's just the way I'm hearing it. And did he call me *Kenz*?

"I'm here." I bounce my shoulders awkwardly.

"Come sit, you're just in time. Mom just finished cooking," Hayden says.

I start toward the table and sit in the chair Hayden pulls out like some sixteenth century gentleman. What is happening? What does Hayden have to tell me that merits this? I'm in so much trouble.

"I like your sweater," Holly says as she takes the chair opposite of Hayden's.

"Thank you." I grin, touching the simple thick navy fabric with the snowflakes all over it. It's the first genuine, not horrified smile I've given today. She's so sweet.

"It's cute," Mary-Anne echoes from across the table. "Where did you get it?"

"I, uh…" I have to think about it a moment. Most of my clothes come from Walmart or the local thrift stores around town. This one, though, I think I remember getting last winter at one of the second-hand stores with Mom. She'd said Dad would have liked it, and I wouldn't let it go after that. "It came from a consignment store. I don't remember the name. It's really nothing special."

"It looks great on you though," Mary-Anne says, smiling tightly.

"It does," Super Old Gran agrees. She's bent over in the chair across the table from Mary-Anne, next to Mr. Marcus at the head of the table, all smiles as I've become accustomed to. I can always believe it if she says it. "Shows those hips off good. At least we know Hayden has something to hold on to."

"Granny!" Hayden and Zach say simultaneously.

"Mom!" Mary-Anne reaches across the table. "That's not—"

"Don't be old fashioned, Mary. We know what they're doing. I don't know how they're doing it, but we all know they're—"

"Okay!" Mr. Marcus bellows over my favorite grandma.

The look on Zachary's and Hayden's faces would have been delightful a month ago. The panic. But now, it does little more than help remove the spotlight from me for a moment. I smile with my teeth clenched. I love her. I don't want to lose her, but it's inevitable.

"How about we say grace, and then we can try to have more appropriate table conversations." Mr. Marcus nods and then drops his head to pray.

I bow my head but don't close my eyes. There's always this

How (Not) to Conjure a Boyfriend

part of me that feels weird in these situations, when everyone else is blind and I cautiously look around the table. It's like I'm peeking into something I shouldn't be, but I think it's just knowing people's expectations.

Holly has her hands up in front of her face, fingers clasped together. Jeff is next to Eliza, who to my surprise looks to be praying along. Hayden looks like he's focusing hard. I hope that has nothing to do with me. I say a quick little intention of my own. *Freyja, give me strength. Give me peace. Give me...strength.* I say it again while Mr. Marcus passes the two minute mark of his prayer. Granny looks like she's about to nod out. I bite my lip and hold back a giggle. That's when I notice Zach's eyes are wide open and he's looking at me.

I slam my eyes shut like I've been caught looking at something private. It's absurd, but it's instinct.

"Amen," Mr. Marcus ends the prayer, and a few other amens go up around the table.

"Dig in," Mary-Anne says, and everyone except me starts attacking the food on the table.

Finally I reach for the basket of rolls and pull one out.

"You should have Christmas with us," Super Old Gran yells across the table. "Randall here," she nods toward Mr. Marcus, "always reads from *How the Grinch Stole Christmas*."

"And we watch the movie too!" Holly shouts.

Christmas? *How the Grinch Stole Christmas?* It's a lot at once. Especially since I won't be around then.

"The good one, too, the one with Jim Carey," Zachary says.

"I don't know. I think Mom and I are doing our usual," I tell Gran. It's just staying home and opening gifts, but it's what we do. We used to go to the theater on Christmas Day to watch whatever was playing. It was our tradition. I think it might have been Mom and Dad's tradition first though, but the theater started closing on Christmas last year, so now we just stream something at home. At least we have more options.

"That sounds nice." Mary-Anne nods. "We don't want to take you from that."

"You could do both," Gran steps back in. "We have Christmas on Christmas Eve. The night of. I'm sure Hayden would love to have you here."

I don't know. I mean, we've always done Christmas on the morning of Christmas itself. The idea of opening presents a day early is foreign to me, except back when I'd beg and Mom would let me open one. There's not usually enough to do that nowadays though.

"I might be able to," I say. I can entertain them for a little longer, but I know it's not going to happen. "I'll ask Mom."

"It's really okay if you can't," Mr. Marcus says.

"Oh, we can make it work." Super Old Gran waves him off, and I can't help but let out a tiny laugh.

"And you don't have to bring anything. No gifts," Hayden quickly spouts.

"Yeah, I'm not getting him anything either," Zach laughs across the table at his brother.

Hayden grunts, I think in amusement. I could be wrong.

"What about me?" Holly whines. The pout puts a stake in my heart, so I can't imagine it doesn't tear Zach to shreds.

"Don't worry. I have something for you," he tells her, and nudges their shoulders together.

"Good. I got you something too," she says proudly.

"I just don't want him thinking he needs to." Hayden puffs his chest. I can't help but notice Zachary's eyes flinching between Hayden and me every time Hayden refers to me as *he*. It's really

How (Not) to Conjure a Boyfriend

not a big deal, but I think it truly bugs him.

"Of course *they* don't have to," Zachary says.

Despite how shitty my insides feel, in that moment the way he said *they* does put a smile on my face, which unfortunately I think he notices. He sits back and juts his chest out, those steel eyes beaming.

"It's good," I tell them, sweeping my gaze across the table. "I promise."

I also promise that if this dinner isn't a short one, I'm going to go insane. Like clinically. The thoughts rampaging through my skull, fighting between self-preservation and being a decent human being are going to rip me apart.

"What do y'all say we play some Old Maid after dinner?" Mr. Marcus suggests.

Old Maid? What's that?

"Oh that would be fun," Mary-Anne agrees.

"I'm going to bed after this," Super Old Gran says.

"Couldn't we play something less…kiddy?" Zach asks.

I nervously raise my hand like I'm at school before Zachary can have his request answered.

"Yes?" Mr. Marcus asks. I think he's confused by my hand being up. "You don't have to raise your hand, Kenzie."

I yank it back awkwardly and smile to cover my embarrassment. At least it's getting my mind off what's been flying around inside it the past day.

"What is Old Maid?" I ask.

"You don't know what Old Maid is?" Zach practically comes across the table, he's so surprised.

"Uh, no." I jump back.

Is it one of those games kids grow up playing with their dads that I never really got? Like football or something? Mom would always play baseball with me. Sometimes basketball, but we never dared try football, except the international variety.

"Whoa!" Zach howls.

"Not everyone knows what it is," Hayden defends me, even though part of me likes that Zach is roasting me. "It's sort of an old person game."

"Hey now!" Mary-Anne yelps. "I am not old yet. Thank you!"

"Right, right," Hayden looks my way and mumbles, laughing.

I lean closer and laugh so his mom can't see, and both Zachary and Holly have their mouths covered.

"Y'all are grounded," Mary-Anne jokes, and I don't even bother pointing out I'm not one of the children.

"Don't worry, babies, I'll bring you candy," Super Old Gran says.

The table breaks out in comeback after comeback, but it's all a hushed mumble in my head as time slows and I'm left in my own little universe, looking from one person to the next. Left looking at the family I almost had. Eliza and Jeffrey, the aunt and uncle. Mine are thousands of miles away in Germany, and while I think they like me, they don't make a point to call. Holly, the little sister I never had. Super Old Gran, the awesome grandmother that sneaks you candy when your parents ground you and says exactly what she's thinking no matter how dirty it is. I have a grandfather on my mom's side left, but I've only seen him like twice, and my grandmother, my Oma, died when I was ten. Then there's Mr. Marcus. My first impression was that he's stern, but there's a softness in his eyes when he talks to Hayden, Zachary, or Holly. I can imagine them playing catch in the yard, or him spinning them in circles on that metal death contraption at the park. I can see the smiles, hear the giggles, and almost feel the hugs. He's the closest I've ever come to having a dad, and I didn't take advantage of it.

How (Not) to Conjure a Boyfriend

I think I was scared to, but I mean, I should have been, right?

I'm slammed back into the here and now with a pat on the back.

"You okay?" Hayden's still giggling. Zachary's peering across the table at us. I swear he's eyeing Hayden's hand on my shoulder.

"Yeah, I'm good. Just zoned out," I tell him. I can't keep going on like this. I have to tell him and get this over with. I can't stand sitting here, enjoying the love and warmth all these people offer me so freely. It has to stop. I need to get away. I need to break the news to Hayden. "Can we go outside? I need some air."

"Yeah, sure." Hayden nods and stands. "Before we go though…"

He looks around the table, all eyes glued to him. He looks directly at me just as I'm getting to my feet. I almost stumble. Hayden reaches out and grabs my hand to steady me.

I go to pull away but remember that's still a no-no. It doesn't matter though. Hayden's already pulled away like he touched something slimy and nasty.

"Kenzie." Hayden's eyes drill into mine. He brings his fist up and clears his throat. His smile feels fake. It's too big, too wide, too something. What is happening? Just don't get down on a knee! Please! "I, uh…uh…I wanted to ask. You know, uh…"

My forehead lowers and I try really hard not to widen my eyes, but I think they do a little. At least the attention isn't all on me now. Still, I'm nervous, because if something is crazy enough to get him like this — to get Hayden Dean Marcus, Mitchell High's star basketball player, the boy who had me nearly drooling a month ago, to hardly be able to speak — then I'm done for.

"He's just—" Mary-Anne starts, but Holly is on it before she can get two words out.

"He wants you to go to the dance with him!" Holly blurts a hundred miles an hour, then gasps. "See! It wasn't that hard."

"Yeah, that." Hayden gives Holly the evil eye. When his eyes return to me, they don't stay there. It's like he's too scared to see me.

"Uh, I —" My words won't come, eyes shooting between Holly and Hayden, then Zachary and Super Old Gran, then back to Hayden.

"The Winter Formal at Mitchell," he specifies.

His mom gasps like she didn't have a clue. Holly squeals and claps her hands. Mr. Marcus is simply smiling. He seems proud.

"Marry them!" Super Old Gran yells.

"Granny!" Hayden whips around and scowls, but he's laughing, sort of.

Just out of view is the one I wish was asking me the same question. The thoughts scatter through my head, bouncing haphazardly about, making me want to crumble onto the floor. I wish it were Zachary asking. I'd say yes. I'd yell it again and again. I'd grab him up and kiss him and ask what we're wearing, if he wants me to wear a dress or a tux, when we're going to get sized or if we even need that. But it's not him. It'll never be him. I've made certain of that with the stupid things I've done. Instead, he's frozen to his chair.

I squeeze my fist and try to speak.

"I, uh, I mean…" I keep trying, but it's not working.

"Say yes!" Holly yells.

I can't do this. It's too much. The dam breaks. It starts as a single tear, streaming down my cheek, probably carving a path through my eyeliner. I sniffle, trying to hold it back, but that deep dread inside my chest keeps building. It starts as unease and grows as embarrassment and sadness weave together while I take in all the eyes around me. Then it breaks, boiling over with fear and self-hatred.

Why the hell did you do this, Mackenzie? You lied to all of them, to all these amazing, kind, and wholesome people. You lied to Hayden. You lied to Zachary. You fell in love with a person you didn't know existed. And I thought somehow it'd be okay, that I'd keep up the ruse and it'd all work out. How could I have been so foolish?

"I can't!" My voice pierces the yells of, "Say yes," and "This is so sweet!"

The room goes silent.

"Huh?" Hayden visibly jerks back.

"I can't." I whisper it this time. This ends now. Whether I'm okay with it or not, they don't deserve to be lied to.

"Really?" Hayden seems confused, but there isn't any of the hurt I'd expected.

"I just...I can't. I was going to tell you after dinner, but-but..." I'm struggling to get everything out between sobs. I can barely see.

"Honey, are you okay?" Mary-Anne starts to get up, but I put up a hand to stop her.

"Tell me what?" Hayden's confusion becomes tinged with suspicion.

"I..." My voice catches. This is happening. I'm not letting anything get in the way of it. Freyja! Odin! Thor! Balder! Heimdall! My gods! Give me even the tiniest sliver of a Valkyrie's strength to just be honest with them.

Zachary stands. "Are you okay, Mack?"

I put up a hand again and shake my head. *Mack.* He's the only person who calls me that, and I love the way it sounds when he does, but please not now. I wipe my face and try to sniffle back the flood. A huff of air expels from my chest and I grunt to clear my throat. It's now or never.

"I'm not your enbyfriend, Hayden. I never was," I blurt. At first, I squint, eyes closing, but I open them again when he doesn't say anything. Is he in shock? I'd be in shock if my boyfriend told me we'd never dated. I'd be mortified.

"Excuse me? But you sa— You said we were dating before the accident." Hayden stops and looks up at the ceiling in thought. "But we're not? This all makes so much more sense now."

"No," I whisper, surprised by the crescendo in Hayden's voice.

"What do you mean?" Mary-Anne is up from her seat again. I can't tell if it's confusion or anger in her eyes.

"You said at the hospital you two had been dating," Mr. Marcus says.

"I know," I say. My whole body shakes. I'm shivering from head to toe with nerves. "But it's not true."

"What?" Zachary's voice goes up an octave.

"It's not true," I repeat.

"So we're…" Hayden points between us. "We're not dating?"

"No." I shrug. "And you don't have amnesia. I don't think."

"Oh," isn't what I expect him to say, but it's what he says.

For a second it distracts me from the feeling boiling inside me, but it comes back like a brick wall rightshe says, finally getting up after Hayden slaps his hands over his mouth like he just let out a secret.

"I need to go, I made a mistake. I…" I stop, I just need to get out of here. There's no point in rehashing the whole story to them. They were there, and I'm sure they can put the pieces together now that they have the truth. "I'm sorry. I didn't mean to hurt anyone."

"Mackenzie," Zachary calls after me as I start for the door. "Wait!"

Hearing him use my whole name causes me to freeze in place. Somehow it feels like a punch in the gut. I'm about to burst into a run, but he's on his feet and next to me in a moment.

"I'm sorry!" I sob, but refuse to face him. "Why did you have to be so great?"

They're not the words I expected to come from my mouth, but at least it's the truth. I finally allow myself to look at Zachary. His steel eyes beg me for answers, and a smile twitches across his lips, or maybe I imagined it. Either way, for a fleeting moment I allow myself to remember how he made me feel, to remember what I'll never know again.

"Huh?" Zachary asks.

How can I answer that? There aren't enough words to apologize to him and at the same time express how I feel about him. How cruel it is to both of us, but I guess that's my fault too. I nod and try to smile, but my heart is so broken I don't think I can. I break our gaze and look around the table.

"I'm so, so sorry. I didn't want to hurt anyone. It seemed so innocent back then, and I swear I meant well, but it was wrong. I understand if you all hate me," I say, and the tears rush back in, pouring over my cheeks.

"Kenz—" Mr. Marcus starts, but Mary-Anne talks over him.

"How could you do this, Mackenzie?" Her words pierce into my heart. "You've lied to us this entire time?"

"Maybe we—" Eliza steps in, but Gramps joins in on the onslaught.

"You thought you could come into this house and—"

I can't deal with this. There is no world where this ends well. There never was. No scenario with a nice little bow on the end of it. I came tonight knowing that, prepared. At least, I thought I was prepared.

"Mack," Zachary starts, but I can't do this anymore.

I twist away from him and sprint for the door, yelling my last apology as I swing it open. "I'm sorry!"

28

THE BELL RINGS AND I flinch. The buzz of conversations and banging of chairs is barely a murmur in the back of my head.

"You coming?" Kaitlynn tugs at my shoulder.

"Yeah," I groan, and scrape the notepad and pens scattered on my desk into my pack. One pen misses and bounces on the beige carpet. "Shit."

I huff and lean over and pick it up. I drop it in my pack with the rest of my junk, and reluctantly my feet drag me away.

"Today maybe?" Kaitlynn says.

"I'm coming." I shoulder the backpack and let her tug me into the hallway.

I feel like a drone. Mindless and numb. I thought school might have been better than home because I'd have distractions, but I was wrong. It felt like work. The constant need to put on a mask or face the barrage of questions from Julieta and my classmates, or worse, my teachers wanting to know if I'm okay. I mean I'm glad they care, but not now. Even a fake smile doesn't come easy with my gut in knots and my heart being rent into tiny shards over and over again every time Zachary crosses my mind. Or Super Old Gran. Or Holly. Gods, any of the Marcus family, but going home to just sit on my bed, staring aimlessly at my altar isn't sounding much better.

Nothing about last night went the way I'd hoped. It was going to be a debacle either way, I knew that, but it was *so* much worse. It literally happened at their dinner table, in front of all of them, all at once. Dinner and a show. Except I was the show, and the

How (Not) to Conjure a Boyfriend

ratings were rock-bottom zeroes. Would not recommend. And I even ran out crying.

Then there's Hayden's reaction. I've mulled over it about as much as I have Zachary's surprise. He didn't seem heartbroken. He actually sounded relieved, and I don't know exactly how to process that. And then the others' faces, and the way Zach called after me. I keep hearing their voices. The *why*s and calling my name in shock and disbelief. I don't think my stomach can sink any lower than it is now.

I don't talk the entire way through the building. My mind won't shut up, so I can barely think to speak, and I think Kaitlynn's had enough of it. She stops in front of me.

"Kenzie. Talk to me." She plants her feet and stares me down. "You can't just keep it all up in there."

"Wanna bet?" I quip, and try to get around her.

She isn't having it. Her hands grip both my shoulders and her nails dig into my skin.

"Nope! We're not doing that." Kaitlynn squints at me. "What's going on up there?"

There's a lot going on in my mind, but somehow it feels empty and drugged yet buzzing with thoughts at the same time. I keep wondering if Mrs. Marcus, or even Holly, is going to hate me. And my head says yes, but I'm begging them not to, and at the same time I feel numb and weighted. I try to weave around the doubts and thoughts to say something useful.

"It's…just…" It's not working, that's what it's doing. What I really want to do is yell at the universe for letting me so very royally fuck everything up. I want to scream at the gods, whichever ones will listen, and thank them for not helping me any. I just want to scream. "This sucks, Kaity. I-I, uh…I effed this all up so bad. I just…I don't know."

"Kenz," she says. "You have to stop beating yourself up. You can't change it. It's over. It's done."

"It was last night," I remind her.

"But it's done," she says again.

"Yeah," I huff.

"It sucks, I know. But you knew it was going to happen," Kaitlynn says. "You've still got me though. Well, you're actually stuck with me. The only way you'll be done with me is if you off me."

It elicits a giggle from me, so that's progress.

"See, you can laugh," Kaitlynn says. "In all seriousness though, I know it sucks, and it's going to take time, but it is my job to make you laugh. So get ready."

"Yeah." I manage a grin.

"There we go!" Kaitlynn says, and throws an arm around my shoulders and drags me through the parking lot.

My first step doesn't go so well. My shoe snags on the ledge of the pathway and I almost end up facedown on the concrete. Almost. Thankfully Kaitlynn tightens her grip just before the momentum can drag us both down. And then, just as my spirits are finally a tiny fraction bit better, I see Julieta running across the lot in our direction. I do my best not to sigh as she walks up.

"Hey! Y'all coming tonight?" she asks.

"Coming to…" Kaitlynn answers exactly like I'm thinking.

What's happening tonight? Not like it matters. Once I get home I'm going exactly nowhere except my bed, where I'm going to stay until morning. And who knows, I might even stay after that.

"The bonfire. At Daniel's farm! Everyone's going!" Julieta gushes. Guess I'm not everyone then. "Kadin's coming! Oh, Kenzie! You could bring Hayden."

"Maybe…" I grumble.

How (Not) to Conjure a Boyfriend

I see the news hasn't spread. I'm sort of hoping it doesn't and people just forget. I don't want more questions.

"We'll think about it," Kaitlynn jumps in. Her eyes sweeping from me back to Julieta. "Just send me the address."

"Will do!" Julieta gives the thumbs-up and races away, disappearing into another group of our classmates.

"Not thinking about it," I mumble to Kaitlynn, and start back down the path to my car. Not in a million years. And obviously Hayden wouldn't be coming with us if we did go, and the person I'd want to take surely hates me now. The thought makes me even sadder. Getting to ride with Zachary up to Daniel's farm and sit cuddled by a fire, almost like that night in the woods…

I huff and try to erase the stupid idea from my head. It's pointless, even if I was hoping he'd text me last night when I got home, which was also pointless. He never did. I don't know what possessed me to hope he would. It's outrageous to think Zachary would even consider speaking to me ever again.

"We obviously don't have to go, Kenzie," Kaitlynn says, but a thought blossoms behind my dull eyes.

"Bonfire means alcohol, right?" I ask.

"Uh…maybe," Kaitlynn says. "Why?"

I don't say anything. I've never had a drink, but why should that stop me?

THE SKY IS SO clear tonight. No clouds, just a dusting of little diamonds obscured only by the massive twenty-foot flames shooting skyward from a mess of logs and branches. Even from Kaitlynn's car its heat reaches my skin. It's just a touch, but it's welcome in this winter chill. And it smells so good. That scent of burning pine needles, which thankfully overpowers the area's other competing scent: a light skunky stink that can only mean one thing. I guess I should have expected that.

"You sure about this?" Kaitlynn asks.

"Yes," I say, then shiver. "I *need* this."

"Do you though?" she asks.

This isn't my usual scene, or hers. It's too big and loud. I'd prefer a few friends around a little fire, a movie night, maybe a group at Hammy's. Not half of Mount Laurel's student body screaming and making out around a massive campfire that could consume half the mountain if it hadn't rained recently. And the sight of people I don't know isn't making it any better. That means other schools! Oh shit! Mitchell High? Hayden or Zachary might show up! No! I hadn't prepared for that possibility. What would I say if they did come? Or would I just avoid them? What if people think we're still dating and we have to break the news?

"About to find out." I shrug like I'm not freaking out inside. "At least we're not home."

"Sure." Kaitlynn doesn't sound so confident.

"Let's go," I groan, and start toward the fire. "Remember the signal if you see them."

It's simple. The signal is to repeatedly say *run* while pushing the other in the opposite direction and eventually to the car. It was Kaitylnn's idea. She didn't think she'd catch anything more subtle quickly enough.

"Got it," she says.

There are so many people. A lot of the faces are familiar, if only vaguely, but most of them don't know me, or they didn't before everyone heard I was "dating" Hayden. Which hopefully means they only know my name and couldn't match my face to it. I'd really like to avoid talking to anyone but Kaitlynn, maybe Julieta, or Landon if he shows up, but that's it. And I really don't want to talk to anyone who just wants to ask about Hayden.

All things considered, as much as being here is so not like me and I currently hate it, tonight's goal is simple. Avoid people, bask in the fire, and find some alcohol. There has to be some; this is Daniel's bonfire. The only reason he hasn't been suspended for selling weed at school is because he's on the starting lineup of the school football team. Everyone knows he's where you go for gas. Surely, that means there will be alcohol too.

"Oh, by Freyja, that feels amazing." I exhale, letting the heat from the bonfire flow over my skin. "I could stand here all night."

"I know," Kaitlynn says. "You could be a bubbling human marshmallow and you'd be okay with it. No wonder you're not afraid of hell."

I shrug. The crackle of the fire blends smoothly with the sounds of voices, hoots, and yells, a mixture of people and wildlife in the surrounding forest. There are people everywhere in huddled groups, which is where most of the noise is coming from, mostly teens around my age gathered in big circles. Some have piles of smoke rising from their center, others just puffs of steam. I think I see Geraldine. Kaitlynn, she, and I were friends in middle school. Then she got to Mount Laurel and decided it wasn't cool hanging with the enby. Her family isn't exactly queer friendly. She's in full conversation with Elana, her replacement for Kaitlynn and me. Most of the football team is in her huddle, some even in their numbered jerseys. If half of them weren't gorgeous, I'd hate them for how much they think of themselves. It's repulsive.

Still, I'm not finding what I'm looking for. No bottles or plastic cups. There are joints being passed around everywhere, and I think I saw a few soda and energy drinks in some hands, but not what I'm looking for. Where is the junk I always hear about? Are the parties not like I've been told?

"This sort of sucks," I say.

"We just got here."

"Still sucks," I repeat.

"Oh my God, calm down," Kaitlynn says. "You're being dramatic."

"Me? Dramatic?" I act offended. It's the most sarcasm she's getting from me tonight.

Someone yells, "It's here!"

I jump and sweep my gaze in the direction of the voice.

"What's here?" I ask Kaitlynn.

"How should I know?" She shrugs.

"Let's find out," I say, and start off.

"Fine," Kaitlynn grumbles and follows after me.

There's a truck, a rich kid's big Chevy. The tailgate is down and a couple guys are lifting box after box from the back and handing them down a line. I follow the trail until it stops at a table where they're stacking them under a tiny lantern next to a cooler. I step closer and see it's filled with ice, and a stack of red plastic cups sits on the foldout table next to it.

"Jackpot," I say.

"What?" Kaitlynn asks.

"Follow me." I rush the table, but I'm still not the first.

Before we get there, one box has already been ripped to pieces and emptied. The person in front of me grabs another and rips the top off, revealing can after can after can. I grab one, and then grab one for Kaitlynn.

"What's th—" she starts to ask but stops. "Seriously?"

"Yeah." I shrug, but suddenly I'm feeling less certain about it.

"You've never drunk." Kaitlynn eyes me, and then it hits. I might not have explained my full intentions for being here. My bad. "Oh. I..."

"You haven't either," I say. "Right?"

"No, I haven't," she says, and takes the can. "I hear it's nasty."

"Then why are they drinking it?" I wave my hand behind us.

Half the boxes are already empty and the sound of cans popping open is like a little musical cymbal being dinged across the field. They like it.

"I dunno. Maybe they just hate life so much they don't care?" Kaity shrugs.

"Perfect, then." I nod and pop the cap on the first can. "Me too."

"Fine. A taste, but I don't think I'm going to drink it," she tells me.

I can vibe with that.

"Bet," I say, and lift the can in time with Kaity.

We both take a few deep breaths and then have a tiny sip. At first it's just liquid, then it hits my tongue and I gag, immediately spitting it back out.

"Shit." I keep spitting but the flavor lingers on my tongue. It's so bitter, like a bag of stale coffee beans mixed with dirt and piss.

"Yuck." Kaitlynn starts spitting too. "Oh hell no!"

"Yeah, no. Me neither." I throw my can in the big plastic bag tied around the table. How can they like that? "Guess I'm never getting drunk."

"Probably best," Kaitlynn says. "That tasted like piss."

"You've drunk piss?" I ask.

"You know what I mean," she says.

For a moment we stand there, not a word said between us, watching everyone else rioting around the campfire, screaming, and yelling, and dancing. It's wild, but I feel so out of place still. Even with my mind numb and somehow still racing, it all feels foreign to me. They look so thrilled and excited. It's like they're having the time of their life out here under the stars in their crowds of people, with their nasty pee beer, but it's just not me.

"You want to leave?" Kaitlynn nudges my arm like the mind reader I swear she is sometimes.

"Yeah. Yeah, I do," I agree, and without a moment to spare we're both off to the car. "We could go back to the Harrel House!"

"Why?" Kaitlynn whines, sliding into the driver's seat.

"Why not?" I ask. "At least it's not getting drunk at a bonfire. So much more fun."

"But is that really a good idea?" Kaitlynn leans toward me. "Like that's where, uh…you and…you know? Plus, your mom hates it when you go places like that."

I sigh. She's right. Maybe it's not a great idea. The whole point of tonight was *not* to think about him. That won't happen there.

"What about that abandoned house near downtown?" I ask. That should be okay.

"Did you only hear half of what I said?" I don't answer, and she throws her head back all dramatic. "Fine. Whatever. Which one?"

Okay, that's fair. There are a few.

"The green one next to that oil change place," I tell her. It's the best I've got. Directions are not my forte, and I can't for the life of me remember the name of the oil change place.

"Jiffy's?" Kaitlynn asks.

"Uh…I don't think so," I say. "It's the one with the blue sign."

"You mean Helton's Muffler shop?" Kaitlynn shakes her head.

"Maybe," I say. Maybe it was Helton's. I thought that was an oil change place. "Is that the one with the ATM out front?"

"Yeah, you're talking about Helton's."

I shrug. "Sure, that house."

"That's a little public, isn't it?" Kaitlynn asks. "What if someone sees us?"

Okay, another valid point. Why is she being so logical when I need her to just agree? I need something to get my mind out of this slump, and there is nothing like slinking through the dark, empty halls of an abandoned house. The adrenaline of it all, wondering if you'll get caught, or if there's something scary inside—it's invigorating. I *need* invigorating.

"Run?" I suggest.

"I hate you." Kaitlynn groans.

"Sweet, let's go!"

29

KAITY'S TAILLIGHTS DISAPPEAR AS I take a right into my driveway and turn the volume down to a reasonable level. The lights are off inside the house, so I'm betting Mom is asleep. At least, I'm hoping. I don't really have a curfew per se, but I'm supposed to tell her if I'm going to be out past midnight. I didn't, and she started texting asking where I was and when I was going to be home. I told her I was okay but didn't answer the rest.

Tonight was needed. After ditching the bonfire, we made it to the house in downtown. It felt good—better—being there. We snuck around back to get in. The main entrance faces the road, and with the prominent *NO TRESPASSING* sign posted out front, it seemed safer. Inside we found the first empty space, plopped down, and ended up just sitting and talking for hours surrounded by dusty cabinets and large cutouts where ovens and refrigerators used to be. We talked about everything. How surprised we are it hasn't snowed yet, the games we used to play in middle school, what color we want to get our nails next—Kaity wants pink with red tips, and I think I'm going back to matte black—and the time I fractured my ankle running up and down the bleachers in middle school. We'd been racing. It was an all-around bad idea. Anything and everything, except *them*.

Okay, there was the one time Zachary came up. That was my fault. I thought he might like my nail color choice, but it was a dumb thought. Otherwise, I did good.

I twist the key in the ignition, and the engine dies *and* my heater cuts off. I squeeze my jacket to my chest to hold in what little heat

I can before jumping out and rushing the porch. I slow just enough not to make a ton of noise unlocking and opening the door, and slip inside.

It's dark. I can only make out the silhouettes of potted plants by the entry, the frames on the wall, and the doorways. I tiptoe down the hall, cringing every time the wood beneath the carpet creaks. I simply need to get to my room and jump in bed.

"Mackenzie Nicholas Jackson." Mom's voice jumps at me from the living room.

I quake and freeze. She's sitting in the dark on the couch with her arms crossed, but her eyes are clear and bold, and locked on me. Shit.

"Hey," I say.

"Where have you been?" she asks.

For some reason I step past the doorway into the living room. I guess there's no real point in trying to get away.

"I was with Kaity," I say. She always complains it's dangerous when I go to abandoned places, so I omit that part. "I told you I was okay."

"That's not the question. What were you up to?"

She's not happy. It's rare we get into arguments. I'm still not a fan.

"We were…" I start. "We were in downtown."

Her brow raises, but she doesn't say anything. Which means she's not convinced that's where it ends. I huff, then spill the truth.

"We went to an abandoned house."

"In downtown?" She gets to her feet. "There could have been squatters, homeless people there. The police could have come. You could have gotten hurt. You know I don't like it when you go to places like that."

"Yes," I whisper and dip my head. "I'm sorry."

"So you weren't at the bonfire?" she asks out of the blue.

"We went, but only for a few minutes and then we left," I tell her. How does she know about that? I didn't tell her. "It was lame."

"You haven't been drinking, have you?" Mom asks.

"What? No!" I stand taller. I mean, I about did, but I didn't. I only took a sip. Why would she ask that though?

"You're not lying to me, are you?"

"No! I swear it!" I say.

"Please don't lie to me, Mackenzie. The police busted the bonfire because there was an accident," Mom says.

"An accident?" I ask. Who? What happened? "Did someone get hurt?"

"No. But they could have," she says. "But you didn't drink there? And you left early?"

"I promise, Mom!" I say it yet again.

"You scared me, mein Schatz!" she says. She rushes over and gives me a hug. "Why didn't you answer your phone?"

"I…" A lie nearly escapes, but I grab it and pull it back inside. I didn't answer her call, I just gave her a vague text response. I shouldn't have, but I did. And now my heart can't handle it anymore and it quakes, and I begin to sob. "I'm sorry, Mom!"

"Sit down, Kenzie," Mom says and sits, patting the cushion next to her.

I do as she says and take a seat. The room is still dark, and I sort of want to ask to turn the lights on, but I don't.

"Is this about the Marcus boys?" she asks, repositioning to face me.

Of course it's about the Marcus boys. Everything is about the Marcus boys lately. That's where all my problems have come from. I mean not them, me, but still.

"Yeah," I mumble.

"Honey, you did what you had to. You told them the truth." Mom puts a hand on my shoulder. "That's never easy. You really liked Zachary, I think."

Loved maybe. I want to correct her, but I'm still debating it. Did I love him? I thought all I wanted was Hayden until I met Zachary. I actually got to know Zachary, and there was something there that I couldn't find in Hayden when he woke up, but it was only weeks. Is that enough time to know you love someone? That's what has been running through my head ever since Thursday night. Do I? I mean, did I?

"I did," I agree instead. "And now I think he hates me."

"Do you know that?" Mom asks.

"I lied about dating his brother. I outed Hayden before he was ready." That one really hurts. I know how scary that can be and how personal a decision that is and should be, but I took that away from him. "Then I pushed him away because I didn't know what to do. Even if Zach doesn't hate me, there's no way his mom and dad would allow it."

"That might be true, but you're *almost* an adult." Mom shakes her head in disbelief. "Mein Schatz is *almost* an adult. You never know what could happen though."

I nod. Why is she giving me hope?

"Mackenzie," Mom sighs my name. "It's going to be okay. You're young."

"But I could have ruined Hayden's life!" I burst. "Do you know how scary being outed is? I didn't want to hurt him!"

"I know, honey." She looks at me knowingly, probably remembering when I came home from school after being outed in eighth grade. "I know."

"And Zachary! How could he like me after all of this?" I ask. "I lied about how I felt about him. I lied, again. I would be so angry if I were him."

"And that's okay. It's not fun, but he has every right to be angry," Mom agrees. *You weren't supposed to agree with that one.* "But it doesn't mean he'll always be angry at you. You're a kind person, Mackenzie. You care. A lot. And sometimes caring puts you in hard places."

"That's for sure," I say. "I just feel awful. I'm angry at myself."

"You're going to have to let that go eventually," Mom says. "It's not easy, but I know you'll manage. You're mein Schatz, of course you will."

I huff. I wish it felt that simple. I wish it was just a matter of time, but I think it's more than that. I need to deserve it.

THE SCENT OF SAGE hangs in the air as I grind yellow yarrow blossoms into a fine blend with a handful of mugwort leaves. I move the pestle clockwise around the bowl, mixing the two flowers together. I try to focus on the rhythm, but a tear drops from my cheek into the bowl. I hold back a sob and keep stirring. It's a truth spell, and I can't think of anything more truthful than a tear.

I considered a spell on Zachary to make him love me, but no, blot on magic and all, *and* obviously my love spell on Hayden didn't go to plan either. Probably also something to do with offending the order of things. So instead, a truth spell on myself, something to help me accept reality and move forward. If the past few weeks have taught me anything, it's that as cliché as it may sound, truth is the best option. It's still so freaking hard to accept it. Every time I think of Zachary it's like a rusty dagger buries itself deep in my chest. The way I hurt him and his family. The lies I told to stay close, get closer to them. The way I ruined any chance I might have had with him. Wanting to kiss him again. The warmth of his hand on my cheek while he looks in my eyes. Gods, those eyes.

Forgetting Zachary isn't an option. Forgetting any of them is impossible. No magic is going to do that. It's just not how it works. It only works that way in the movies, not real life, and even if it could, I'd be left with either chunks of memory missing or a bunch of blurry faces and weird moments "alone." The thought of that is even more haunting.

"Calm, Kenzie," I say to myself and wipe new tears from under my eyes.

Spells are powerful things, but they're also fragile. I've learned a lot about that lately, unfortunately. My intent, the way I think about it, how I frame it, the way I feel in the moment, the vibes I send out into the universe to make *it* a reality mean everything. One off thread can pollute the whole into something unintended and…well, problematic.

I look down at the words scrawled on a simple piece of paper. I'm supposed to speak them while the flame eats away at the tall white chime candle set at the center of my altar with my mixture sprinkled around it. I just have to focus. I stop grinding the mixture and take a long slow breath. Then I sprinkle the blend clockwise around the base of the candle. I reach for the pestle again and my mind wanders. It always comes back to him, to Zachary. What is he doing right now? Is he angry with me? Did he actually feel the same or am I imagining it? Oh my gods, *did I* imagine it? I've done it before. Why not this time?

There was Tanner Blackbourn my freshman year. He smiled at me once, and I thought he loved me. He didn't. That was my first actual crush, but it ended when I saw Hayden. And now there is Zachary. *Was* Zachary. Not anymore. Gods, he has to hate me.

Focus, Kenzie. I sprinkle a little more yarrow and mugwort around the candle and pick up the lighter. *Breathe*. But a quiet sob breaches my lips. *Focus on your spell*. My tears don't stop, but I ignite the lighter anyway. I stare at the flickering yellow flame a second. It dances above the wick, ready to spark a new flame, but I stop short of lighting it. I suck my lips in and sigh. My nerves are on edge, and my chest is so heavy. I need this, but I don't know if I should.

No. Stop. Just stop, Kenzie. This is how you messed all this up in the first place. I sigh and wipe my face — it seems like that's all I'm doing tonight. Crying. My chest is tight, like it's retracting in on itself, squeezing my heart into oblivion. It feels like it's cracking under the pressure, wilted and black beneath all this chaos and pain, drowning me in my head. It's unbearable. I swear it's going to drive me insane.

I need to forget. I need to go back to that person who fawned over an unreachable boy with no real hope of obtaining him. The one who didn't let it drag them across the coals and bite at their thoughts every waking minute. It was normal. It was just a crush. That's where I want to be again. I don't want to remember that moment they thought I was Hayden's enbyfriend. I don't want to remember the rest.

I release the lighter's trigger, and the flame disappears as I shake my head. This isn't the time for a ritual. Not with the way I feel. There's no way on Odin's green Earth my intentions would be pure now. My grief, self-hatred, disgust — it'll find a way to seep in and pollute it, and if that happens it'll be a distorted and twisted version of my intent, just like all this was.

I lean back and let out a slow breath. *Just slow down, Kenzie. Breathe.*

My phone vibrates, and my eyes dart to the screen. I deflate a little. It's Kaitlynn. She can wait. Actually right now, everyone can wait. *Breathe*.

I look up at the ceiling and close my eyes.

"Freyja." I force my eyes open. A simple prayer will do. "Odin. Balder. Thor. Hodor. I need your help."

But what do I ask for? Forgiveness? Clarity? Forgetfulness? Is it selfish to keep wanting to forget? Sometimes being selfish isn't a bad thing, but when?

I sigh and make a decision. "I know forgiveness wasn't really a common concept back in your time, but if one of you could find it in your plan to forgive my…" I pause. My what? My intentions? My lies? My deceit? My fear of losing all of them? I swallow back the lump in my throat and wipe new tears from my face. I have this. "My lies. Please forgive my lies and let me find peace in what's left."

30

I JERK TO LIFE as something blares in my ear. What the... Oh. It's my alarm, TXT's "Frost." I slap at my phone once I find it strewn on the bed, finally prying my eyelids open. I don't remember falling asleep. My last memory is sitting in bed, crying, and the smell of incense wafting about my room.

I sit up and check my phone. Eleven o'clock on the dot and...I have two texts from Zachary. Please stop.

ZACHARY: Hey
ZACHARY: Can we talk?

"Nope," I say directly at the phone. I'm not sitting here and texting back and forth about how much I screwed up and ruined everything. And even if it's not that, I can't deal with anything else right now.

I drop my phone back onto the ruffled comforter and lie back down. I don't want to go to work today. My eyes are too heavy, complete with dark bags. *If* I had enough motivation, I could probably use a little makeup and make them not so noticeable, but not today. Can't I just stay here and be sad alone, at home, and in bed? What better place?

I let my eyes close, but the dark is replaced by him. Those intense yet kind steel eyes, looking at me. It sends a twinge of pain straight through my heart knowing I'll never see those again. Not in the same way, at least.

I shake back to life, trying to lose him from my head, and suddenly my watch reads 11:20 a.m. Shit. I pounce—well, more like slouch—out of bed and take a much-needed shower before putting on a thick black shirt and brown skirt, then layering my thickest jacket over it all. I don't want to face people today. I need everyone to be nice and not complain — the impossible I know, but please! I can't deal with the junk.

At least Kaitlynn is going to be there, and I think Dawn. I need them to distract me, to get me out of my head. Maybe it's better to be at work than here at home, staring at a wall. I still don't want to leave though.

I scoop my keys from the little table next to my bed and drag my feet into the hallway. Mom's waiting at the other end, arms crossed in a tan blazer. If I didn't know better, I'd think she was heading out for church.

"Morning," she says. "I made you some of those orange cinnamon rolls you like."

To my surprise, my mood lifts the tiniest bit and I manage a gentle smile.

"Sweet," I say, trying for her to be a little more myself, and move faster down the hall. "A reason to live."

"How'd you sleep?" Mom asks, shaking her head at my response.

"Fine, I guess," I say, and follow her into the kitchen.

Four rolls sit on a plate, slathered in a fresh warm orange glaze. I breathe in their citrusy aroma and pick one up.

"Is it all right if I take this on the road?" I ask. "I'm running behind."

"Sure," she says, and gets a little plastic container from the cabinet. While she packages the other three, I say a quick thanks to Freyja for my mom. "Now be sure to give at least one of these to Kaitlynn, okay?"

"I'll give her half of one," I joke.

Mom grins and shoos me toward the door. "You better be

joking. Now go on, don't be late. I love you, mein Schatz."

I grin and give her a kiss on the cheek before heading out the door with a "love you, Mom" thrown back toward the kitchen as I walk outside with a bit more jazz in my step. Still though, today is going to suck.

"REMEMBER TO CLEAN BEHIND the mixer and fridge before you leave tonight," Dawn says, looking over her checklist.

We're closed tomorrow for Christmas Eve and the next day for Christmas, which means today is deep cleaning time. When I got here, it was the prep table in back, underneath it, behind it, above it—everywhere. Oh, and the drink cabinet. Dawn and Kaitlynn are about to leave, so I'm getting the closing tasks for the day. Yay me. All by myself.

"Got it." I nod, trying to put on a smile, but I think it comes off more as a straight line. "Can I do some of that before close?"

"As long as you keep an eye out here," Dawn says, and walks into the back, leaving me with Kaitlynn.

"Sucks to be you." Kaitlynn grins.

"If you only knew," I come back.

"Cheer up, bitch." She winks. Had it been anyone else, I might have crawled across the counter.

It's slow right now, but we're expecting a little rush right before we close. That's how it usually happens on Sundays. Church people coming to get their pre-night service coffee and not tipping so they can tithe.

"You could smile a *little*, you know." Kaitlynn shrugs and squints at me. "You look like you hate life."

"Maybe I do," I suggest.

"Valid," she says.

How (Not) to Conjure a Boyfriend

I try anyway. It's part of the job. Don't put my feelings on the customer, so I will my cheeks to rise for Kaitlynn. "Better?"

"We're...getting there," she laughs.

"I'm going to start cleaning," I tell her. It's more to distract myself than anything. I pick up a washcloth and start patting down the display case. There are no customers left in the building, so I move from there to the little bookshelf with its collection of Woodsy Café & Cakes shirts and hoodies, tumblers, and even a few popular fiction titles up top. *Everything is fine*, I tell myself. *Just think about cleaning.*

Freyja, please help me keep my mind off him. I don't even want to think his name. It means too much.

The door chime rings, and Kaitlynn announces, "Mr. Franz."

"Hello there, Miss Kaitlynn," Mr. Franz says.

I stop and turn around. I have to say hey, he *is* my favorite customer. I'm surprised when there's a woman about my mom's age and another, who I think is probably a little younger than me, with him. Her hair is gorgeous, blonde and silky, and hangs over her shoulders.

"Hey, Mr. Franz!" I say, moving toward the counter.

"Mackenzie," he says with his usual broad smile lifting his wrinkled cheeks. "Meet my daughter, Anna, and granddaughter, Isla."

His family! I've always wondered if he had family around. I sort of felt bad for him on days like this and Thanksgiving that most people spend with family. Guess I don't need to.

"Good to meet you both." I nod at them. They're pretty, and I think I can see some of Mr. Franz in Isla. It's the nose, I think. It has the same raised bridge.

"They're here for Christmas," he says. "All the way from back home in Poland. It's been almost a year."

"Aw!" Kaitlynn sighs.

"I'm so glad y'all could come. Your dad and grandad is my favorite customer," I tell them. "Don't tell anyone else."

Just his presence lifts my mood. I've never seen the man look anything but grateful and peaceful, and something about him feels like he was sent from the gods themselves to calm me.

"Can we get you all something?" I turn to his family.

Mr. Franz nods and moves to the counter. I look for a second more, watching the way he cups his hand on his daughter's back at the register. It melts me, and for a moment, Christmas sort of feels like Christmas.

Ding, ding.

I rush behind the counter so Kaitlynn can finish helping Mr. Franz and I can go ahead and help whoever just walked in. I wipe my hands on my apron and look up. Immediately I freeze.

"Zach?" I say before thinking.

"Hey." He grins, but he looks nervous with his hands balled up together.

"W-what are you…uh… doing here?" I finally get the words out, and I'm already wincing. That probably sounded so rude to Mr. Franz and his family.

"I, uh…I wanted to see you." He steps closer and finally stops at the counter and puts his hand on the wooden top.

"Oh," I say, unable to stop my lips from skewing off to the side and showing my anxiety at his mere presence.

What is happening? Why does he *want to see me*?

"Maybe this isn—" I start, but Zachary literally puts his hand over mine and stops me. That familiar warmth shoots up my wrist and pulses to my brain, and I'm met with both a calm and fear I don't know how to pull apart.

"Stop, Mackenzie," he demands in the kindest tone, and I can't help but listen. He gives me a crooked grin and starts up again.

"Maybe this *isn't* a good idea, but *this* is *my* choice."

I'm unable and unwilling to argue, stuck in his gaze again. He pauses and looks into my soul for an eternity, or maybe it was a few seconds, I don't know. I lose track of everything around me. It's like the room melted away until he brings me back to reality.

"I'm sorry."

"Excuse me? Wh—" I blurt, but he frowns at me and squeezes my hand, which manages to shut me up.

"Hold on. Give me a second," Zach laughs. I shrink a little. My bad. He says it again and pauses before explaining. "I'm sorry. For the other night. I should have run after you. I shouldn't have let you go without saying something."

"Oh," I say. I don't know why I say it. I don't even understand why he's apologizing. Why would he have run after me? What I did was horrible. "Zach, no—"

His eyes pierce me, and I go silent. He drops his head and lets it bob a few times like he's really thinking about what he wants to say next. When he looks back up, he locks his gray eyes on me, but they're not what I expect. It's not anger that occupies that steel gaze. There's not a bit of malice in them, none. No. It's kindness. Compassion. Warmth. That's what I find instead, and somehow it seeps into my body and lights a little part of my heart all over again. I try to stop it, but it's already there.

He grunts and inhales a massive breath like he's about to blow into a trombone. I brace. *Stay calm, Kenzie. Just listen and it'll all be over soon.*

"I love you, Mackenzie," he says.

My chest falls, shoving all the air from my lungs, and my mouth gapes open. What did he just say? There's no way. Absolutely no way that can be true. Eyes wide, I brace my gaze onto his beautiful eyes. *You love me? How?*

"I was sort of hoping you'd say something after that." His voice shakes, and he laughs to cover some of the anxiety.

"I-I, uh…" I want to say it back, but this feels like a fantasy. I must have heard what I wanted to instead of what he really said. That's it.

"I know you think we all hate you and don't want anything to do with you, but that's not true," he says. "The others were shocked. Hayden was just excited he wasn't losing his mind."

"What?" I ask.

"Yeah, Eliza sat us all down afterward and told us everything. She said you'd been wanting to tell us, but she said to let her," Zach fills me in, and it's weirdly comforting. Maybe it's just because it's him, or maybe it's just because it's not the end of the world. Either way, somehow this is happening right now.

"Yeah," I say, and look down at the counter.

"It's okay though," he says.

"I don't understand. How is it okay? How is any of that okay?" I ask.

"You admitted it." Zach shrugs.

"Like weeks after the fact, and after diving headlong into your family," I remind him.

"Well, lucky for you my family adores you," he tells me, which I'm having a hard time understanding still. "Plus, you only had me convinced for like a week there at the end."

"Really?" I ask.

"Yeah, I know my brother…mostly," he tells me. "And why else do you think I kissed you?"

"Oh!" I yelp, and then we're both laughing. "I'm still sorry though."

I've forgotten other people exist, let alone those in the shop with us. Suddenly I feel so small and embarrassed as Mr. Franz

How (Not) to Conjure a Boyfriend

and his family, Kaitlynn, and Dawn all appear in my periphery.

"*We* know, and *we* forgive you," Zach says.

"We?" I ask, glancing at Kaitlynn, who's wide-eyed and stunned staring between the two of us. She doesn't have a poker face, so at least I know she wasn't in on this.

"Yeah, *we*. *All* of us," he says. "Hayden actually said to thank you. Apparently, he was talking to one of the guys on the basketball team but was afraid to come out, so they'd broken it off. You helped him come out, so they're back together."

"Really? He's not—"

"He's oddly glad," Zach says. "It helped him."

"I...uh...well, that's good, I guess." I grin, but I'm still having a hard time looking at him or making sense of how anything good could have come from all this.

"It is. I promise," he says.

"But you? You don't hate me?" I twitch when I ask.

"No! I don't think I could. Well, I mean I did for like a day when we first met, and maybe a little when I realized I liked you but you were fake dating my brother." Zach laughs. I try not to take it as a punch and laugh quietly too. "Oh! Can I come behind the counter a second, Mackenzie? Just a second?"

"Sure," I say before thinking about it. Technically the rule is employees only, but I spoke before that flashed in my head. Sorry, Dawn. "But stop calling me Mackenzie. It sounds weird from you."

He smiles and practically bounces around the corner and walks up to me. Without a word, he scoops up each of my hands and holds them between us.

"Well then, *Mack*! I know I already said it, but I need you to hear it and believe it," Zachary says, and if I weren't already nervous, I am now. "I love you. I think you already know that, but I have to be sure."

He stops and looks at me expectantly. My heart is screaming and beaming red through my cheeks. I want to jump him and kiss him and tell him he's everything, but I keep calm and think about my words before I say them this time. Guess that's the new me—thinking a little more before I speak.

"I do. I know, and I lo…I like you. I like you a whole lot," I tell him. It feels pathetic not to match his *I love you*, but I don't want to lie again. I do like him. Gods, do I like him. Everything about him. But it's time to start being very honest, and that means maybe I have to hold back a little. "I hope that's enough for right now. I'm having to reevaluate what it means to love someone at the moment, you know."

I want to kiss him so bad, but I don't. I'm going to let him lead for the moment, even if it's killing me.

Zachary grins at me. "Of course it's enough. Honesty is always enough, Mack. Oh! I have one more thing."

"One more thing?" I ask, and look back to Kaitlynn. She shakes her head and throws her hands up.

Zach steps forward. If he were wearing a hat, the brim would be dangerously close to my head. Well, over the top of my head. He pulls my hands up higher and squeezes my fingers gently.

"Mackenzie Nicholas Jackson," he says, then stops.

"Whoa, the middle name is coming out, huh?" I joke. "How do you even—"

He lets go of my left hand and presses a finger to my lips. "Shh."

My eyes blossom at his touch.

"Did you just shush me?" I say once he removes his finger.

"Yes, now let me get back to what I was saying."

"Oh, sorry." I give him an amused grin. My bad again.

"So again. Mackenzie Nicholas Jackson." He pauses and a

thought strikes my brain. *Oh my gods, it's way too early for a proposal! Please tell me you know that! Please don't ask that!* "Would you do me the honor of being my date to the Winter Formal?"

My eyes bolt open. The dance! A tear pokes from the corner of my eye and I'm sort of grateful I didn't put on makeup this morning. It's a happy tear though. This boy sees me beyond my mistakes. I don't know how he does it when *I* can't even do it, but he does. He sees who I want to be. He sees my heart. I've never known what that feels like until this moment, and it's better than our first kiss. It's a joy that I don't know I'll ever be able to express.

"Say yes!" Mr. Franz yells, now across the shop.

I'd forgotten about them being here, and retract a little, but Zachary doesn't let go. I give Mr. Franz a nervous grin.

"Listen to that man," Zach laughs.

"Uh. Yes! Of course!" I finally say it. "Yes, I'll go to the dance with you!"

"Awesome," he giggles. "Oh and, would you maybe be my enbyfriend too?"

Excuse me? Why else would I go with you to the dance?

"I thought that was evident." I stick out my tongue.

"So that's a yes, right?" he chuckles.

"*Yes!*" I say so he'll stop asking.

"Thank you, Mack," he says, and pulls me toward him.

Just like that night in the old, empty, dark house, everything quiets and I swear his eyes close in slow motion, or maybe it's everything else that's going slow. I don't know which, and I don't really care, as our lips touch and I lose myself in his kiss. That same vanilla-mint soothes my senses while his warmth pushes through my skin and he squeezes me closer.

"Thank *you*, Zach," I say when we part.

Not ten minutes ago I felt like my life had ended, but here I am in the arms of the most genuine guy I've ever met, and he said he loved me, and more importantly I believe it. But there's always something else; it's not just him that I lied to.

"What about your family?" I ask, bringing some tension back into the situation.

"Oh yeah! About them..." He grins mischievously, and taps his phone a few times.

"Huh?" I purse my lips, but before he can answer, the door chime rings and my eyes light up.

It's Mary-Anne and Mr. Marcus. Holly, and Eliza, and Catina, and Jeffrey. They're all smiling, rushing into the store, hands up and yelling, filling the tiny shop with a raucous laughter and joy. Then there's Super Old Gran hobbling in behind them, yelling, "Kiss them again!" and my heart practically melts all over again. I love her so much. Gramps and Kiki are behind her, helping her get through the door. Then at the end of the entourage is Hayden. He's the only quiet one, but he's grinning.

"Kenzie!" It's said so many times by so many people I don't know who's talking until Mary-Anne rushes around the counter and engulfs Zach and me in a big hug.

"I want you to know that you *are* family, Kenzie," she tells me, looking between us. "You have been for weeks. We just didn't know how to react."

"It was a lot to take in, you know?" Mr. Marcus admits. "But you really *are* part of the family."

I'm awestruck. I don't know what to say. How do you handle such unconditional love?

Hayden walks around them and stands across the counter the way he has so many times before. It's weird seeing him, really seeing him, but even more so now that the obsession is gone. I squeeze Zachary as the thought puts a grin on my face.

How (Not) to Conjure a Boyfriend

"Of course we wish you would have told us earlier, but you really grew on us," Mary-Anne says.

Eliza cocks her head to the side and smiles with bright white teeth. "I told you you were family."

I laugh and nod back at her.

Yeah, I effed up. I shouldn't have let all this happen. I should have told the truth at the beginning. I'm not trying to excuse that, but somehow, it all worked out. It's beyond anything I could have imagined. Maybe Freyja is smiling down on me right now. Maybe it's fate. Maybe it's something to do with my spell. I don't know, and honestly I'm not sure it really matters.

"Kiss them!" Holly screams.

I look at Zachary and smile. He's laughing right back.

"Yes! Kiss them," Eliza echoes and winks at me. I couldn't have made it without her. She's my saving grace. My witch mother. I hope she doesn't mind that she's going to have to teach me everything now.

"Oh, come on! Kiss them before I die," Super Old Gran croons.

I giggle and look at Zach again. He's smiling. It's something I want to see as long as I can. I don't want to hurt him ever again, or any of them. I want them all just like this.

Finally, Zach leans in and kisses me. His hand falls to my lower back and he pulls me in closer. It just feels right. Eyes closed, taking in the taste of his mouth, the feeling of his soft lips gliding against mine, and a warmth that I don't think I could ever get enough of. A few seconds go by with hoots and *get its* playing as background music, before we part again. My eyes open and it's all I can do to pull my gaze away from his.

"I love y'all," I say once we break away, and I'm rushed by a mob of people I now can truly call family. Even Kaitlynn joins in.

Warmth takes over, and I stare into Zach's steel eyes as they look back with not a doubt in the world. Moments ago I thought my little world was over, and now I'm standing in the middle of a brand-new family who loves me despite my flaws, with a boy I never expected to come into my life, who simply watches me with love in his eyes.

"Okay, back off. Back off." Zach squeezes between Eliza and me, and wraps his arms around me. "Give them some space."

I giggle, and his eyes find mine. This is what I was missing. What's truly amazing right now is that I thought if a day like this ever came, it would be with Hayden. I was stuck on him, maybe even a little obsessed, but he's on the outside watching. He's not the guy holding me. Not the one I can't stop giggling at. And yeah, I know this isn't the way most love stories go. Honestly, it's probably the exact opposite of how you should fall in love, but I did. Somehow, some way, against all I thought was going to happen, I did. Honestly, maybe that's the beauty in all of this weird chaotic world. I thought I knew what I wanted, but life said *hold on and watch*.

ACKNOWLEDGMENTS

IT'S HARD TO CATEGORIZE and weigh out who helped here and who helped there. And in the end, to every single person who had even the tiniest hand in this story, I thank you.

That said, first, I'd like to thank my alpha and beta readers: Jen Upright, Hazel Franz, Jo Casto, Jordan Webb, Jacob Baker, Nicole, and yes, even you, Jaiden Lighthouse. You all helped take this story from the idea I had to a story worth telling. Thank you to Amanda Bryers and Jo Casto (again) for their indispensable help bettering my understanding of real-life witchcraft. Thank you to Marcia Roseman for her medical expertise. Thank you to Yayira Dzamesi for such a beautiful cover! Have you seen it? I'm assuming you have, but look again, it's amazing.

Thank you to two of my favorite people in the world, who I've never actually met in person because y'all rudely live in other countries but every day make my life a little better on Instagram. Kristyniel Isabella, my K-pop and BL bestie from afar—not only have you encouraged my possibly unhealthy addiction to K-pop, J-pop, and T-pop, you've been a constant aid and confidant in both this story and life in general. Love you, K! And of course you, Charlotte Kinzie, there's no way I can forget you. You've been with me since the beginning, or at least it feels like it. Thank you for listening to my incessant questions about whether something is good enough, and letting me send you random snippets or promos to see if they're okay. At least it's broken up with hilarious memes, reels, and talking about our crazy lives.

Obviously, I would be remiss to forget my editor, Christie

Stratos. You are amazing, and you are kind, and you are patient, oh so patient. Thank you for being my editor and giving me the kind yet useful feedback I need to bring these stories to life. I'd also like to thank Laura Zimmerman, Cale Dietrich, BK Clark, Bob Clark, and Leo Samworth. You each have done so much to support me, from reading proposals, to helping with better representation, to proofing my work early, and more. Thank you so much.

Last, I want to thank Dawn Evans. You've been a second mom to me for years now, and a constant supporter. Your shop, Editions Coffee Shop & Book Store, has been an indispensable part of my writing since I first discovered Kannapolis existed. It's where I've done so much of my writing, but also smiling, laughing, crying, and hoping. And thank you to you specifically for always being there for me. Actually, also thank you to Kannapolis. There's something about this little town that I just love.

ABOUT JORDON GREENE

Jordon Greene is the author of *A Mark on My Soul* and *Every Word You Never Said*. An alumnus of the University of North Carolina at Charlotte, he works as a senior software engineer. Aside from work, Jordon can usually be found at his favorite little coffee shop or a local baseball game annoying his found family, or obsessing over Asian-pop music and the newest BL drama. He lives in Kannapolis, NC with his cats Genji & Freyr.

VISIT JORDON GREENE ONLINE AT
www.JordonGreene.com

www.ingramcontent.com/pod-product-compliance
Lightning Source LLC
LaVergne TN
LVHW030342070526
838199LV00067B/6404